Braking Points

Books by Tammy Kaehler

The Kate Reilly Mysteries
Dead Man's Switch
Braking Points

Braking Points

A Kate Reilly Mystery

Tammy Kaehler

J met —
A fellow chocolate lover!
(thanks for the recipes :ü)

Tammy Kaehler

Poisoned Pen Press

First Edition 2013

10 9 8 7 6 5 4 3 2 1

Library of Congress Catalog Card Number: 2012910494

ISBN: 9781464200991   Hardcover
       9781464201011   Trade Paperback

Poisoned Pen Press
6962 E. First Ave., Ste. 103
Scottsdale, AZ 85251
www.poisonedpenpress.com
info@poisonedpenpress.com

Printed in the United States of America

To An Lachat-Harmsen,

For friendship across the miles, years, and generations.

Acknowledgments

As usual, I've mixed the real and the imaginary for my own purposes. I have no affiliation with real locations, entities, or organizations—especially the American Le Mans Series or the Breast Cancer Research Foundation—only admiration for their work.

This book is my tribute to the style of racing I first encountered in 2004 and grew to love, as well as all the talented and friendly competitors and staff in the American Le Mans Series. I hope the 2014 season will yield a new, exciting world of sportscar racing with increased competition, drama, and success for every participant and fan of the sport.

I owe thanks to a wide variety of experts for information, including Dr. Jason Black, Adam Rogers, Aaron Nakahara, Tina Whittle, Tom Leatherwood, and Ray Taylor. In the racing world, thank you to Patrick Long, Joe Foster, Kevin Buckler, Andrew Davis, Nick Fanelli, Charlie Cook, Dr. Gregg Summerville, and Bob Flohrschutz for information and advice. Extra special thanks and appreciation to racing gurus Doug Fehan, Beaux Barfield, Shane Mahoney, and Pattie Mayer for answering question after question after question with enthusiasm and humor.

Thank you also to the real Leon Browning for your generous donations to the Austin Hatcher Foundation and allowing me the use of your name. In the writing arena I owe great debts to Christine Harvey, Wendy Howard, Cary Sparks, and Tracy Tandy for valuable feedback and keeping me part of the writing group, even from 400 miles away. Huge thanks to Rochelle Staab for review, critique, and cheerleading. To Julia Spencer-Fleming, Hank Phillippi Ryan, and Hallie Ephron, I value your advice, support, and blog more than I can express. To my agent, Lucienne Diver, thank you for having my back and for ongoing guidance. And to Jessica, Annette, Barbara, Rob, and everyone else at Poisoned Pen Press: thank you for being wonderful people and for allowing me the opportunity to be here.

To my family and friends, thanks for forgiving late birthday greetings, little contact, and infrequent responses during the writing months. Special thanks to Gail, Roger and Aggie, and Linda and Jerry for being unflaggingly proud, excited, and encouraging.

Finally, to Chet, thank you for making this book possible. Without you turning off the television, making dinner for months on end, and valuing this book as much (at times more) than I did, it wouldn't have happened.

Road America

Elkhart Lake, Wisconsin

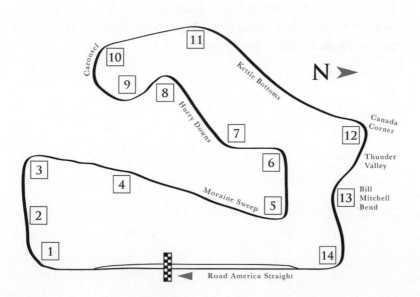

Chapter One

Sunday evening

It's one thing to see the man you're dating lurking in the shadows with another woman. It's another when the woman is dead.

I walked up the fire lane behind Siebkens Tavern and Inn, my goal, the bottle of ibuprofen in the glove box of my car. As I reached the street at the north edge of Siebkens' block, a noise caught my attention. I turned my head to see what looked like two moving bodies on the ground next to a building.

Two people and a dark space away from the bustle of the courtyard indicated drunken assignation—even if the participants were next to parked cars and mini-dumpsters. I almost averted my gaze and left them to it, but as my eyes adjusted to the dim light, I understood more details of the scene ten yards away.

If it was a romantic encounter, it was one gone wrong. The woman lying on the ground was limp and unresponsive. The man bending over her was the guy I'd been dating for five months, Stuart Telarday.

I gasped, and Stuart looked up, the weak light from a street lamp showing me his stricken face. I froze.

He spoke, hoarse with shock. "Kate. It's—she's dead."

I ran four steps, weighed down by the knot of dread in my stomach, then sank to my knees next to him. I could barely draw breath for the sadness blooming in my chest.

I looked at Stuart. "What did you do?"

Chapter Two

My world started going to pieces at 120 miles per hour. That's when I lost control of my racecar and ruined my team's race at Road America. It wasn't clear if I'd also ruined our season in the American Le Mans Series…or another driver's life.

My co-driver Mike Munroe qualified and started the number 28 Corvette fourth in the Road Race Showcase at the famed track in Elkhart Lake, Wisconsin. He moved the car up to second in his hour-and-a-half stint, and then I took the wheel during a full course caution. In my first thirty minutes, I did everything a professional driver should do: hold my position, put pressure on the car ahead, and stay out of trouble.

The car felt so good, balanced in the braking zones and powerful on the long straights, I forgot my concern about the slate-colored clouds that had teased us with sprinkles all day. But the heavy, swollen skies were ready to unload.

In minute thirty-three of my stint, I got a radio call, "Rain starting, Turns 8 through 10."

I didn't respond. Focused on braking for Turn 14. Clip the apex. On throttle gently. More. Unwind the wheel. Don't run off the outer edge of the track into the grass. Stand on the throttle. The Corvette's 491 horses pushing me up the hill.

Hold the car steady. Foot to the floor. Over 170 mph. on the front straight. I relaxed for a second. Considered slippery track ahead, took two deep breaths. Pits flashing by on my right, cars in for wet tires already.

Then hard braking for Turn 1. Downshift to third. Wheel right. Apex the corner. Feed throttle back on. Braking early for Turn 3. They say "slow in, fast out" to a corner, and I wanted all possible speed down the Moraine Sweep. Right through 3, on the throttle quick. Up to sixth gear, flying. Big, fat drops of rain on my windscreen. Dive past a Porsche from the slower class. A wiggle as my slick tires struggle for grip on the damp track. Brake hard for 5. Down to second gear, slower than my usual 60 mph. Tires holding, turning left. Only a little curb on exit.

Up to Turn 6, still light rain. Through Turn 7—into a downpour. My single exterior wiper blade barely made a dent. I was blind, slowing, trusting the blue LinkTime Corvette five lengths ahead of me wouldn't stop. Trusting I remembered where the track was. Brake slowly, carefully. Pray my tires hold. Search for my marks for Turn 8—there. Turn left, unwind the wheel. Throttle gently out of the turn.

The deluge was over at the turn-in for the Carousel, Turns 9-10, a single, sweeping, 210-degree right-hander. Barely sprinkling there. I shook my head as I held the car steady through the first apex, then the second. There was no way to tell how wet the track was from one corner to the next. Any minute, I knew I'd be called to the pits for wet-weather tires.

I played the next moment over and over in the hours, days, and weeks to come, analyzing split-second impressions and trying to determine the cause. I still didn't know what I should have done differently. How I could have saved it.

I'd followed a blue Corvette for some laps, always a few car lengths back. Coming out of the Carousel, my momentum carried me forward and the other Corvette faltered. I was right behind him.

"Miss a shift there?" I muttered under my helmet. I wasn't looking to pass yet, but I didn't want to be behind a car in trouble.

I knew to be careful. We were headed for the Kink, one of the toughest corners in racing—not much of a turn, but flat, blind, and fast. With concrete walls on both sides. Everyone knew taking the Kink flat out took guts.

Midway between the Carousel and the Kink, I pulled my front wheels ahead of the blue Corvette's rears, laying claim to the inside line for the right-hand bend of the Kink. I saw a few drops of rain, but the track wasn't very wet.

The problem started at the apex, where it was clear he wasn't slowing. Wasn't giving me room. Was squeezing me off the track. In a heartbeat, our racecars, clinging to the limits of adhesion and speed in a turn—pulling one and a half Gs at 120 mph—touched, rubbed, and broke loose. At the limit in a racecar, any change in grip can be disastrous—and it was.

We crossed paths: me going left, him going right. I felt the balance of my car changing through the steering wheel. I felt contact with the track slipping away through the chassis and my seat. Sliding. I tried to point the car down the track as I headed for the outside wall. Stomped clutch and brake to the floor. Once I'd lost traction, there was no regaining grip. No ability to stop or turn or control the car in any way. Only desperate prayers to scrub speed.

The car didn't respond to me. The wall was too close.

Save it. No. Spin the other way—and I hit the wall. I turned the steering wheel left at the last minute and caught traction somewhere, tipping the car around, softening the impact because the Corvette hit concrete with the right front corner instead of straight on the nose. But it was still big.

Wham. I slumped right against my belts, legs lifted off the pedals, arms curled to my chest so I didn't break a wrist when the wheel jerked around. Tried to breathe after the impact. A helpless passenger as my car rebounded onto the track, still moving. Speed maybe cut in half. I closed my eyes against the dizzying blur outside. A second to consider reaching for the wheel to control the car—then another crunch. I was tossed right again, collapsing against my belts, arms tucked to my chest. For the second time, my helmet smacked against the high side of my seat.

I opened my eyes, gasping for breath, and discovered the world was still. My ears rang and my vision cleared with the smoke around me. I uncurled my arms, set my feet on the floorboards. I faced forward in the middle of the track—a terrible location, proved immediately by a Porsche whizzing past, kicking up debris that thumped my car. I knew yellows were waving, and I hoped subsequent cars wouldn't hit me. I looked down. No visible blood. I flexed toes and fingers, squirmed under my belts. Nothing felt broken. I looked right and saw the other Corvette in the grass against the wall.

I knew I'd gone left. The LinkTime Corvette must have gone into the inside wall. We'd obviously bounced back onto the track and slammed into each other, stopping our momentum.

External sounds percolated through the dull roar in my head—which I realized was more than my thundering heartbeat. I looked at my dash. The engine still valiantly turned over.

Two prototypes and a Ferrari swept between our cars and ran through the debris field. The outside world returned in a rush.

"Get out of here, Kate, keep going!" I shouted. I needed to follow those cars, to limp back to the pits. To reverse time. Anything to fix the car and salvage points, a finish, some pride out of the disaster. The power of my rage alone should have been enough to move the car.

I put the car in first gear and engaged the clutch, hearing the engine labor to respond. I only moved a few inches. Through the misty rain I saw safety workers appear, and I waved at them to help me. They paid little attention.

My radio squawked. Not for the first time.

"Kate, repeat, are you all right?" Jack Sandham, team and car owner, spoke.

I pressed the transmit button. "He squeezed me. The car might be OK, I'm not sure. I'm sorry." My voice came out higher than usual, in short, gasping breaths.

"Are you hurt, Kate?"

"I'm fine. Why won't they help me?!"

I pounded the wheel in frustration as I watched more safety workers arrive and ignore my car in favor of the other Corvette. Finally, a safety worker opened my door.

"You hurt?"

I waved a hand and yelled, "No. Clear my front wheels!"

He shook his head. "Front right's gone. Rear suspension's broken. Better get out."

I wanted to argue with him, but he was impatient and unyielding. I shut down the engine and unbuckled myself, feeling shame heat my face. If I couldn't get the car back to the pits on its own power, we couldn't finish the race. Our day was done. *Dammit. Why did I let that happen? Why didn't he leave me room? That asshole.*

I stood on wobbly legs next to my car studying the other Corvette. My anger at the other driver for wrecking me was tempered by a fizz of unease in my gut. The blue car was in shreds, the hood buckled, both sides caved in, the rear crumpled. My own still looked car-shaped in comparison. He'd gotten the worst of the accident by a long shot.

A medical worker held my shoulders and watched my eyes while I shouted answers to his questions. "Yes, I'm OK. Nothing hurts," "What happened is he squeezed me and we wrecked here in the Kink," and "I had a turkey sandwich and some barbeque potato chips for lunch." After that, he started pressing against different parts of my body—my upper and lower back, my sternum and abdomen, my shoulders, my legs—to be sure nothing was broken or causing me pain, indicating internal damage.

I was unhurt, and the medic was distracted, glancing behind me to the other car. I followed his gaze to see a half-dozen safety workers clustered around the crushed driver's side of the racecar. I couldn't see which of three blue Corvettes it was, but one of six men was undoubtedly hurt.

I should have been moving to a waiting ambulance for my obligatory trip to the medical care center, but instead I watched the paramedics painstakingly extract the other driver, strapping him to a back-board, then a stretcher. The driver gestured weakly with his left hand as five workers wheeled him to the ambulance, each one busy over his body.

I could barely breathe for the frustration I felt. My car was wrecked. I was angry at myself and furious at the guy on the stretcher. But it was hard to be mad at someone while being worried he was seriously hurt. It might also be hard to be mad at *that* driver.

I'd recognized the helmet as belonging to the crown prince of racing, our version of the Beatles, Mickey Mouse, and Dudley Do-Right, all rolled into one attractive package. The nation's favorite driver was guest starring in our ALMS race on a rare weekend free from NASCAR duties. No one, anywhere, didn't like Miles Hanson.

Except maybe me.

Chapter Three

The rain stopped while I was in the medical care center being pronounced non-concussed, but likely to be bruised. No surprise there. The only update on Miles Hanson's condition was the sound of the life-flight helicopter taking off, transporting him to a hospital.

The doctor held me an extra ten minutes, making me drink some apple juice, saying I looked shaky. An understatement. I barely kept a lid on the emotions swirling inside me: fear, anger, disappointment, defensiveness, concern, and guilt. I started to feel strained muscles and bruises—especially my left hand and wrist, which must have hit the something. Juice alone wouldn't fix my problems.

I sorted through my reactions. I wanted to—*did*—blame Miles. I also knew I'd need to see a replay of the accident to be sure that wasn't my guilt or ego talking. Most likely it was a "racing incident," a no-fault (or shared-fault) mishap that occurs when racers push the limits hard. Particularly in the rain. But I wasn't ready to accept responsibility yet—easier to blame him, however much I worried about his injuries.

I was upset for my team. Jack Sandham and Ed Swift, the owners of Sandham Swift Racing, would have to buy a lot of new car parts. The crew would have to tear down and rebuild new assemblies in a tight timeframe, because the next race—Petit Le Mans, the season-ending endurance classic—was only two weeks away.

I replayed the accident in my mind. *Did I screw up? No, not my fault. I could have done things differently, but my job is to pass cars and drivers, particularly when they're begging for it. And he was.*

I rubbed my sore left wrist, sure I'd replay the event and the conversation with myself for days to come.

My juice was finished and my knees had stopped shaking. Time to face the music. I squared my shoulders, thanked the medical personnel, and headed for the exit door as Stuart Telarday walked in. He was as perfectly pressed as always, but his wavy, sandy-brown hair flopped onto his forehead and he was frowning—signs of high distress to someone who knew him. Which I did.

Over the past year, I'd gone from thinking Stuart over-starched, stuffy, and lacking in humor to finding him appealing. To dating him. Our five-month history totaled scores of telephone conversations, six dinners, and a few dozen kisses that made me tingle in memory. But I was still in the cautious stage of our relationship, unsure about how we interacted at the track.

He saw me and visibly relaxed. "You're all right, Kate?"

"I'm fine. What's the status on Miles?" My voice was abrupt to keep myself focused on business. To keep my emotions dammed up.

"Nothing yet. Let's get you back to your team."

I let him take my arm and guide me outside, wondering why he'd appeared at the medical center. He was the VP of Marketing and Operations for the American Le Mans Series or ALMS. Plus we'd been dating. Neither role explained why he'd escort me back to my paddock.

The crowd of more than fifty racegoers in the parking area outside did.

I expected the media, and I'd been mentally preparing politically correct sound bites in which I pointed no fingers, as much as that galled me. The outlets covering the race—Radio Le Mans, print publications, SPEED Channel, SportsGroup TV, and even the on-track announcer—typically converged on drivers after accidents to ask what happened. Those reporters were up front, and I answered multiple versions of the same question with one statement.

"It got wet really fast and we were still on slicks. The other car missed a shift or something, and I got close enough to him that I either needed to pass or risk being stuck. I thought we were clear and clean. I haven't seen a replay yet, but I'm guessing it was a racing incident. One of those things that can happen when we're all pushing hard all the time. I'd like to thank my team, Sandham Swift, and our sponsors, BW Goods, Racegear. com, and Leninger's Auto Shine, who prepped and gave me a fantastic Corvette today. My thoughts are with everyone else's, hoping Miles Hanson's injuries are light and quickly healed."

As I spoke into microphones and mini-recorders, Stuart hovered behind me, a six-foot wall of protection. Though grateful, I didn't understand why until we cleared the media and encountered the fans.

Fans? Do I have fans like this?

No, I didn't. Miles Hanson did.

Men and women of all ages surrounded me, shouting questions, some openly weeping. *Wait, weeping?*

"What happened?"

A tall man, all round edges and beer belly, thundered, "Was he OK?"

"Didn't you see Miles?"

"How *could* you?" This from a bleach-blonde wearing a Miles Hanson half-shirt over cantaloupe-sized fake boobs.

"Why did you hurt him?"

*They all blamed **me**? But it was his fault!* I faltered on my way through the crowd.

Stuart urged me forward, repeating over and over, "We don't have any information yet, but a statement will be made when we know something."

People continued to press toward me, many wearing the yellow and orange flames of Miles' NASCAR livery, some pleading with me to give them positive news of Miles, a few glaring, even snarling, at me. I was too stunned to speak, grateful for

Stuart's presence. We got through the scrum and found Tom Albright, my team's media guy, waiting in a golf cart.

As we pulled away, I saw my friend Zeke Andrews pop out of the crowd, looking worried. He'd been in the ranks of reporters I spoke to, the lone representative of SPEED Channel now that SportsGroup TV had taken over ALMS broadcasting rights. Zeke caught my eye and made a "call me" gesture, then waved in response to my nod.

Tom cleared his throat as he navigated paddock traffic. "Kate, we're all relieved you're OK. The accident looked nasty."

"Thanks. It wasn't fun. I'm really sorry to the team and the crew."

He slowed the golf cart. Directly in front of us was the flat-bed tow truck with Miles' crumpled car. Every body panel was crumpled, some half torn off, and every tire was askew. I shuddered. I really wanted to see the replay of the accident.

A new thought struck me. I whirled to face Stuart. "Is Miles still OK?"

"He's hurt, but alive."

I faced front again as a skinny woman with gray hair grabbed the front roof support on my side of the golf cart. Tom slammed on the brakes in response, dragging her two steps. Decked head-to-toe in bright yellow with orange flames, her tank top and baseball cap were also emblazoned with Miles' number 92 and the Chevrolet logo. But more shocking than the riot of color were her sobs. She hiccoughed, and I smelled sour beer breath as she spoke. "How could you? Who are you, anyway? You know you'll never be as good as Miles, so you wrecked him? You should rot in hell!"

She released the golf cart to wipe her eyes, and Tom drove on.

Stuart put a hand on my shoulder, and I flinched. "Ignore it, Kate."

I tried. No matter what happened, I knew a driver's staunch-est supporters would always blame the other driver in a wreck. If Miles threw someone to the ground, unprovoked, fans would ask what the victim had done to upset him—such was the nature of the fan world. The cause of our wreck seemed obvious to me, but it was clear Miles' fans and I wouldn't see eye-to-eye. On anything.

As we rolled through the paddock, we encountered more crying faces, more anguished questions, more swear words. I even heard a threat, someone promising to "Hunt you down if he ain't OK!"

We reached the Sandham Swift garage, where a small knot of spectators gathered to await the arrival of my own wrecked car. Stuart whisked me behind the rope barrier that separated the public from our team's space before anyone could react to my presence. He stayed outside our motorhome, shutting the door behind me with a thud, and I wobbled up four steps to collapse on the couch, breathing hard. For the first time, I felt uncomfortable in the ALMS paddock, even scared for my safety. I didn't like it.

Tina Nichols, Hospitality Director for Sandham Swift Racing, sat down next to me, a bottle of cold water in her hand. She kept the four Sandham Swift drivers organized, fed, and wearing clean, dry racing gear. Everyone in the paddock knew her, loved her, and called her Aunt Tee.

"Kate, sweetheart, are you all right?"

My smile felt rusty. "I'm fine, thank you." I took the water she offered and looked at Mike Munroe, dressed in street clothes and sitting on the couch opposite me. "For now. We'll see when Mike gets through with me. Or Jack."

Per ALMS rules, Mike and I shared the number 28 Corvette for Sandham Swift Racing—one of two cars the team fielded in the GT or Grand Touring class—each of us driving roughly half of each race. Drivers, teams, and car manufacturers all competed for race wins and season championships, and until I'd taken us out of this race, Mike and I had been neck-and-neck with another duo for second place in the GT drivers' standings.

Our points total was especially impressive because of the reconfiguration in the American Le Mans Series GT ranks this year, which combined former GT1 and GT2 classes into

GT—resulting in double the competition. Mike would be justified in being angry with me for dashing his championship hopes.

But Mike merely shrugged. Large and muscular, with olive skin and brown hair and eyes, he could look imposing and angry, especially behind the wheel. At heart, however, he was as gentle and mellow as a giant teddy bear. "You were due. You hadn't wrecked all year. I banged the car up some, remember?"

"I sure as hell haven't forgotten, since I got the bill." Jack's steps shook the motorhome as he walked from the back room through the kitchenette. "And you, Kate."

I swallowed and looked up at him. Up and up and up.

As was his habit, Jack stood in the middle of the room, feet wide, fists to hips. Tall and reed-thin, his attitude and power made him as intimidating as men twice his bulk. He was fair and direct, and he didn't believe in sugar-coating. Today was no exception. "Screwed that one up, didn't you?"

I winced. "I don't know how it happened. Coming out of the Carousel, Miles did something—or didn't do it. I was on top of him. It was hard *not* to pass. I was afraid I'd get stuck if I didn't get around. I couldn't tell it had rained hard there, and he squeezed me in the corner." I paused, remembering. "Maybe I hit paint, too." I looked at my feet. *Shit, I **did** screw up.*

"Your hands on the wheel."

I looked at Jack again. "So my fault. I'm sorry." He didn't care what other cars did, only what we'd done—if my hands were on the wheel, to him any accident would be my fault even if I couldn't have avoided a wreck with a miracle. I felt less anger and more shame as I realized Miles and I shared the blame.

Aunt Tee patted my knee.

Jack snorted. "Damn right it is. I don't pay you for rookie mistakes like that."

I hung my head, feeling my face burn. The silence lengthened. Jack wasn't likely to fire me for a single accident—every driver wrecked at some point, and I'd been pretty clean so far that season. But "wasn't likely to" didn't equal "for sure wouldn't." My stomach fluttered.

"But I'd be a fool to expect you'd never make them—either of you." He looked from me to Mike.

Mike winked at me and addressed Jack. "Doesn't that conflict with your 'Don't hit shit' mantra?"

"Little known corollary, 'Shit happens when you're racing.'" Jack shrugged. "Just don't let it happen very often."

My stomach settled and breath came more easily. Some of the weight I'd felt pressing on me lifted.

"You're mellowing," Mike said.

"Think I'm being too easy on her?" Jack turned to me. "Am I?"

I fumbled, looked at my feet. Finally met Jack's eyes. "Maybe?"

"You'll be disappointed in yourself enough for both of us. Besides, folks outside the team will be harder on you. Least you'll know we've got your back." He looked from me to Mike. "You two square?"

"Sorry again, to everyone." I made a point of meeting Mike and Jack's eyes.

Mike pulled me off the couch for a hug. "Hell yes, we're square. Kate's my wingman."

"I only helped get you a date once." I smiled and pushed him away. "Let me go change." I finished the bottle of water as I headed to the back room.

"It was a good date. And I've got other plans." Mike's voice carried as I closed the door behind me.

I sank down on the bed, feeling like a fraud for going out to race and returning without the car. The buzz of race engines outside taunted me. I clenched both hands into fists, wanting to punch something. The need to be out there, for the wreck never to have happened, was a physical ache in my chest. My frustration brought tears to my eyes.

No hitting, Kate, and no crying. Male drivers don't cry, do they? Don't give anyone the idea a female is too emotional or weak for this job. Any crying happens at home, not at the track, no matter how upset you are.

I sat up straight and took three slow, deep breaths, staring myself down in the mirror inside the closet door. Small female, strong enough for racing and handling this fallout. Shoulder-length black hair in a ponytail to go under a fireproof hood and helmet. Fair skin, now flushed with frustration, shame, and disappointment. Blue eyes mirrored the same. Not a single injury to be seen. No infirmities. Only a pity party going on inside.

The positives. I wasn't hurt. Hopefully Miles wasn't—*no, don't think about him until you know he'll be OK.* Jack wasn't mad at me and wouldn't fire me. Mike didn't hate me. That left the crew, who worked three days perfecting the setup of the car to earn us prizes, bragging rights, championship points, and media exposure—though I'd gotten us plenty of the latter. My next step needed to be a round of apologies and thanks to our team mechanics and staff.

It's racing, Kate, not competitive knitting. Equipment gets broken, people make mistakes. It was my turn, and now I was getting over it. Besides, I was a damn good racecar driver.

I changed from my fireproof gear into jeans and a team polo shirt. I was closing up my duffle bag when I felt the front door of the motorhome slam shut and heard Stuart's voice, "We've heard from the hospital."

Chapter Four

I banged the bedroom door open in my haste to reach the front room, where Stuart and Tom stood.

"Well?" I demanded.

"He's OK," Stuart said. "Severe concussion and a broken collarbone. They'll monitor him a day or two to make sure there's no serious brain injury."

I swallowed. "The words 'brain injury' don't sound good."

"He's alive," Tom pointed out.

Stuart nodded. "And not in surgery for anything yet. They think it's a concussion, nothing more serious, and rest will fix that. Of course, it's a month or more out of the racecar, but he should make a full recovery."

I sat down in a kitchen chair, sorting through my emotions. Miles would be fine. Probably. I could be mad at him for his role in the wreck. A little. But he wouldn't race in NASCAR for a while, wouldn't win his third championship this season. I wondered how that sobbing woman in the paddock would react. Wondered how much worse the fan reaction might get. Being unpopular wouldn't get me fired, but it wouldn't help me attract sponsors either.

"About the media." Tom pulled up the chair facing mine.

I took a deep breath and smelled cookies baking. "Cookies? Now?"

"Never the wrong time for cookies," Mike put in from the couch.

"A touch of comfort," Aunt Tee said. "You only now smelled them?"

"I was preoccupied before." I squeezed my eyes closed, then looked at Tom. "Let's do it."

"Kate?" Stuart's expression softened as he studied me. "I'll talk to you later?"

"Sure. And thanks—" I broke off, choking up. Two deep breaths and I was back under control. "Thanks for before."

"Any time you need me, Kate." He exited the motorhome, and I wondered who else understood he meant more than his professional support.

Tom brandished a notepad and pen. "I'll do our usual release, and we'll make a statement about Miles. Then you should talk to the press waiting outside."

I was entering the acceptance stage of racing accident recovery. I'd felt denial and anger sitting in my wrecked car. Remorse I'd been working on since the medical center—and would continue to chew on. Blame was an optional stage, depending on the wreck. I hadn't dwelled long there, because the person I wanted to point the finger at exited the track on a stretcher…and I knew better. In my case, acceptance meant it was time to take on unappetizing responsibilities. I nodded at Tom. "I'm ready."

Twenty minutes later, after a quick call home to my grandparents—the only parents I'd ever known—to assure them I was fine, I stepped out of the motorhome with Mike and Tom. Tom went to placate and prep the reporters waiting at the rope barrier. Mike went with me to talk to our crew. Fortunately, our sister car, the number 29, was celebrating a best-ever finish of fourth in class, so the team was in good spirits. No one acted like my best friend, but no one was hostile either. Distributing Aunt Tee's chocolate chip cookies along with my apologies didn't hurt.

Then it was time for the press.

The crew from SportsGroup TV had run down the paddock to catch someone else, so I spoke with the Radio Le Mans reporter and a group of print journalists first. They asked the same questions I'd answered outside the medical center: what happened, how I felt about it, was I hurt, and how did this affect our team going into the last race of the season. I gave them a bare-bones explanation and the basic platitudes.

Then the SGTV team returned—a cameraman, a pit reporter I hadn't met because he'd recently moved to the ALMS from another series, and an assistant or junior reporter, a woman. She was six inches taller than my five-foot-four, curvy in her required SGTV firesuit, and a knockout blonde. Seeing her brought a smile to my face.

"Juliana Parker?"

"Kate Reilly! There you are!" Her voice was halfway to a squeal as she threw her arms around me.

I laughed and hugged her. "Where have you been the last few years?"

She pulled back and smoothed a stray lock of hair into place. "Representing Alabama, doing broadcast news, and working my way to this gig. But look at you!"

The pit reporter with her cleared his throat.

I turned to him. "Sorry. I'm Kate Reilly."

"Felix Simon." He clasped my outstretched hand like a man fifty years his senior. It was usually men my grandfather's age who shook as if afraid I'd be hurt by their strength. As if I didn't race cars for a living.

"Kate." Juliana touched my arm. "We'll catch up later."

"Tonight at Siebkens Tavern?"

"Perfect." She moved back, out of the camera's angle.

At a nod from the cameraman, Felix stepped close, smiled at me, and started speaking. "I'm here in the Sandham Swift paddock talking with their young, rookie female driver—certainly a better looking driver than most teams have—Kate Reilly. Kate, what happened out there today?"

He tilted the microphone to me as I fought to keep a pleasant expression on my face. In two sentences, he'd reduced me to the level of perky high school cheerleader, undermining my talent and racing credentials with every syllable.

I squeezed a response through my clenched jaw. "Hi, Felix. What happened today was an unfortunate racing incident, compounded by rain and two drivers misjudging conditions and space on the track. I'm so disappointed for my team and also the LinkTime Corvette team." I stopped as Felix pulled the microphone away from me.

"A racing incident, Kate? How do you respond to those who have called it one hundred percent error on your part—one you shouldn't have made? Or those who call you dangerous on the track?"

The glee lighting his eyes and face as he asked his awful questions disturbed me. I reminded myself to stay calm and professional.

"I still call it a racing incident. I may have misjudged the wetness of the track there, but I was well up on his car and had the inside line, so he could have left me more room, not crowded me so much. We're racecar drivers, and in the moment, we're going to push, regardless of the weather conditions."

I read the intention in Felix's eyes and grabbed the mic above his hand, keeping it close to my face as I went on. "Did I mean to do it? No. Is this single incident—which is all I've had this year, aside from a couple solo trips into gravel—enough to label me dangerous? I don't think so."

Felix looked less happy when I released the mic than before I started—which didn't fit with the stories I'd heard of him being a great guy.

Especially when his smile resembled an animal baring teeth at its prey. "And how do you assess your chances at the next and last race on the schedule, Petit Le Mans, as well as in the championship?"

"I think we're still in with a fighting chance for the top three. The team's still looking good—"

A new voice cut through whatever response I might have made. A man shoved close to me against the rope line. He was in his forties, of medium height, build, and Southern drawl, remarkable only for his red face and overabundance of outrage.

"Did I hear right? You think Miles *crowded* you? *His* fault? How dare you!"

Tom got in between us, offering a hand. "I'm Tom Albright, and you are?"

"Don't matter. She better understand correctly." The red-faced man hadn't taken his eyes off me. "Miles did nothing to you. You plain ran him off the road!"

"It does matter." Tom spoke firmly. "You know who we are. Who are you?"

He looked at Tom. "Nash Rawlings, president of the Miles Hanson fan club."

That explained a lot.

"Mr. Rawlings," I began.

"Bitch!"

Oops.

Rawlings leaned around Tom, shouting at me. "You got no right to talk about someone with more talent in his pinky toe than you got in your whole body. No right! You drive so bad you can't stay on the track by yourself—so you ran into him. And hurt him. They should take away your driver's license."

It wasn't the time to point out my driver's license only worked on the street. I had a racing license to race cars.

"I think we're done here." Tom again stepped between us.

But Nash Rawlings kept ranting. "Why do they let you damn girls drive? You're just decorations—" he looked me up and down "—you ain't even good looking. Shouldn't be allowed on the track. You weren't there, more *real* racers could compete!"

I froze. Not letting that one go, no sirree, Bob.

I pushed Tom aside. "Mr. Rawlings. I don't know what century or backwater town you're from, but in case you haven't noticed, women—*women and girls*—have been racing and winning for decades. If you want to talk about decorations, look at the pretty-boy backmarkers who have seats because they sell products well. I have *earned* my way here, and I am tired of being treated as second-class in the racing world because I don't have the right equipment between my legs—and I'm not talking about the car.

"I am a *racecar driver,* and I know sometimes I get hurt. Your favorite driver got hurt today because we both tried to be in the same place at the same time—he *did not* get hurt because I'm a woman. Now take your misogynistic, redneck views and get the hell out of my paddock!"

I flung my hand in a dramatic, sweeping gesture. Only then realizing the SGTV camera had captured every moment on tape.

Chapter Five

Two hours later I sat at a table in the main room of Siebkens Tavern with Tom, Mike, and my best friend, Holly Wilson, a petite, polished redhead from Tennessee. A dozen members of the Sandham Swift team and crew were elbow-to-elbow in the crowded room with at least a hundred other members or fans of the racing world.

My head hurt. "Please tell me I didn't really say 'redneck.' Tell me I didn't lose my temper at a fan for the first time ever."

"You sure did." Mike smacked his lips as he polished off his second Leinenkugel lager.

Tom nodded. "It was quite a speech. As your team publicity guy, I have to say it was ill-advised."

I dropped my head into my hands and groaned.

"But as your friend," Tom went on, "your response was magnificent."

I looked up in surprise. "Really?"

"I have to agree, sugar," Holly said. "It was a moment of glory. I wish I'd been there to see it, though at least I've caught it on the news three times—make that four." She pointed a red-tipped finger to a television mounted above the bar. "In some ways it's a feminist battle cry. In other ways…you called him a redneck."

"I didn't, exactly." I caught her look. "Maybe no one will notice."

To ignore their pitying expressions, I studied the history around us. "Siebkens" referred to the Siebkens Inn, where I was staying that weekend, a collection of white, two-story clapboard buildings, originally built in the early 1900s and clustered together on a single, large block. But Siebkens also referred to the Tavern, properly the Stop-Inn Tavern, famous as the best bar on the racing circuit.

Drivers and fans had come to Elkhart Lake, Wisconsin, since the 1950s for great motor racing, and they'd been showing up to Siebkens every bit as long. Newer, trendier hotels and resorts appeared over the years, but the racing world had never deserted Siebkens and its Tavern. Everyone in racing had been to the bar at least once to meet friends, order a pub meal, and down a beer or two—and everyone at a race weekend showed up there, too.

The Tavern's décor bore witness to its colorful history. The walls, ceiling, and pillars were plastered with bumper stickers, flags, signs, and any other racing-related item that could be stuck or pinned. I liked to sit where I could see the "Sandham Swift Racing" sticker Mike and I had posted and signed the previous year.

But this time I was glad to be sitting with my back to the Tavern's north wall, near the steps leading to the screened porch, able to watch the room. The reception I'd received so far from the racing world was mixed. Some people were openly supportive, such as the other drivers and crew from Sandham Swift and my friends sitting with me. Two or three individuals, including a prototypically East Coast preppy guy, were outright angry. If looks could kill, I'd be bleeding on the floor of a thousand wounds. I tried to ignore those.

Much of the response was cautious, with the most speculative looks coming from four guys standing together: Felix Simon, two print journalists, and Scott Brooklyn, who reported for SPEED when he couldn't drum up a driving gig. The public might think I'd wrecked Miles on purpose, ignoring or not knowing wrecking was the last thing a racer set out to do. But other drivers and teams in the ALMS—even the media—would know I didn't crash deliberately. Instead, they'd be asking themselves if

I was good enough. If I'd been unable to handle the pressure, the weather, and the celebrity driver. Was this a one-time thing, or had Kate choked?

I'd finally seen a replay of the accident, which showed Miles and me in our cars, ricocheting like pinballs between the concrete walls of the Kink, racking up damage instead of high score. The video confirmed my growing suspicion, and race control's determination, that Miles and I shared fault for pushing too much in the wrong conditions. I knew I hadn't lost my nerve or faltered under pressure. But only time and more racing would convince my peers.

A gust of warm air reached our table, bringing with it hints of a humid summer night. Somewhere on the other side of a score of bodies, I heard the screen door leading to the Tavern's lawn and patio slam shut.

"Kate!"

I snapped out of my daze at the sound and sight of Juliana in front of me.

"Jules." I jumped up to hug her.

The woman with Juliana flashed a large diamond wedding ring set as she pushed her honey-blonde hair behind her ears. Her face was familiar, but it wasn't until her smile revealed the single dimple in her left cheek that I recognized Ellie, or Helen, our friend and former racing competitor.

"Ellie Grayson, how are you?" We hugged each other.

"It's Prescott now, and I'm great. No need to ask how you are. Our Kate!" She held me at arms' length and reached one hand out to Juliana. "Can you believe, the three of us together again? Almost like old times."

I felt the tightness of regret in my chest. "It's been so long."

Juliana looked from me to Ellie. "Seven years."

We'd been an unlikely trio. At twenty-two, Ellie had been the mature and responsible one, innately kind, moving through the world secure in herself and confident in her actions and choices. Juliana, at twenty, was the stop-traffic gorgeous one—adept, controlled, racecar-driver Barbie, with a generous heart and fierce loyalty under the perfect exterior. I'd been the eighteen-year-old tomboy, a serious, focused, and emotional perfectionist. I studied them now. Seven years didn't seem to have changed us much.

The only females racing in a Skip Barber Formula series, we'd been forced together more by circumstance than choice. But we quickly became friends as we grumbled to each other about the lack of facilities for females at racetracks, as well as how the boys who were our competition treated us. By the end of the season, we traveled in a pack to and during race weekends and confided every slight, every racing tip, and any bit of gossip to each other. At the championship banquet, we swore undying friendship and vowed to keep in touch as the season ended.

Our resolve lasted only a couple months, until Ellie bowed to the pressures of her family to focus more on college than racing, I took the racing seat both Juliana and I had been vying for, and Juliana went off to compete in beauty pageants. I'd always been sorry about how our friendship ended.

I squeezed their hands before turning to introduce them to Holly, Tom, and Mike, who exchanged greetings and then left. Mike and Tom went to talk to friends a few tables away, and Holly left for dinner with Western Racing, the team she worked for as hospitality director. It felt almost like old times as Juliana, Ellie, and I sat down together—though in our past life we'd never done so over a clutter of empty beer bottles in a bar.

"I can't believe we're all here." I couldn't stop smiling. "What have you been doing?"

Ellie gestured to Juliana, who spoke first. "Y'all know I'd always done both pageants and racing? With mama pushing on me, I started taking off in the pageant world and spent a year as Miss Alabama."

"How did I not know that?" I gasped.

Juliana waved it off. "The racing world doesn't pay much attention to pageants, though I did sing the national anthem at a Talladega NASCAR race that year. I made the top ten in Miss America—almost won the talent and congeniality portions. I still say that girl who won congeniality was a faker."

Ellie's eyes twinkled, and I burst out laughing.

"She was!" Juliana insisted.

Ellie covered Juliana's hand with hers. "And now you're working for SGTV?"

"That's right. I did a lot of on-camera work as Miss Alabama, and I got hired as a features reporter for a local station in Mobile. Then a network affiliate, then a bigger market, another bigger market. I was in Dallas for the last three years, until I went knocking on SportsGroup's door three months ago."

"Really?" I wouldn't have called that a step up.

"I wanted to get back to the racing world," Juliana said. "Their mix of racing and other sports coverage suits me. They've had me jumping around, covering different kinds of events, but I'm convincing them I belong in sportscar racing—and in the booth, not only in the pits."

I'd forgotten how beautiful Juliana was. Looking at her polish and poise, it was easy to see her as a star in broadcast media. "I'm so glad you're back in racing, Jules."

"It wasn't the way I meant to do it—thought I'd get here in that racecar you took from me." I caught my breath as she wagged a finger my direction, though she was smiling. "But I'm here. If I learned anything from mama, it was determination."

"Determined" didn't begin to cover Juliana's mother. "Demanding, iron-willed, and intolerant of mistakes" might.

Ellie must have remembered her also, because her smile was grim. "How is your mother, Juliana?"

"She passed on early this year. It's been a difficult time."

Ellie and I both offered sympathy, and after a respectful pause, I turned to Ellie. "And you, Mrs. Prescott? What have you been doing with yourself?"

Ellie glowed with happiness. "For the past six years, I've worked part-time for a company that drives pace and safety cars for the IndyCar series, as well as being an instructor for a couple racing schools. My husband Ethan is the national sales manager for Dunlop Tires—"

"I met him last week," Juliana explained. "That's how Ellie found us again."

"We thought we'd surprise you this weekend, Kate. Ethan and I have been married four years now. Two years ago we had twins, Samuel and Chloe." Ellie reached for her phone and showed us a photo of two adorable toddlers.

She went on. "I'm here this weekend for a couple appointments and because the ALMS is interested in the program my group provides for IndyCar. Wouldn't it be fun if we were all back together next year?"

Juliana nodded and turned to me. "There's little need to ask how and what you've been doing, Kate. Setting the racing world on fire."

"I'd hardly call it that," I protested. "Especially after I lost my temper today."

"You've always worried too much, Kate," Ellie soothed. "Everyone will understand you're a good person."

I wanted to feel her optimism. I turned to Juliana. "Tell us about the cities you've worked in and what it's really like in broadcasting."

As Juliana shared stories of newsroom antics and described her favorite neighborhoods across the country, Stuart joined us, a beer bottle in one hand, a drink in the other.

"Kate. Ladies." He nodded to them as he set the glass in front of me, saying, "Orange juice, hold the vodka." He knew I preferred water or juice to alcohol after a race—even an aborted race like this—to get my body rehydrated. His appearance, and the beverage, meant at least one American Le Mans Series official wasn't mad at me for ruining Miles' foray into sportscar racing.

I performed the introductions, though it turned out Stuart and Ellie already knew each other. Juliana batted her eyelashes, and like every male I ever saw, Stuart responded with a smile. "Can I get either of you ladies something from the bar?"

"Some orange juice, like Kate," Ellie said. "If you wouldn't mind."

I stopped him. "Ellie can take this one, if that's all right with her. I've had three already, and I'm feeling waterlogged." At Ellie's nod, I excused myself to the bathroom.

As I fought my way back to the table through the crowd, the SPEED journalist jostled me on his way out the door. I couldn't tell if his roughness was deliberate or a function of the packed room, but I decided to ignore it. I heard Gramps' voice in my head, "Don't go borrowing trouble."

Juliana sat alone at our table. I looked around to see Stuart talking to someone at the bar, but no sign of Ellie. "They left you by yourself? I'm sorry, Juliana."

"Not to worry. Stuart apologized but was pulled away by some people from Audi corporate headquarters. And then Ellie got a call from her kids—her husband, I suppose—so she stepped outside."

"Still, it wasn't nice of us to leave you. You don't have any headache medicine, do you, Jules? Or ibuprofen?"

"Nothing with me, sorry." She held up a stylish leather bag barely large enough for money and a cell phone, then stood as Ellie returned. "I was only waiting for you both to come back so I could say goodbye."

We exchanged e-mail addresses, phone numbers, and hugs, vowing to keep in touch. Juliana indicated she'd be working the pits for SGTV at the last race of the season. Ellie wouldn't be there, but we knew we'd see her the next year at race weekends the ALMS shared with IndyCar.

"Or maybe at all of the ALMS races," Ellie said, after Juliana left.

"Something you want to share?"

She smiled, flashing her dimple again. "Not yet, but I'll let you know."

Stuart returned a minute later and pulled up a chair next to me. Tom also drifted over, bringing with him a friend named Buddy who drove for a GT Porsche team.

I rubbed my forehead. "I need to hunt down some painkillers, if you all will save my seat here for a few minutes. Don't go anywhere. I'll be right back."

Stuart pulled my chair back for me, and Ellie waved as I headed for the door.

Twenty minutes later, I knelt behind the Tavern next to her dead body.

Chapter Six

"What do you mean, 'What did I do?'" Stuart demanded. "How could you say that?"

"You're here—it slipped out." I tried to swallow past the lump in my throat. "Are you sure she's…"

I reached for Ellie's arm, but Stuart stopped me.

"She's gone, Kate." His voice broke in a rare show of emotion. "I've been doing CPR for five minutes, but I can't get a pulse."

"Shouldn't we keep trying? Call paramedics?"

"I called nine-one-one." He slumped, hands on his knees. "She's been gone from the Tavern almost as long as you have."

My brain felt numb. "She—but—what are you doing out here?"

Stuart put a hand on my shoulder, to support us both, I suspected, and rubbed the other over his face. "Andy, one of the Michelin tire reps, joined us right after you left. Ellie started looking pale, nauseous maybe. She said she wanted some air, she'd be right back. When Andy left a few minutes later, I realized she was still gone, so I came outside to see if she was OK. I thought maybe she was in her car."

I couldn't stop looking at her. Willing her to breathe. But her lively green eyes, which had recently beamed with pride and happiness, were dull. The vibrant friend I'd spoken with only a few minutes ago was gone. I heard sirens in the distance, and I felt tears roll down my face. The only other dead person I'd ever seen was Wade Becker last year. This was harder. This was a friend.

"Kate."

I saw tears in Stuart's eyes also. He stood and helped me to my feet, folding me into his arms. I sagged against him, my breath hitching in my chest.

The sirens got louder. I stepped away and took a deep breath, smelling the moist, earthy air laced with the stink of the trash in the bins behind me. *Things shouldn't seem so normal if a friend is dead.* I focused on the details, avoiding the grief. Ellie lay on her back on a mixture of grass and gravel in an area the size of a parking space between the building and a dark sedan at the curb. Beyond her head was a rolling mini-dumpster with a large, white van parked on the other side of it, nose up to the Inn.

Except for her lack of movement and the hint of anguish I imagined in her expression, she looked the same as in the Tavern. I felt the lump rising in my throat again, and I concentrated on her clothing. Her mint-green silk blouse was tucked into her gray trousers and secured by a thin black belt. Both black flats were on her feet, though the shoe had popped off her right heel and hung twisted on the toes of that foot. Something was off, but I couldn't place what. I saw no wounds, no blood. No sign of life.

I stifled a sob. "Ellie, I'm so sorry. You were loved." I turned around as the sirens grew deafening, then quieted. Two police cars and an ambulance turned the corner.

The following minutes blurred together in a whirl of flashing lights and questions from men in different uniforms. The paramedics arrived and went away again. Police secured the area. The low murmur of a crowd gathered in the fire lane penetrated my daze, and I watched one of the cops move to keep spectators away. Stuart and I were separated to speak to different officers while the police chief and coroner were summoned.

Officer Michaels was tall, blond, handsome, and not above using his considerable charms to get answers to his questions. He expressed his sympathies as he took my statement about the events I'd been part of and witnessed. Though I had nothing to hide, I felt nervous talking to him. I'd been blameless the last time a dead body was concerned, and I ended up chewed up and spit out by the rumor mill. *Get hold of yourself, Kate. There's no blame here, just a sad loss.*

My eyes filled again. Officer Handsome whipped a pack of tissues from his back pocket and seemed to read my mind. "You've had a busy day, haven't you, Ms. Reilly?"

I blinked up at him. He was most of a foot taller than me, though he was doing his best to slump, ducking his head to be less intimidating.

He smiled. "I saw you had an accident today, and then a… verbal altercation with someone?"

And now I'd found a friend dead. A friend who was one of the good people on the planet, whose generous spirit hadn't changed over the years we hadn't seen each other. I remembered photos she'd shown us of her husband and children, and my heart broke. I couldn't stop the tears.

With an arm around my shoulders, the officer guided me to a folding chair at the corner of the building. We were far enough from the line of caution tape strung across the end of the fire lane that the dozen people gathered there couldn't hear us. As I tried to stop crying and breathe, I noticed Tom was part of that group, keeping an eye on me. I blew my nose.

"What else do you need to know, Officer? Yes, it's been a rough day." I rubbed my sore wrist.

He glanced at his colleague—a shorter, rounder, balding man, talking with Stuart on the other side of the police cruiser in the street—then squatted in front of me, elbows on knees. He looked at his notebook. "What is your relationship to Mr. Telarday?"

I hated answering that question under normal circumstances. "We're dating. I drive in the ALMS. He works for the Series."

"ALMS, American Le Mans Series?"

I nodded.

"Is that a conflict of interest?"

"He doesn't make race decisions, and he stays out of decisions about marketing that would involve me—what does this have to do with Ellie?"

"You never know what might be relevant."

"How did she die?"

He shook his head before I finished the question. "We don't know. Did she have any medical conditions or allergies?"

"She didn't seven years ago." I swallowed hard and looked around at tall trees to stop thoughts of Ellie's dying moments.

"You were with her in the Tavern. Did she have a purse with her? A cell phone?"

That's what was missing, her handbag. "A small, black, leather satchel. I think she'd hooked it over her chair—at a table against the far wall, near the bar. A phone in a green case. She showed us photos of her kids." The thought of them sent me reaching for tissue again.

He gestured to an officer standing nearby and explained what to look for inside the Tavern.

"Did you see her eat or drink anything?"

"No, but I left a few minutes earlier to get some headache medicine. Stuart bought a juice for me that I gave to her, but I don't know if she drank it."

After a few more questions, Officer Michaels was done with me, except for asking when I planned to leave town.

"Tomorrow afternoon, after a brunch meeting."

"Please check in with us after your meeting in case we need to have you talk to someone else."

"Someone else?" I held up a hand to stop him from responding, as logic finally broke through the fog in my brain. "You think this is murder?"

He didn't comment, only verified he had my cell number correct and released me to Tom, who was ready with a hug. Stuart's face showed relief as he looked my direction.

Tom and I cut through the dozen people standing at the perimeter of the scene watching the police activity—a mix of teams and fans who'd spilled out of the Tavern—and I ignored questions directed my way. We went down the lane and around the corner to the tavern green and had settled at a table when a man I didn't recognize approached.

Tom moved to intercept him. "I'm sorry, we're not talking to press right now."

Of course, the media. I was surprised there weren't video cameras recording the activity, though thinking back, not all the bright lights and camera flashes had come from police devices.

"I'm not press, just a fan of Kate's. I'm sorry to interrupt, but I'm not sure when I'll have the chance. I wanted to ask her to sign something."

"This isn't a good time. If you'll send—"

"Tom, it's OK." I stood up and stepped around him, addressing the fan, a skinny guy with pasty white skin, a prominent Adam's apple, and dark blond hair in a close-cropped Caesar cut—the style George Clooney revived in the nineties. "I'll sign it if you'll excuse us after that. What is it you have?" I didn't see a book or a card in his hand, but he did have a canvas bag.

"Thanks. It's so great to meet you." He shoved a hand at me, which I shook. "It's a piece of your car's bodywork I picked up in the Kink today."

Tom carefully kept any reaction from his face as he pulled two permanent markers out of his pocket and handed me the silver one.

"Always prepared, Tom, thanks." I murmured. Then to the fan. "Where should I sign, and do you want me to sign it to you?"

He swallowed audibly. "Yes, please, to George. That's me, George Ryan. Anywhere is fine."

He helped me steady the one-foot-by-two-foot chunk of carbon-fiber—given the strip of metal along one finished edge, it came from a wheelwell. I signed "To George, stay out of the walls! Kate Reilly" and thought this had been the strangest day of my life.

George left, with head-bobbing gratitude, assurances he was my biggest fan, and apologies again for interrupting us. Tom and I sat down at the picnic table, and I put my head in my hands.

"That was weird," Tom said.

I laughed, quick huffs of breath that became gasps as I started crying again. I got myself under control quickly this time. "Will this day ever end?"

"And here's the real cavalry—I mean, the media." Tom pointed to a van disgorging camera crew and reporters on the main street in front of the Tavern.

"I can't face that now, Tom. Can't do it."

"It might be casier now than—" he saw my face. "Later. No worries."

"Thanks."

"What's your schedule tomorrow?"

I had to concentrate. "I have brunch with—a distant relation." The meal and meeting was with my father, but Tom didn't know the full story and I didn't feel like explaining I had met my father, James Hightower Reilly III, for the first time two years ago and had only been willing to talk with him for more than a minute during the past six months. Brunch the next day was a milestone in our relationship. I didn't feel equal to the task, but I'd rescheduled twice already and I couldn't do so again.

I went on. "The cops told me to check in before leaving town. Holly and I are driving to her place in Nashville for a couple days before heading to Atlanta."

"Can we talk tomorrow? I'm driving home then also, but it might be good to have a statement ready about this. I can write it up for you tonight." As the media, PR, and computer guy for Sandham Swift Racing, Tom didn't specifically work for me, but he'd send out any releases I needed.

"I'll call you after I check in with the police. At this rate, I'll be lucky to get out of here by next weekend."

I looked up and saw Stuart headed my way, past reporters surging toward him and shouting questions.

Tom looked from me to Stuart to the reporters. "I'll head them off so you guys can get out of here. Call me in the morning."

"I owe you one."

As Stuart reached me, I grabbed his hand. "Let's go, Tom will buy us time." We made it to my room on the first floor of the Inn overlooking the pool, and I broke down. He held me for many hours while I grieved.

Chapter Seven

I went for a short, easy run the next morning to loosen stiff muscles from the accident and to clear my head, which felt achy and thick from my crying bout the night before. I was still sad, but the jog through town and around the lake buoyed my spirits. Until I checked my e-mail.

The account I used for correspondence with the public, fed by a contact form on my website, had 897 unread messages. I assumed the number was due to spam, until I read subject lines and opened messages at random to find them full of vitriol about wrecking Miles and insulting his fans. One called me "lesbian devil-spawn," and another, a "NASCAR-hating Nazi." I stopped reading, sick to my stomach.

In the account I used for personal correspondence I found an e-mail from Tom telling me the police questioned everyone at the Tavern the night before, collected every container of food or drink from four different tables, and took copies of digital photos from any phone or camera they could find. Tom attached the photos he'd taken of Juliana, Ellie, and me, but I couldn't face opening them.

Another e-mail from Tom contained a press release about Ellie, and I responded by thanking him, but asking him to hold it, since the media hadn't mentioned me yet in that story. I also sent a note to Holly explaining what happened the night before and how Ellie's death, plus my needing to talk to the police, might affect our plan to hit the road that afternoon.

I left my hotel room to meet my father for our first meal together, hoping I was done with surprises for the day. For the month. I walked down the fire lane to the edge of Siebkens that faced Elkhart Lake feeling a familiar mix of curiosity, pleasure, and dread as I thought about James Hightower Reilly III.

After my mother died in the hospital two days after my birth, my maternal grandparents raised me to believe my father's family had "washed their hands of me," to quote my grandmother. My father proved my understanding wrong last year, which made my grandparents' house less a sanctuary and more a battleground. Grandmother still refused to discuss the topic, leaving me unsettled.

My father had overcome my initial desire to keep him at arm's length with persistence and understanding. I wasn't ready to fall into his embrace, but I liked the man, maybe cared about him. Something about him tugged at me.

I walked into Otto's Restaurant at the Osthoff Resort, a large complex adjacent to Siebkens, and once again experienced a shock of recognition. I'd gotten my coloring from my father, quintessential "black Irish," along with his average height and nose.

"Katherine—Kate." He approached, hand outstretched, and leaned in to kiss my cheek. That was new.

"Good morning, James." Using his first name was as far as I'd gotten. I wasn't ready for "Father," and "Dad" wouldn't ever happen.

"You're feeling no ill effects from the accident?"

"Some stiffness. Nothing major."

He spoke again after we were seated and perusing the menus. "I understand there was some excitement at the Tavern last night as well?"

"It wasn't exciting. I was there."

"I'm sorry." His face fell, and he leaned forward. "I didn't hear what happened, only that police were called."

I outlined the events in as few words as possible, and he exhaled through pursed lips. "I apologize for sounding insensitive. I had no idea. And I'm so sorry for you, Kate." His hand fluttered in the air before patting mine on the table.

Smooth corporate executive that James was, he turned the conversation to other topics, including my plans for the coming off-season and next year. I could only tell him I'd have big news in a week.

He raised his eyebrows, but didn't press the issue. "You'll go home to New Mexico for a time? Do you have many close family members on your mother's side?"

"Not really." I paused as the waiter delivered our meals. "It's strange you don't know this."

"Your mother and I fell in love at university and married in the courthouse, thousands of miles from her family. I knew the basics about her—she was an only child—but not a lot of details. We never had a chance for me to meet her family."

I held up a hand to stop his story, my emotions too raw from Ellie's death to risk a discussion about my mother. "There are distant cousins, grandchildren of my grandmother's siblings, out in California. But we're not close."

"The lack of other family will become difficult, as your grandparents get older."

"Yes." I dug into my ham and Wisconsin-cheese omelet.

"You do have other family. Mine."

I set my fork down. "I should make our situation clear. My grandparents and I don't have other blood relations around Albuquerque. But we're part of a strong community. When I was a kid, my grandparents joined the local Unitarian church, and that's been our family for twenty years. Members of the church check in on my grandparents a couple times a week while I'm gone, and I have friends my age as well as surrogate parents I'm in contact with. I have a different kind of family."

"Understood." He took a bite of his pancakes. "You have other blood relations. Maybe some day you will consider them family."

I started to speak, but he shook his head. "Maybe you won't ever see us as family. We'll take it as it comes."

We let the topic lie for a minute while we ate. Then I sighed, admitting curiosity. "Tell me about them."

"My wife is Amelia. I met her after I finished college—I'd returned to Boston University for my final year after your mother." He cleared his throat. "She's a lawyer."

"In a big Boston firm?"

"No. She worked part time while our kids were young, but she's been in the non-profit world, primarily representing abused women and children, often donating her time. It's her crusade."

Damn it, I didn't want to like the woman. "And you have children?"

"Two, a boy and a girl. Eddie is the oldest—four years younger than you. He just turned twenty-one, and he's in his last year at Boston University. Lara is nineteen and in her second year at Swarthmore College."

"You didn't make Eddie 'James Hightower Reilly the Fourth'?"

He smiled. "Three was enough. I felt he should find his own identity, though in every other way he's a carbon copy of us—a bank and finance man already. When he was five, he announced he'd run the family business, and he's never wavered."

Half-siblings. Family with generations of heritage and stories. Foreign concepts. Better to change the subject. "Tell me about the banking business."

As the waiter cleared empty plates and topped off our coffee, my father explained how his ancestor three or four "greats" back founded a bank in Massachusetts, which survived market ups and downs, expanded nationally, and prospered. It was no longer privately owned, but my father still sat on the board and held an executive role. It was a fluke that another board member, entranced by the number of "eyeballs on racing," proposed corporate sponsorship of automobile racing eight years prior— leading to my father's path crossing mine.

My father was paying the check, at his insistence, when he dropped a bomb that had "family" written all over it. "The bank will be hosting an invitation-only party the night before Petit Le Mans, and I hope you'll attend. All of the owners and corporate representatives will be there, as well as Series staff, many drivers, VIPs."

I made a non-committal noise as he lit the fuse. "As well as my wife and children. Plus other family members who work for the bank, uncles and cousins and such."

Jitters hit my stomach. "Do they even know about me?"

"They know about you. Amelia and the kids are eager to meet you."

My heart pounded. *This is ridiculous. I don't need this extra stress in my life.*

He looked hesitant. "I need to make you aware of something beforehand. It's not entirely relevant, but I don't want you to misunderstand or be caught unaware."

I stiffened, sure I didn't want to hear what he had to say.

"Even if it pushes you away again." He sighed. "My father put you in the family trust, which no one knew until his death early last year. There is some…consternation in other branches of the family about you—do you have a legitimate claim, who are you, and so on." For a moment he looked angry. "They're blowing hot air. Legally, it was my father's choice, and they can't change the trust. None of us can. I hope the family will have more class than to engage you directly about it, but I felt you should know."

"I'm in the will? I have an inheritance?" When he nodded, I continued. "I don't want it, so take me out. Problem solved."

He rubbed his chin and waved away the waiter offering more coffee. "That's not how it works. You can keep the money or give it away, but you can't remove yourself from the trust."

"Then tell whoever's cranky about it I don't want it. I'll give it back."

"Kate, I hope someday you might feel part of the family. That you might…" He paused and watched me.

I focused on refolding my napkin and aligning my coffee cup and water glass on the table, trying to mask my panic.

He wasn't fooled. "Never mind. The question will only come up after I'm gone—which will be many years, God willing. If anyone mentions it, you can explain your stance. But know I only have hopes of you, not expectations. Please."

I gave him a grudging nod, annoyed with myself for acting like a surly child, but uncomfortable with what he offered. *My head tells me to push him away. But my gut feels a connection. I'm fighting my upbringing. Fighting my grandparents.*

He put away the reading glasses he'd used for the bill. "I'd appreciate it if you'd attend the party. I know it might be stressful, but a brief social situation could be an easier environment for a first meeting. Please consider it?"

I nodded again. As we left the restaurant, I tried to explain. "I know I must seem ungrateful, but I'm used to my life. This is a big change. I don't know if I can give you what you want from me, and I won't insult you by pretending to feel something I don't."

I didn't add I wanted to run screaming from the thought of his established, extended family, because he wouldn't understand why. I wasn't sure I understood, myself.

Chapter Eight

I walked back to my room at Siebkens with one more weighty matter on my mind. When I checked in with the police, I discovered they wanted to talk to me at the station that afternoon, which meant Holly and I weren't leaving Wisconsin that day. After making arrangements with the Inn to keep my room, I called Holly to apologize.

"They've got a spa at the Osthoff, don't they?" A rhetorical question. "I'll be fine," she'd continued. "I'm worried about you and Stuart."

"Stuart?" I hadn't spoken with him yet.

"I talked to him earlier. He's been at the police station since ten this morning."

I looked at my watch. Noon. "I've got a bad feeling about this."

She sighed down the phone line. "Sugar, you've got some bad juju."

Didn't I know it.

We agreed to meet for dinner, and she told me to bring Stuart if I could "spring him from the pokey." I tried to find that funny.

I never saw him in the four hours I spent at the police station answering questions on two specific topics: what I knew about Ellie, which was precious little and a decade old, and what and who I'd seen in the Tavern. I'd given the same information to Officer Michaels the night before, but this time I talked to a

Sheboygan County Sherriff from the Criminal Investigations division. I had to ask Lieutenant Rich Young point-blank about Ellie's death before he admitted they weren't sure it was natural.

"That's…disappointing," I sighed.

If he'd had antennae, they'd have quivered. "Only 'disappointing?'"

"Look, when you wanted me to talk to you again, I expected this. And given my life has run to chaos in the last twenty-four hours, I'm numb to shocks."

The sheriff reminded me of my father, short for a man, dark haired, slight build, and peering at written material through reading glasses. "Yes, you were in an accident in the race yesterday?"

"Then I made an ass of myself on national television. Then I reconnected with two good friends from my youth and found one of them dead an hour later. By this morning, most of the NASCAR community has e-mailed me to say they hate me. I've got long-lost family trying to claim me—never mind, that's not relevant. Suffice to say, unless you plan to arrest me or Stuart Telarday, I'm shocked-out."

"Hmm."

"You don't, do you?"

"Not quite yet, but we appreciate your continued cooperation."

My insides churned. I'd have preferred a definite "no."

As the detective wrapped up, he confirmed what Tom told me. The police questioned everyone in the Tavern before allowing them to leave the night before—though it wasn't clear if anything there was related to Ellie's death. They'd also be contacting anyone they knew of who'd been in the Tavern earlier in the evening.

Back at my hotel room shortly before five, I arranged dinner via text message with Stuart, who'd left the police station only minutes before me. Then I sat on the side of my bed and stared at my phone. I'd made my apologies to the LinkTime Corvette team in person after the race, but I owed Miles Hanson a call—driver to driver, no teams, media, or assistants in the way.

I admitted to myself that I dreaded reaching out because I didn't know how he'd respond.

I cracked the knuckles on my free hand while I rang the number I'd gotten from his team. My heart was in my throat, which annoyed me. *He's simply another driver, and the accident was his fault, too.* I slumped in relief when voicemail picked up.

"Hi, Miles, it's Kate Reilly. I, uh, wanted to call and see how you were doing, and apologize for my part in this. Seemed to me like a racing incident—like we both should have known better in the rain, right? Anyway, I hope you're healing well, and I'm really sorry to hear you're going to be out of your Cup car for a couple weeks. Take care."

That duty done, a little more weight dropped off my shoulders.

Zeke Andrews, my long-time friend, surrogate big-brother, and racing mentor, was the next person I dialed. He'd messaged me earlier in the day wondering if I was free for lunch and saying he'd seen me the night before at Siebkens talking to the police. I reached him waiting for a plane at the Milwaukee airport and explained the situation.

"At least I'm not a murder suspect this time around," I assured him. *I hoped.*

"I should hope not. I'm sorry we couldn't grab lunch, since Rosalie's with me."

"I can't believe I missed her." I hadn't seen Zeke's wife in three years.

"She was only around last night, but you can see her at Petit."

I was surprised. I'd never seen Rosalie at the races. "I thought she hated crowds."

"So did I." He didn't elaborate because he was called to board. We agreed to talk later in the week.

While I was in an explaining mood, I called my grandparents. They'd caught the news item about a death in Elkhart Lake after the race, but they hadn't realized "Helen Prescott" was the Ellie Grayson we'd all known.

"That poor girl," Gramps muttered. "Vivien, you remember little Ellie?"

I heard Grandmother saying indistinguishable words in the background.

"I know she was an adult by then, but they were all little to us. Besides, she was the sunniest little thing."

"Gramps." I reclaimed his attention. "She was taller than you."

"You know what I mean, Katie. How are you taking her loss? I don't remember you seeing her recently. Did you keep in touch?"

"I hadn't seen her since we all went different directions. I was the only one who kept racing. I'm sad we won't have a chance to be friends again. Sorry for what could have been."

"Well, now, that's life you're talking about. You keep your head up, Katie. Don't let those turkeys get you down." Gramps' parting shot made me smile.

I had enough time to shower before meeting Holly and Stuart at the Siebkens restaurant on the other side of the green from the Tavern. The place was deserted with all the racegoers gone home, and we sat in their screened-porch room with a bottle of wine. Stuart and I held hands under the table, while Holly pretended not to notice.

After twenty minutes of comparing notes on the questions Stuart and I were asked by the sheriff and local police, we agreed we had no idea what happened and put the topic away for the rest of the meal. The next most interesting subject, at least to Holly, was my wreck. I hadn't seen the news since I discovered the avalanche of e-mails. According to her, I'd missed a number of developments.

"Tell me." I drained the wine in my glass and filled up again.

"Racing news sites had articles this morning," she said. "Race reports, covering the wreck, Miles' injuries, and your rant at that stupid fan."

"That's not so bad." Stuart squeezed my hand.

I watched Holly's face. "There's more."

Her red, corkscrew curls bounced as she nodded. "The racing sites did a follow-up interview with Nash Rawlings, adding the information they'd gotten from Miles' camp that he'll be out of his car for four to six NASCAR Cup races."

I covered my eyes.

"That means no championship this year, which everyone, especially Rawlings, blames you for." She tapped a fingernail on her wine glass. "The racing sites are full of Miles' lost championship hopes, and the major networks are picking up the fan story now."

"What do you mean, the fan story?" I glanced at Stuart, who shrugged.

"From the non-racing media's perspective," Holly explained, "the story is an individual who's so fanatical about his hero he'd get in your face, crying and ranting. Your story is the focal point for illustrating how far fans will go, along with coverage of the growing NASCAR fan community, hero worship, and so forth."

I blinked. "I'll go down in history as the instrument of destruction. Like Sterling Marlin tipping Dale Earnhardt into his fatal slide and pitchers giving up home runs to lose the World Series." I sighed. "Stuart, how much does the Series hate me?"

"No one hates you. Officially, the Series is disappointed in how Miles' participation in the race turned out. Personally, anyone who understands racing—who isn't blindly, emotionally attached to him—understands that this was a racing incident." He paused, softening his voice. "This will pass, Kate."

"There's another thing." Holly chewed on her lower lip. "Have you heard about Racing's Ringer?"

"Heard the name."

"I forgot, you're the queen of social media avoidance. Stuart, you know it?"

He nodded as a waiter arrived with our food. I wound pasta around my fork as Holly explained.

"It's a blog, started this past summer, with a fast-growing audience. An insider's perspective on racing. Anonymous. Loaded with gossip, innuendo, and rumor—and usually dead-on correct. Whoever's writing it is well-connected and can clearly get people to spill secrets for publication."

"But he's no bastion of journalistic objectivity," Stuart put in.

Holly nodded. "He's opinionated, even passionate about his likes and dislikes. Vicious sometimes, when he takes someone to task for poor behavior—which he likes to do. He's funny, unless you're in his crosshairs."

I looked at Holly. "The punchline?"

"He's going to town with the story of the wreck, the fan, and your 'redneck' comment." She grimaced. "He's being pretty nasty."

"How nasty is nasty?"

"He's calling you a no-talent, whiney crybaby and suggesting people who agree with him write letters to Jack telling him to fire you." She looked at Stuart quickly before delivering the final blow. "I'd say 'who cares?' except I checked with Jack, and he's already gotten three hundred and seventy-eight e-mails."

Chapter Nine

I'd lied to Lieutenant Young when I told him I couldn't be shocked again that day. Holly assured me Jack laughed the whole thing off, declaring he had zero intention of firing me. But the story shook me.

Stuart raised a glass. "Here's to a better week ahead."

"To Petit," said Holly.

I touched my glass to theirs. "To fewer people hating me tomorrow than today and yesterday."

We finished the meal talking about plans for the next week and a half—life would roll on, as much as I wanted to run away from it for a few days. Afterward, Holly and Stuart walked me back to my room, Holly loitering down the hall while Stuart kissed me goodnight. They headed back to their rooms at the Osthoff, and I went inside and sat down on the bed. I'd held bewilderment and distress at bay throughout dinner, but now I felt adrift, unfocused. Disheartened.

I was mystified at how my life—personal and professional—had gone from business-as-usual to a minefield in the space of two days. I might despise myself for the weakness, but I was emotionally overwhelmed. I caught myself repeatedly trying to crack the knuckles on both hands and sat on my fingers to keep them still.

On the positive side, I knew I wanted to be racing and I was good at it. As far as I knew, I still had a job and sponsors—including the new contract I'd inked.

But every other area of my life was out of control. I didn't know what to do with my father and his family or how to reconcile that relationship with my grandparents' feelings. I didn't know how I felt about Stuart. Didn't know how to deal with public doubts about my racing ability and widespread questions about my character. I was angry at myself for not handling crazy-fan Nash Rawlings well.

I ignored the voice in my head telling me to toughen up, because I needed to be honest with myself. I was also devastated that legions of racing fans hated me—hundreds of them feeling so strongly they'd send an e-mail saying I should be fired. I wanted to pretend I didn't care what anyone else thought—hell, I wanted to *not* care. Aside from my personal reaction to being hated, being likable and salable were important components of a driver's skillset. I feared for my career.

Gramps usually kept me from drowning in self-doubt, and I heard him in my head, "Remember what is important to you, Kate, and pursue that with every bit of your energy, because we never know how much time we have." My mother hadn't known. Neither had Ellie Prescott.

That was the problem. My emotional upheaval had its roots in grief about Ellie. I got up to open the casement window for the night breeze. *Then take control. Don't sit here feeling helpless. Make a decision, just one.*

Fine. I'd think about Stuart.

He'd become important to me. But I held back, only responding to his invitations, not taking initiative. I didn't ask myself what I wanted or how I felt about him. Through the window I saw his hotel rising above the trees.

I knew the reason for my detachment. I didn't trust him or myself. I'd had two serious relationships, and both had ended when the man wanted me to change my life and goals to suit his. The first was my high school sweetheart, who supported my racing until he understood I planned to make a career of it—wherever in the world that took me—instead of settling down in Albuquerque with him. He never understood how hard I was willing to work to achieve my dreams and the miles I would travel to fulfill them.

The other was Sam Remington, a former open-wheel driver currently having a breakthrough year in NASCAR's Cup series. He took me under his wing at an on-track test day, and we spent every spare minute together for the next six months, falling in love. Then he got the call to move to NASCAR full time, and he asked me to go with him. Not as a driver, with my own career and identity. As his fiancée.

After that, I avoided relationships and focused on my racing. The two weren't compatible in my experience.

Stuart Telarday had snuck under my guard, annoying me first, then challenging me. I still found him mildly irritating and uptight in his role as Series VP during race weekends. But on a personal level, he made me laugh, encouraged me, and supported me. He was attractive, successful, smart, and, for some reason, really into me. We had chemistry. Were we in a relationship? I supposed so. Was I ready to take the risk and embrace him emotionally? I realized I already had.

I shook my head. *What the hell was I thinking? Grab the reins.* The only question remaining was why we were both alone right now.

I quickly brushed my teeth, dug a sample vial of perfume out of my bathroom kit and dabbed it in strategic spots, and put jogging gear on over the only set of lingerie I owned—which Holly coerced me into buying on our last shopping trip. My heart pounded as I hurried out of Siebkens, over to the Osthoff, and through the hallways to his room. My whole body vibrated with the thudding of my pulse as I knocked on his door.

He answered, shirtless and in sweatpants. He looked good, better than good, and my throat went dry. He hid some muscles under that Series attire.

"Kate? What's wrong? Come in—let me get a shirt." His voice trailed off as he retreated to the bedroom of his junior suite.

I shut the door behind me, setting out the "do not disturb" sign and flipping the deadbolt. I leaned back against it, kicked off my shoes, and had my hands on the zipper of my hoodie when he returned, decently covered by a polo shirt. That was a shame.

"Kate?"

I hadn't said a word, not to be mysterious, but because my extensive media training hadn't prepared me for this. In the end, I said nothing, simply stepped toward him and pulled the zipper all the way down, revealing black and red lace and a lot of skin. It was the first time I'd seen him speechless.

I shook the jacket off my shoulders and slipped it down my arms. Two more steps and I stood an inch away from him. His eyes darted furiously from my lace-covered breasts—small, but showcased in a push-up bra—and my face. His mouth opened and closed, but no sound came out.

I rose on my tiptoes, put my arms around his neck, and planted my mouth on his. It took him half a second to respond, and then he all but inhaled me, his arms crushing me to him. Seconds or minutes later, I couldn't tell, I freed one arm and reached down to untie the drawstring on my sweatpants. Once that was loose, my sweats slipped to the ground. I tore my mouth free long enough to whisper, "Lift." He picked me up, and I wrapped my bare legs around his waist.

He groaned deep in his throat and cupped my butt. Still kissing the breath out of me, he staggered to the bedroom, stopping to lean against the doorway.

"Kate, are you sure?" he murmured, leaning his forehead against mine. "This isn't because you need comfort after trauma? You're not drunk, right?"

I pulled his head up by his hair and looked him in the eye. "I'm confused about other stuff, but not you. How about you? This isn't because I showed up in fancy underwear and you need comfort, is it?"

His face grew serious. "I have loved you from the minute you swaggered into the ALMS paddock, making every other woman look dull in comparison. You just had to catch up."

I had a heartbeat to think, *Too much, too soon, too fast.* And then he kissed me like no one and nothing else in the world mattered. I stopped thinking. He stepped forward and gently lowered us both to the bed.

Chapter Ten

If I gave Stuart the shock of his life the night before, he returned the favor the next morning. I woke up to hear him in the bathroom, brushing his teeth. He walked back to bed, sweatpants riding low on his hips and unruly hair sticking up in one spot.

"Good morning." He smiled at me.

"Stuart, you look sloppy!"

He pulled my pillow out from under me and propped it against the headboard with his own, leaning back and ignoring my protest. "The image you have of me."

I stayed on my stomach, chin in my hands. "It's different now. But you always look so neat, clean, and—unmussable. I always feel sweaty and rumpled and…."

"Mussed?"

"Never polished next to you. It's intimidating."

He tipped my chin up. "Three things. One, you're a racecar driver. You sweat and wear horribly hot clothing to do your job. No one cares that rock stars are sweaty and mussed. You have the same mystique. Two, you shouldn't be intimidated by anyone or anything."

He paused, searching my face.

"Three?" I prompted.

"Three can wait." He scooted himself down and pulled me up, and we were lost in each other again.

Over room-service breakfast later, he said, "Three is you should get yourself a crisis PR specialist to handle media fallout."

"That's for people with real problems." I heard myself and stopped. *It always happens to other people, not you, right?* I frowned. "You expect media reaction to be that bad?"

"Might be already." He tapped a finger on the sports section of the *USA Today* that had been waiting outside his room. A one-inch sidebar at the top of the left column read, "Did Female Racecar Driver Wreck Fan-Favorite For Media Attention?"

I made him write down a referral before he ate another bite.

By ten o'clock, Holly and I were on the road to Nashville in my Jeep. She tipped down her sunglasses and peered at me from the passenger seat. "You finally did the deed with Stuart."

"We've been in the car three minutes. What are you, psychic?"

She faced front again, the cat-got-the-cream expression on her face matching how I felt inside. "It's the way you look. More relaxed than last night—than you should be for how much garbage is going on. Happy."

"I am happy. Except he thinks he loves me."

"Sure he does. It's been written all over his face for months." She saw my frown. "What's the problem? You like him, too."

"I like him. I don't know if I love him. Now I feel guilty I haven't said it back and worried he feels more than I do. I can't deal with this."

"Tell me what's really wrong."

I took a deep breath, held it for a count of five, then released it. Felt calmer. "I don't know where to start."

"It's an eleven-hour drive to my house, sugar. Lay it on me. We'll work it out."

By the time we reached the outskirts of Chicago, we'd talked through my litany of problems and what my plan of attack might be for each: the accident and the racing world's subsequent doubts about my driving ability ("kick ass at Petit," Holly said), pressure from my father to meet and be part of his family ("go slowly," I decided), my stupid response to Miles Hanson's fan ("apologize and ignore it," she said), my concern Stuart was in love with me (Holly shook her head), and the grief I felt about Ellie. There weren't any solutions to my sadness over Ellie—or for my confusion about Stuart—but Holly let me talk about my memories.

At one point, soon after she'd taken over driving duties, I looked at her. "You're the only one I talk to about this stuff."

"Your emotions, you mean?"

I considered. "Put that way, I sound like an idiot."

"No, you sound like a guy. It's no surprise, Kate. You work with guys, hang out with them. The racetrack isn't a place to get all Maury Povich and talk about how you *feel*. But sometimes you have to. For those times, I'm here for you. Also to drag you shoe shopping."

I laughed. "Thanks."

After that, I was ready to face the music. Using Holly's smart-phone—and swearing to get one of my own the next day—I checked racing news and blog sites, and found my name had gone from mud to something lower. I was being trashed in the comments on articles, with one in two comments on every article using the word "bitch"—when they were being polite. Any supportive voices among the mob were vilified in my stead. It took me two hours to gather my courage to look at the Racing's Ringer blog.

Racing's Ringer, whoever he—or she—was, posted information in two categories. "Eyewitness accounts" comprised two-thirds of the blog posts and contained anecdotes, incidents, or stories he or one of four trusted sources saw or heard personally. Those were marked with an icon of the word "eyewitness" under a cartoon of a pair of eyeballs in a car. "Unconfirmed reports" were little more than gossip, apparently gathered from any and all sources via a prominent "Send Me News!" link on every page. Those were prefaced with the word "unconfirmed" and followed by the Ringer's spin and judgment. All posts were accompanied by a photo or video.

I read through two dozen short entries, many of them unconfirmed, about past accidents I'd been in (whether I'd caused them or not), reporters or fans I'd snubbed (by mistake), and assorted misdeeds and misbehaviors (everything from wearing sweats while picking up dry cleaning once, to gloating over another driver's misfortune that allowed me to win a race…when I was twelve). He used two unflattering images of me in rotation.

By the end of five pages containing multiple blog posts, I wanted to pound on the dashboard, throw something, or scream. Each story from the Ringer and every comment from a blog post or article felt like another pebble placed on top of my chest, making it hard to breathe. Crushing my spirit. I was exhausted, yet frantic—and I, too, thought this Kate Reilly person was lower than pond scum.

I twisted in my seat to face Holly. "Why does Racing's Ringer hate me? Some of this is true, but most of it is willful misreading of situations. When do I catch a break for being human?"

"Maybe you should ask him. I don't mean defend yourself. But ask why he's so set against you."

"He'd make fun of me. Then again, how could he get worse?"

I faced front and wiggled the seatbelt to a more comfortable position, sifting through my emotions. I was furious at being falsely accused and made a spectacle of, as well as scared about the drama damaging my career. I felt helpless, at the mercy of faceless hordes who only saw or read part of the story, which made me mad again. Underneath it all, I was hurt that someone I didn't know—I assumed I didn't know—hated me that much.

I stuck with rage, because dwelling on the pain might make me curl up into a whimpering ball of self-pity.

"I'm doing it." Before I changed my mind, I typed a note in the comment form: "Dear Racing's Ringer, Why do you dislike me so much? You take delight in reporting mistakes and missteps in my career, and I'd very much like to know why. Kate Reilly."

Maybe I'd get something to work with.

The next task was my voicemail. After the first two post-race calls from reporters, I'd sent my grandparents and other key people e-mails telling them I was fine, but not to call. Then I'd put the phone on silent—checking for text messages, but ignoring calls. I knew there'd been dozens of attempts and messages, and I dialed voicemail via speakerphone, so Holly could hear also.

From eighty-three missed calls, there were twenty-five messages, mostly requests for comments or interviews. Nineteen from
media outlets I'd never heard of, and five from publications or
reporters I knew. All referenced the accident in the race and Miles'
injury; half of them also referenced Ellie's death. One was Juliana,
devastated about Ellie and asking how I was doing. She also warned
me her SGTV bosses hoped I'd do an on-camera interview with
her. Holly agreed that might be the best tribute to Ellie.

The single non-media message was from a man claiming to be
Miles Hanson's biggest fan and telling me I would burn in hell
for what I'd done. Hearing a stranger's voice saying something
so hateful was worse than vituperative comments on a blog, and
my hand shook holding the phone. It took fifteen minutes of
deep breathing to regain my equilibrium.

The last hurdle was my professional e-mail inbox, which I
pulled up on Holly's phone. I clicked through seventy-three
of the 1,238 unread messages. Six offered support of the "you
go, girl" variety. Sixty-seven were complaints or hate messages
about Miles. His injury was my fault, of course, but I was also
blamed for other problems he'd had in his NASCAR races, for
making people quit being fans of racing, and for the cost of
race attendance. Moreover, I was proof women don't belong on
the racetrack. One guy called me the devil. A couple of them
threatened personal harm, should I show my face around Miles
again or should he suffer lasting injury. Five wished I'd die in
a wreck, one said I should have died instead of Ellie, and three
threatened to kill me themselves.

Once I stopped hyperventilating, I called Stuart's crisis public
relations company, which turned out to be a husband and wife
team based in Los Angeles. Matt and Lily Diaz had written
the book on crisis management, marketing, and publicity after
steering two pro basketball players, a golfer, three NFL players,
and a tennis ace through the media minefields of misdemeanor
and felony accusations. Even a couple trials. Someone with a
problem in the motorsports world was new for them.

I explained who I was and started to describe my recent image problems, mentioning the death threats. Matt stopped me, instructing me to hang up and call the police, then call them back. I started with Lieutenant Young at the Sheboygan County Sheriff's office, who took down the details and advised me to notify the police wherever I stopped, so local authorities had record of the situation. He made it clear no agency could do much based on threats alone—unless someone acted on them. I assured him I'd contact Nashville and Atlanta police when I got to those cities.

After I hung up with him, I called Matt and Lily again. Before I could resume my explanation of the problems I was having, Lily interrupted me. "Tell me, are you an 'aggressive hothead out to succeed over men at any cost?' Or not?"

Chapter Eleven

"Lily," Matt Diaz spoke before I gathered my wits. "Give the poor girl a chance."

I cleared my throat. "You've been reading blog posts."

"We looked around while we waited for you to call back," Lily said. "But we'll get totally familiar with your situation over the next couple days. By Thursday night, we'll have a plan."

I gave them websites, blogs, and news outlets covering the story—covering me—especially those whose representatives had left me voicemails. I gave them my e-mail login information so they could see what they were up against. And I promised to send a schedule of my sponsor and team obligations for the next two weeks, as I had a full calendar starting Friday. When I hung up, I felt better than I had in days. They were expensive, but having them on my side was worth it. A call to give Tom the latest news, a quick stop for lunch, and it was my turn behind the wheel again.

We were eight hours in when Holly looked up from her phone. "Uh oh."

I glanced away from the road to her worried face. I took three deep breaths and a sip of Diet Coke. "I'm ready."

"First of all, you're trending on Twitter."

"I'm not even on Twitter."

"I know, but you're trending with a couple hashtags."

"Hash-what now?"

She sighed. "Sugar, really, social media? What generation are you from? Hashtags are for search terms or topics. Hashtag 'Kate

Reilly' is getting some use, and hashtag 'blame Kate' is making the rounds. You need to join Twitter."

Before I could comment, she held up a hand. "There's more. Racing's Ringer responded to you—complete with the creepy eyeball graphic. He's a jerk and he's wrong, but he explains his problem with you."

"Read it to me?"

"'An open letter to Kate Reilly. Dear Ms. Reilly, You wrote today asking me why I dislike you. Why I have such fun repeating tidbits about your career. I'm happy to explain to you and my Ringer Readers.'"

"'Ringer Readers?'" I broke in. "That's dreadful."

"Agreed. He continues, 'It's not true to say I dislike you. I have no use for you and, honestly, I don't get the hype.'"

"Hype? I have hype?"

"Let me finish reading. 'So you've done nothing of value, particularly off the track. Like so many others, you can drive some. But color me unimpressed, because you have a growing voice in the racing industry and the sports world you don't use. You're a role model, do something about it! Give back to the fans and little girls who admire you. Contribute to a cause, speak out for an organization. Stand up for something! You're a public figure and it's your responsibility to inspire those around you. So until I see you stepping up to your responsibilities, you don't get my respect. Signed, Racing's Ringer. P.S. One thing that's outright unforgivable is your lack of response to Ellie Grayson Prescott's death. Sources tell me she was a good friend of yours back in your formula racing days, and you found her dead, but can't be bothered to comment or show remorse. If this is how you treat friends, how do you treat your enemies?'"

For three miles down the road, I had no words to express the injustice.

Holly broke open a bar of dark chocolate and handed me a piece. "You did ask."

"When was I supposed to make a statement about Ellie? The night it happened, when I was in shock? Don't I get time to cope? Do I call a reporter today and make a statement? I don't get it." I ate the chocolate square.

"He's holding you to a higher standard than most drivers. Shoot, most boys steer clear of DUIs and speeding tickets, and they're golden. I wonder if the Ringer is a woman, and that's why she—he? it?—is so hard on you."

"On one side I've got people threatening to kill me because I *did* something. On the other, I've got someone berating me for *not* doing something. Damned if I do, damned if I don't."

"You ain't kidding."

We rode in silence another couple miles. One minute I felt like crying, the next I felt like yelling, and the next I thought I could laugh and ignore the whole mess.

"Turn off the brain," Holly suggested, breaking off another piece of chocolate and handing it to me. She popped Garth Brooks into the CD player and for two hours, we sang our heads off and pretended the world of murdered friends, frightening fans, and angry bloggers didn't exist.

Wednesday at her house in Nashville represented an island of calm. We slept late, then I went for a long run, joined Holly for a healthy, home-cooked breakfast, and worked out for more than an hour with the weights I carried in the back of my Jeep. We left the house only for me to purchase a new smartphone—the last person in the world to get one, Holly declared—and for both of us to take a yoga class at a local studio. By the end of the day, I felt great. I'd worked out all the kinks and stiff muscles from the accident, stress, and long drive. My wrist felt fine. My body felt normal again. We did lots of laundry and thoroughly ignored media, e-mail, and blogs. No one even called us.

Thursday I woke up rejuvenated. That's when the peaceful feeling ended.

Lieutenant Young from the Sheboygan County Sheriff called to tell me they had a preliminary determination in the cause of Ellie's death.

"I appreciate the information, Lieutenant, but why are you telling me?"

"Because we believe what caused her death was nitroglycerin located in the orange juice identified as her drink."

"Nitroglycerin—the stuff for hearts? That can kill someone? In Ellie's—but I gave the juice to her. I mean, Stuart gave it to me and he brought it from the bar. He wouldn't put anything in it. I didn't."

"We don't think you did, Ms. Reilly."

"There were a hundred people in that room, anyone could have...but why would they want to hurt Ellie?"

"We're not sure yet, but we also can't rule out the possibility that you were the intended victim."

"Oh my God." My knees turned to jelly, and I crumpled onto Holly's sofa.

He offered tips for protecting myself in case I was still a target, but I couldn't concentrate on his words. Dangerous physical situations I could handle, but the way I lived life on the road made it difficult to guarantee my food and drink weren't tampered with. Maybe a logistical impossibility.

I hung up and pulled myself together, relating the information to Holly, who was alarmed to find me motionless and dazed in her living room. Then I called Matt and Lily for a scheduled planning session, upsetting them with the news.

"The randomness of life on the road might be your best defense," Matt said.

"At least until I'm having team meals during the next racing weekend."

Lily made me promise to stay alive, then offered to hook me up with her favorite service that would ship poison-free meals from Los Angeles. I hoped it didn't come to that.

Then we got to work discussing the media campaign they'd planned, which, they vowed, would improve public perception of me. We walked through the press releases they'd send out, via an e-mail media blast and by reaching out to key contacts personally. Then they drilled me on clear statements about the events of the prior weekend, including specific phrases they wanted me to use in reference to Miles, my "redneck" comment, and Ellie. I paced through Holly's house, gesturing with a free hand, emphasizing different words each time until the cadence felt natural. In the end, the rehearsed lines rolled fluidly off my tongue.

"I want to apologize to anyone who took offense at the language I used while my emotions were high. My intent was not to disparage anyone."

"I have reached out to Miles Hanson and the LinkTime Corvette team…"

"An unfortunate racing incident…"

"I am very sad about the death of Helen Prescott, who I raced with years ago and considered a friend. It was too difficult to speak about her before this time."

As we talked, Matt and Lily sent copies of schedules, releases, and talking points in e-mail, and I promised to alert them to any new development—though I didn't know how things could get worse. I hung up feeling relief as a lightness in my body. Bringing them in to fix my image and reputation was one of the best decisions I'd ever made. I owed Stuart for that.

After one last call—to Tom to update him and Jack on threats, my PR team's activities, and my location and health—Holly and I left Nashville mid-afternoon and rolled in to the Westin Peachtree Plaza hotel in downtown Atlanta around nine that night. My hotel room was being paid for by the new sponsor I'd be meeting with on Friday, so Holly shared with me. She was a night owl, and I was nervous about the coming meetings, so we were up late.

"I don't see why you're worried." She pulled open the drapes of our room on the forty-seventh floor to see the lights of downtown Atlanta.

"Number one, new sponsor, new people, and my reputation isn't the best these days. That's enough. But number two, it's a *beauty company*."

Chapter Twelve

I'd landed the kind of deal every young, unknown athlete dreams of, one that would bring me sponsorship money, national exposure, and the chance to be tied to a great cause. Beauté was a hundred-year-old cosmetic company selling a full line of products in low- to high-end department stores. Though the name was French for "beauty," Beauté was an American corporation founded in and still run from Atlanta, with a long tradition of supporting women's health efforts and non-profits.

They were launching a new line of products—"Glorieux," pronounced "glor-i-oo," meaning "glorious" in French—tied to a new initiative: promoting breast cancer awareness and research through a partnership with the Breast Cancer Research Foundation or BCRF. To support the campaign slogan of "Active, Healthy, Beautiful," Beauté chose six young, up-and-coming female athletes from a variety of sports as models. One was me.

In return for Beauté sponsoring me for the next two years in whatever car I drove, I'd participate in their advertising campaigns, make appearances for the company, and get involved with fundraising and awareness efforts for BCRF.

Holly sat cross-legged on her double bed, filing her nails. "You're beautiful, Kate."

"I feel like a fraud." I poked at my left wrist, noticing the bruises were mostly yellow now. "Plus the company, the campaign—they're so damn *pink*. So girly. I'm not the most feminine woman around, you know."

She raised an eyebrow at me. "This is the real problem."

"I'll feel out of place. Who am I to represent beauty? I'm waiting for them to decide they've made a mistake."

"Maybe Jack made a mistake too and will fire your behind."

"What? Hell no, driving's what I do."

Holly slid off the bed and stood in front of me, hands on hips, her temper making a rare appearance. "Being female is also what you do. Women come in all shapes, sizes, and degrees of femininity. Maybe they picked you because you *weren't* girly and feminine. Because you're a tomboy. Because you're a female who kicks some ass. Dammit, Kate. Own. Who. You. Are." She jabbed her index finger at me with each word.

"Even if I'm hated enough that someone tried to…" I couldn't say the words.

"Why are you doing this? Why are you racing? Why is this your career?"

"Because I love it, and I'm good at it."

She nodded. "What's your goal?"

"To win races. To drive every kind of racecar and every race-track I can. What's your point? You know this stuff."

She threw her hands in the air. "You didn't tell me you're doing this to be popular. If Jack wants you to drive, do you care what Nash Rawlings thinks?" When I shook my head, she went on. "Then you don't care what hundreds of Nash Rawlingses think."

The extrapolation from one guy to a sea of Kate-hatred was hard. "I guess?"

Her voice was like steel. "Don't let sexist, ignorant fools win because they made you doubt yourself."

I sighed. "No pity party?"

"Say it. Mean it."

"Hang on." I shook out my arms, rolled my shoulders twice, and sat up straight. Took a deep breath. "If people pay me to drive, I don't care what all the Nash Rawlingses out there think. Or if they hate me. I'm female, and I'm a racecar driver."

Holly watched to be sure I meant it, then softened. "Shoot, you respond pretty good to a smack upside the head."

"Sorry."

"What's that again? I can't hear you." She sat back down on the other bed.

"I'm sorry I'm being an idiot."

"I'm used to it."

I threw a pillow at her.

Entering Beauté's corporate headquarters the next day, I held on to Holly's words. Nancy, the head of their public relations staff, met me in the lobby and immediately dispelled my lingering fear Beauté would cancel my contract.

She escorted me to the meeting room, explaining that since we'd talked earlier in the week—when I called to explain the situation and how I was dealing with it—she'd been in communication with Matt and Lily, Tom from Sandham Swift Racing, and even the Elkhart Lake Police. While Beauté wouldn't make its own statement, they were ready to respond with complete support if the question should arise.

Nancy squeezed my shoulder as we paused outside the meeting room. "We're behind you one hundred percent, and we want you as part of this campaign. Let me know if there's anything you need from me." She pressed a card in my hand before handing me off to a marketing representative.

I didn't know what I'd done to deserve this company and this deal, but I wouldn't let anything ruin it. I put on my best "meet the public" face and prepared to be the best tomboy corporate representative they'd ever seen.

Besides me, there were eight corporate staff members in the room and three other female athletes—spokeswomen—a rower, a soccer player, and a jockey. The basketball player and the marathon runner wouldn't arrive until the next day, for the official press event. Once introductions were done, Beauté product experts spent an hour covering the beauty lines the company sold, specifically the new line we'd be representing.

The "Glorieux" products were meant for active women, meaning they were waterproof, sweat-proof, and guaranteed not to run. One of the first rules of our contract was to only use

Beauté products, to be supplied by the company. They loaded us up with facial cleanser, toner, moisturizer, foundation with SPF, concealer, blush, lip stain, eyeliner, eye shadow, mascara, eyebrow gel, and powder in the right shades for our complexions. And stuff to remove it all. They assured us professionals would demonstrate how to use everything.

"We also encourage you to experiment," chirped the vice president of product development, a stylish, flawless woman in her fifties.

After that onslaught of information we got a break, and as we helped ourselves to coffee, I learned the jockey, Tina Burleigh—finally someone shorter than me—felt as out of place as I did. A fellow tomboy in a sea of femininity.

I leaned close to her. "Did you know we needed eyebrow gel? That it existed?"

"If it's not mascara or lip balm, it might as well be from another planet. You know, I'm still not seeing myself as the embodiment of beauty."

"I said the same thing to my best friend yesterday. She told me to shut up and get over myself."

Tina almost choked on her coffee. "She's got to meet my brother. He said the same thing."

We continued chuckling as we settled back into our seats around the long, oval table. Next up, the marketing team explained where ads would be used, how the partnership with BCRF worked, and what phrases we should know and spout at every opportunity. I wasn't sure how I'd feel about seeing my face on a billboard, but I was eager to attend BCRF fundraising events as a Beauté rep—starting with a 5K and half-marathon in downtown Atlanta next Sunday.

Over a leisurely buffet lunch, the Beauté staff asked each spokeswoman to talk about the challenges of being a professional female athlete in our fields. Tina and I had different experiences than the others, given we both used "equipment" to do the work, and we competed on the same playing field as men. But we all had experience being discounted because of our gender, and we quickly found common ground. It dawned on me I'd receive more than sponsorship and free makeup out of this contract—I'd also gain a ready-made network of colleagues for support and friendship.

To end the day, makeup artists sat us down and put eighteen products on our faces. The corporate team handed me a logoed duffel containing a six-month supply of more cosmetics than I knew what to do with, as well as corporate-branded polo shirts, scarves, a windbreaker, and a knit hat.

I staggered back to our hotel room a mere eight hours after I'd left and collapsed face-up on my bed. My head was bursting from the corporate information and new talking points I'd stuffed into it.

Holly leaned over me, inspecting my face. She grinned. "Sugar, you look downright female."

Chapter Thirteen

I finally thought to check voicemail on my new smartphone after thirty minutes of sitting on the edge of the bathtub watching Holly play with the products I'd been given. My new outgoing greeting referred all media inquiries to Matt and Lily Diaz, so I had only five messages to listen to.

The first one nearly made me drop the phone, Miles Hanson, telling me he was fine, agreeing about shared blame, and hoping we'd meet again in better circumstances. "You stay out of the walls, now, hear?" was how he signed off. I felt giddy.

I returned Stuart's call first, only to be shocked by the news he had for me. He hadn't left Elkhart Lake on Tuesday because he'd returned to the police station to answer more questions, including some about his prior relationship with Ellie.

"Your what?"

"We were engaged a number of years ago."

"Engaged?" My voice went up as my stomach fell. "Why didn't you—"

He broke in. "What? Get married? Tell you?" He paused, and I could picture him running a hand through his hair. "We were together a year, and engaged for two months. You know what she was like. Once in a while she'd make a last-minute decision—a complete reversal of what she wanted the day before. And never budge. Our engagement was like that. One day, she didn't love me enough and she was gone."

I was silent, remembering the occasions I'd watched Ellie change her mind like that—about the paint scheme on her helmet, about her decision to go to college instead of going racing. I was surprised she'd done so over an engagement. Over Stuart. *She knew him well. First. Better than I know him now.*

"I never saw it coming. Turns out, I missed a lot about her." He sounded tired. "Why didn't I tell you? It never came up."

I wondered what else I didn't know about him. *Would I have gone to him if I'd known about Ellie? Was he really over her? Did he kill her because she'd betrayed him?* My breaths were shallow, and I realized I was becoming hysterical.

"Kate, the police know I had no reason to kill her—and less reason to kill you."

"You heard about that?"

"Yes, and I'm worried about you."

That was more than I could handle from my new lover who admitted being dumped by a good friend of mine—who'd died from poison intended for me. My head hurt. I don't remember what I said, but I got off the phone.

Holly leaned in the bathroom doorway. "You all right?"

"I'm not sure." I filled her in. "I know the idea is crazy, but… could he have killed her?"

"I thought you were the target?"

"They don't know for sure. Could Stuart kill someone? How can I even ask that? I slept with him, I like him."

She shrugged. "Anyone could kill if they had to, but I don't think he had a reason to kill her—or try to kill you."

"Because she betrayed him? Because he still loved her? To keep me from finding out about their history?"

"You writing for telenovelas now? Take a breath, sugar."

I took three and felt my heart rate slow. "It has to come back to motive. Dozens of people in that Tavern had the opportunity to put something in the juice, but there's got to be a reason."

"We don't know why anyone would want her dead, but we sure know people who want you dead."

"I can't face the idea that Ellie died *for me* because I pissed off a bunch of Miles Hanson fans." I dropped my head in my hands.

"It's the obvious explanation, for now. But it's no one's fault but the person who killed her, remember?"

I nodded.

She spoke again. "Enough of this. Focus on one thing at a time. Deal with the rest later."

I wiped thoughts of Stuart and Ellie from my brain and called Grandmother and Gramps to check in. My conversation with Grandmother was brief, both of us avoiding topics that might lead to my father. Gramps wanted to hear how my "girly day" (his words) had gone.

The other two messages were from Lily Diaz, reviewing various media requests, and from Juliana, officially requesting an on-camera interview. I called Lily first and confirmed I should say yes to Juliana, plus do phone interviews Lily set up with three print reporters. I called Jules to set up the on-camera for the next afternoon, suggesting coffee beforehand.

At that point, Holly forced me to sit at my laptop for a Twitter tutorial. I created my account as @katereilly28, because my name alone was taken.

"What if you aren't driving for Jack?" she cautioned. "The car number won't mean anything."

"My mother and Gramps were both born on the twenty-eighth of different months."

"That works. Now set up Twitter on your phone."

Holly pointed me to a number of people to follow, including her, the Series, other teams, and the Breast Cancer Research Foundation.

"Now what?" I looked at her.

She rolled her eyes. "Tweet something. Figure it out while I play with your makeup again."

Twenty minutes later she reappeared for an update.

I felt like a bear coming out of hibernation. "I haven't done anything. I fell down a rabbit hole of Twitter."

"That'll happen. Tweet something, now."

I typed, watching the character count with fascination as it ticked down. "@katereilly28: Ready or not, here I come. Trying to figure out Twitter. Looking forward to Petit next weekend. See you there?"

I put my arms in the air. "Yesssss!"

Chapter Fourteen

My priorities Saturday morning were a good workout in the hotel gym, a hearty breakfast, and a three-block walk to the Beauté and BCRF press event at Centennial Olympic Park. Holly skipped the workout, but joined me for the second two. We arrived at the park an hour before start time, as camera crews set up tripods and assistants ran around with clipboards.

The tent next to the stage was the preparation and make-up area. Once there, I changed into my pink polo shirt with the twin Beauté and BCRF logos, and a stylist threaded a scarf through the loops of my black twill trousers, tying it in a jaunty square knot. I met the two spokeswomen who'd been missing the day before: the pro basketball player, a tall Asian woman, and the marathon runner, who was short, dark, and wiry.

As the six athletes were prepped and styled, we shared stories of getting the call from Beauté and making the trip to New York for our first photo shoots. After the Beauté social media rep walked by, waving her phone in the air and calling out, "Don't forget to post about this!" we also swapped Twitter names, followed each other, and retweeted BCRF and Beauté posts.

I was relieved to find the others equally nervous about being the face of a beauty line. As Tina put it, "I'm used to the spotlight, but not to looking good in it."

"I'm safe," Carrie, the rower, declared. "If I'm not dripping with sweat, no one will know who I am."

"At least you're used to talking about sponsors, Kate," noted the basketball player. Siena was her name.

"I'm surprised you've gone five minutes without naming names," Tina teased. "Isn't that in your contract?"

I smiled. "They pay the bills, we talk about them. We practice interviews and sound bites about as much as driving. But this is different." I looked around at the others. "This is bigger than my team or sponsors. More important."

Though we were all nervous, each was proud and excited to have earned the chance to affect a larger community. Even without Racing's Ringer chastising me, I knew I was a standard-bearer for women in my sport, a role model for young female racers. The day had finally come when I had the platform to do good on a larger scale.

The irony was that as Racing's Ringer took me to task for not doing more, this sponsorship deal had already been signed. I wondered how he'd take today's news.

"Uh oh." Holly browsed the Internet on her phone while I sat in the makeup chair, a man working on my hair and a woman putting lip liner on me.

"Ut?" I couldn't move my lips.

"He's at it again."

"Ashing'sh Inge?"

"Yes, Racing's Ringer. Do you want to ignore it, or know now?"

I pointed to the floor, meaning "now."

"He dug up old stories of you behaving badly—he's calling them 'unconfirmed,' which doesn't mean much. Three stories now, and he claims there will be more in a series of reports that will 'expose Kate Violent's true character.'" She made air quotes with one hand around the last words.

The makeup artist was dusting powder over my face, so I could form words again. "Kate what?"

"He's given you a new nickname, something he's fond of doing. You're now 'Kate Violent.'"

"But…"

"It's awful *and* catchy. Read the stories." She handed over her phone as the hair and makeup team pronounced me done and instructed me not to mess anything up.

According to the Ringer's first "eyewitness account," I was a poor sport. The story was from my formula days, involving Ellie and Juliana. It was true I'd bumped Juliana in the braking zone for a corner, sending her into the wall and me into first place for the win. What few had seen was Ellie attempting a kamikaze pass and hitting me, to start a chain reaction. Of course, the Ringer told only half the story.

The second incident concerned a specific regional race in which I'd "clawed" my way to the front of the field and "ruthlessly" blocked the faster drivers behind me. When a competitor managed to get beside me, I'd "shoved" in front of him—the Ringer triumphantly labeled this evidence of my violent temper—causing a wreck and ending the other driver's day. I closed my eyes and felt the shame and despair of that moment as a weight on my shoulders—even fourteen years later. I was eleven when it happened.

The facts were correct. My coach that year in the go-kart ranks was working on my toughness, my will to win. I listened to his voice in my head instead of my own and pulled the bonehead move, causing my first bad accident and sending Sean Ellis, now a friend and former competitor in the Star Mazda series as well as karts, airborne in a double-flip worthy of a gymnast. I'd learned that day to trust my own instincts, no one else's. Sean and his parents forgave me sooner than I'd forgiven myself. Now, I felt ashamed all over again.

I scrolled to the last story and laughed so I didn't cry—Beauté promised their makeup was waterproof, but I didn't want to test it. That story, also true, defined selfishness and aggression. I was eight, and it was my fourth race ever. I wanted to win, did something awful to make it happen, and figured out I didn't want to succeed that way the minute I took the checkered flag. I tried to make the race officials give the trophy to the kid I'd wrecked, but they wouldn't. I tried to get out of the winner's circle ceremony, but Gramps wouldn't allow it, wanting the shame of the moment to teach me a lesson. I accepted the trophy with tears streaming down my face, then went straight to the other kid's truck and trailer. Wiping away tears and snot with the sleeve of my racing suit, I stuttered out an apology, thrust the trophy at him, and ran off.

That day, I resolved to win fairly or not at all. But the Ringer didn't want to talk about kids growing up. He wanted to talk about what an asshole I was.

"Holly!" I hissed at her. "What do I do? Should I tell someone here?"

"What did your crisis PR people say about stuff from the Ringer's blog?"

"Ignore it."

"You're prepared if reporters ask, right?"

"I have three responses to deflect the topic, plus I'm loaded with talking points."

"Like my mama always said, if trouble finds you, so be it. But there's no need to go huntin' for it."

I settled back in my chair. "Ignoring it."

"Speaking of huntin' for trouble, when's that sponsor event?" Holly took her phone back.

"Tomorrow morning." I looked around the tent, smelling makeup and hairspray, seeing women and pink. "Can you imagine a more stark contrast?"

I had obligations to Beauté as my personal sponsor, and I also had obligations to sponsors of the Sandham Swift Racing team, such as mentioning sponsor names when talking about the car and participating in events, activities, or photo opportunities with their representatives. At the crack of dawn Sunday morning, Jack, Mike, and I would meet reps from the 28 car's title sponsor, BW Outdoor Sportsman's Supply and Goods, or simply "BW Goods," a national hunting superstore. We'd meet hunters, shoot guns, and—if we were lucky, I was told—pose with fresh kill.

I studied my face in the mirror. I was getting used to being made up, but I was more accustomed to seeing sweat, matted hair, and the creases my fireproof head sock made on my face. This was an enhanced me, closer to the feminine ideal—which made it not quite me. In my mind, "feminine" meant fluttery, giggly, helpless, and being swathed in ruffles and pink. But here I was wearing pink and makeup, looking softer, pretty. Maybe I could find a compromise between sweaty, athletic tomboy and prissy, perfect, can't-get-dirty girly-girl.

I caught Holly's eye as she looked at my reflection. "I'm not sure where I'll feel more out of place, here or there."

"You've got more potential for girly than you let on, sugar, so I'd pin my money on tomorrow being more strange. Then again, maybe you put on your Kate Violent persona and let those guns rip."

Chapter Fifteen

Seven of us in pink polo shirts stood at the entrance to the tent with three black-clad women wearing radio headsets prepping us for our one-by-one reveal. The addition to the six spokeswomen was a breast cancer survivor who radiated energy and goodwill. She went on stage first, after Beauté and BCRF executive introductions and a basic summary of the partnership. Her name was Anne, and she was thirty-three, a survivor of stage four breast cancer, diagnosed three days after she turned thirty. Those of us waiting looked at each other in shock.

Athlete introductions were next, first Siena, then me. I walked up four steps to the stage and shook hands with the row of bigwigs, momentarily disconcerted by the stage backdrop: black and white headshots of each spokeswoman. There I was, larger than life. Turning, I stepped to the microphone and looked out at the audience, seeing a handful of press, a couple dozen staff members from each organization, and at least two hundred breast cancer patients, survivors, and supporters.

We'd been prepped for the statement, warned to keep it to a couple sentences. I was so moved by Anne that I jettisoned what I'd prepared and spoke from the heart. "For months, I have been thrilled and proud to be part of this partnership, and I thought this day would never arrive. But being here, seeing you all, meeting Anne backstage…I am humbled. Humbled and honored. Anne, and all of you out there who are dealing with this every day, you are the real heroes. I'll do anything I can to support you. Thank you." Anne hugged me before I reached my chair.

Considering the work put into making me pretty, the formal part of the program was brief, and after that, the executives took questions from the press. I scanned faces in the crowd, thinking about their courage, but snapped to attention when I heard my name spoken by a male reporter.

"Can you or Kate Reilly comment on the difficulties she's been having lately? I understand she had a run in with another driver and some fans. She's also involved in a police investigation into a possible homicide. Did those issues cause you any concern over her selection to this group of admirable women?"

My breath caught. He'd voiced my biggest fear. I concentrated on not letting tension show in my face and hearing a response over the roaring in my ears.

The executive director of BCRF made way for the CEO of Beauté, Lindsay Eastwood, who stepped forward to the microphone. I'd met her the previous day and decided I wanted to be her when I grew up—though I'd never achieve her degree of poise and polish. She was tall and slender with thick, graying hair cut in a stylish bob, perfect pink lipstick three shades darker than our shirts, and killer red heels.

Better than her style was that she smiled at me, stepped forward, and smacked an answer out of the ballpark. "The reason we're here is to support women, and men, who face a tremendous challenge in life. A challenge that, frankly, makes the variety of other troubles in our lives seem insignificant. Based on the fact Kate is with us today, it's clear she recognizes what's important. As do we. We love Kate, we respect the hell out of her ability to drive a racecar, and we admire her character. So when there's mud being slung around? We're not afraid of getting a little dirty at her side."

I wondered if she'd adopt me.

One more press question, benign this time, and the event was over. I made a beeline to Lindsay to thank her. As she hugged me, she whispered, "We checked you out, Kate. We're not worried."

I felt lightheaded with relief. "I can't thank you enough."

"Feel free to quote me." She winked before turning to greet others.

I reached Holly at the foot of the stage, still shaking my head over my luck, but before I could speak to her, a fan walked up wearing a Sandham Swift t-shirt. He was taller than me, skinny, pale skinned, dark-blond-hair. Average looking, but familiar.

"Hi, Kate? Would you sign these for me?" He held out a copy of the Beauté and BCRF press release and a photo of me driving through the Corkscrew at Monterey's Laguna Seca track.

"Sure. It's great of you to come out today. Do you live here in Atlanta?" I took his pen and signed.

"I do. And I'll see you at the track next weekend."

I looked at him again. Prominent Adam's apple, hair brushed forward, early-thirties. "Did I see you in Wisconsin last weekend?"

"Yeah, I'm George. George Ryan." He introduced himself to Holly and apologized for interrupting us.

I remembered him. "Outside the Tavern, with the piece of my car."

"I'm sorry about the timing and your friend. At least you got to connect with her again, briefly. I used to follow all three of you."

"You did?"

"For sure. It's cool to watch young drivers develop their talent and say I knew you when—I mean, knew of you. I didn't know you, obviously."

"How did you end up a fan of racing?" Holly asked. "Do you race?"

"No, but it's really exciting to watch. My first job was for Cooper Tires, so I found out about racing at lower levels, then I was hooked. I used to go to as many races as I could in the Midwest. It's funny how many of you who I watched racing eight or ten years ago are now in the ALMS—or broadcasting it."

Holly nodded. "You never know where people will end up, do you?"

"That's part of the fun," George said. "Trying to guess where young racers might go and tracking their progress to see if I'm right."

"How's your batting average?" I asked.

"Pretty good, but some still surprise me. I knew Kate would stay behind the wheel and thought Ellie Grayson wouldn't. But I was sure Juliana Parker would be driving—though she's back now in a way. Some people you can just tell will end up in broadcasting, you know?"

Holly raised an eyebrow. "Like who?"

"Zeke Andrews. Felix Simon. Hailey Leamon, over in IndyCar. I messed up on Scott Brooklyn though. I pegged him for all or nothing, racing or leaving, but not broadcasting. What makes it hard is how different a driver's personality is behind the wheel and in the paddock, though I always think if you're a jerk on the track, at some point you're going to be a jerk in the rest of life, too."

I was impressed by his insight. "What do you do for a living, George?"

"Sorry, I'm running off at the mouth." He blushed. "I'm in human resources, corporate recruiting, specifically."

"You'd have to be good at analyzing character for that job."

"I'd like to think so. But for racing, it's only a fun game to play."

Lindsay Eastwood passed, nodding at Holly and George and patting my shoulder.

"Anyway, thanks again for signing these." George held up the event materials. "And for chatting."

We shook hands again and he left.

"A little nervous, but a nice guy," Holly said, after he was well out of earshot. "And how about that gift the CEO gave you? What a response."

"No kidding. I've got to tell Matt and Lily."

"How does she look so good? I checked. She's sixty and could pass for forty."

"Maybe it's time to start using these beauty products after all."

The CEO's ringing endorsement made the press event the high point of my day. My spirits deflated when Holly and I discovered how far the influence of the Racing's Ringer blog had spread. In addition to three more stories about "Kate Violent living up to her name" on the blog, there were a number of stories in the regular media about the Ringer's posts—not reporting my past behavior as fact, but mentioning the accusations as part of a discussion about the power of blogs over cultural consciousness.

I hated being the prime example.

Matt and Lily were encouraging when I called them, telling me to trust them. They set to work getting copies of the Beauté press release and Lindsay's statement to every media outlet they could think of. Certainly the three reporters I spoke to by phone that afternoon—one from the Associated Press, one from CNN, and one of my old friends at *Racer* magazine—all had the information. I hoped the tide was turning.

Chapter Sixteen

Juliana was also prepped with the details of the press event, and she congratulated me when Holly and I arrived at her hotel. We sat at the lobby bar over cups of coffee and quickly mapped out what we'd talk about on-camera, including how I knew Juliana and Ellie back in the day, how we'd reconnected just prior to Ellie's death, and a bare-bones description of finding Ellie's body.

I sipped my coffee as Juliana made notes in a notebook.

"I spoke with the Elkhart Lake PD today," she said, breaking off a piece of the biscotti we'd gotten with the coffee. "They gave me some information I'll use as part of the special report with your interview."

"What did they tell you?" Holly leaned forward.

Juliana glanced at me. "They said Ellie was poisoned—wouldn't say what with—but she may not have been the intended victim. Do you know anything, Kate?"

I nodded slowly. "But you can't use it. I'm not supposed to say anything."

"I can differentiate between business and friendship, Kate." Her voice and posture were stiff.

I touched her arm. "I'm sorry. They think I could have been the intended victim."

Hurt changed to sympathy on her face. "But that's awful. Who'd want to kill you?"

"Beats me. A Miles Hanson fan?"

Holly changed the subject, asking Juliana about her new job with SGTV. "Everyone in broadcasting wants a network job in a top market, right? But you gave one up to move to SGTV. I figure you had a reason."

Juliana laughed. "You're right. I voted myself off the network news island. I realized I wasn't happy, and I missed racing." She turned to me. "As Kate knows, I lost part of my sponsorship, and then she got the job we both tried for."

"I've always felt terrible it made you leave racing," I put in.

"It was the right time. I'd juggled racing and pageants and school, and I knew I'd have to choose. I had some health issues, and the choice was clear. My mother—I was an only child, and she'd always been very involved in my careers," she explained for Holly's benefit. "She told me I'd go farther in pageants anyway. She humored my desire to race, using it to teach me lessons about always trying to improve. 'Be the best!' she'd tell me." She blinked back tears.

Holly handed Juliana a bar napkin to use as a tissue. "A major event like losing a parent can make you rethink where you are in your life."

"Exactly. I realized my life was mine to direct. So I came back to racing, because it's where my heart's always been. And I'll still honor my mother by being the best wherever I am."

We toasted that sentiment with our coffee cups.

A few minutes later we were upstairs in a large suite, microphones attached and cameras rolling. After addressing Ellie's death, Juliana gave me an opening for other topics. "I understand that was merely the last event in an already tough day for you?"

"Yes. I was terribly upset to have played a role in wrecking myself, not to mention another driver and team. On top of that to lose someone I'd only just reconnected with—I was devastated. I must have appeared unfeeling, and I want to apologize to anyone who felt slighted by my actions."

Juliana nodded sympathetically for the camera filming her over my shoulder. "It sounds like a difficult time emotionally. But you had good news coming up, right?"

"It was a weekend of ups and downs. It's hard to celebrate after such sadness, but I know Ellie would be happy for me and tell me to get on with business. I'm honored and excited to be part of Beauté's campaign supporting the Breast Cancer Research Foundation—and especially to promote the idea that every woman is beautiful."

Our interview ended shortly thereafter, and an assistant who'd been helping with lights went out into the hallway. Seconds later, Felix Simon, the pit reporter Juliana had worked with at Road America, walked in, nodding to the crew packing up the cameras.

"How'd the little tea party go, Juliana?" His voice was light, but patronizing.

She rolled her eyes at me. "It was fine, Felix. Kate, I'm so sorry, but I have a follow-up phone interview in two minutes. Will you forgive me if I run?"

"Sure, Jules." We hugged each other, and she slipped from the room.

Meanwhile Felix settled himself on the arm of the sofa I'd been sitting on. "How touching. Her first little solo job for the network. How'd you perform for her, 'Kate Violent?'" He raised an eyebrow at me and crossed his arms over his chest.

My fingers froze on the mic I'd been unfastening from my collar. I looked up, feeling a flush rising in my face. I noticed Holly getting to her feet at the other side of the room where she'd been a silent observer.

He went on, his face hard. "Did our Jules ask you any hard-hitting questions about your pattern of aggression?"

"What is your problem?" I clenched my hands into fists at my sides to keep them from shaking.

He shrugged, smiled. "I'm just doing a journalist's job, asking you questions. I don't have a problem. Maybe you do, if you can't handle the real world. Are you like all the other girls I've seen who try to call themselves racers? You can't take what you're trying to dish out?"

"How do you know what I can take? Why would you judge me based on other people?"

"So far you're exactly like the rest. Looking for attention with whatever underhanded means you can find. I hate to break it to you, hot stuff, but tits and ass only get you so far in the racing world." He shook his head. "But I forgot, you're better than that. You should have taken that meal ticket to NASCAR when Sam Remington offered. You'll wash out of racing soon enough—and like all the others, you'll blame everyone else for the fact that you can't hack it, instead of accepting you're no damn good."

I vaguely heard Holly's voice saying, "Hey, now" through the buzzing in my head, and I felt her hand on my arm, trying to calm me.

I shook her off, stepping close to Felix and looking him in the eye. "Why would you attack me personally? What code of professional ethics or personal honor says that's all right? Or are you afraid, Felix? Are you like some other men I've met, so threatened by a girl you have to lash out, keep me down? Does it make you less of a man because women are racecar drivers? If that's how fragile your manhood is, I pity you."

I ripped the mic off my shirt, yanked the receiver from my waistband, and threw them on the couch next to him. "I'm out of here." I whirled to leave and saw a camera on someone's shoulder. The red "recording" light was on.

Not again.

Holly tugged me sideways, and we left the room.

The elevator doors closed behind us and I sagged against the wall. "Shit! Shit, shit, shit, shit."

"It's not that bad," Holly began.

"I flew off the handle on camera *again*," I moaned. "I never do that, Holly. What's *wrong* with me?"

"He provoked you. That was way out of line."

"He works for the network, they'll edit that out. And the Ringer blog will get it…" My breath caught in my chest.

Holly held up her phone and tapped the screen. Felix's voice spilled out, "…tea party go?"

"You recorded it?" My tears dried up.

"Lily Diaz told me to watch the interview and record anything touchy. When Felix came in and got all smirky at you, I hit record again."

"Have I mentioned lately you're my best friend in the entire world?"

"You can thank me by buying me dinner."

"Done."

I took calming breaths as Holly dragged me into the hotel's gift shop—she couldn't pass one without going in. After trying on dozens of rings, she finally settled on one with tiny crystals in the shape of a ladybug, and once she paid for it, we exited the hotel to walk to the corner. While we waited to cross, I admired the moody, twilight skies and watched pedestrians.

"It's like Felix wasn't even talking to me, but to other women from the past. That's some deep-seated resentment there."

"He certainly expects female drivers to behave only one way." Holly stood to my right, head down, studying her new ring.

Traffic sounds changed, and I looked up to see the light was green for us to cross. I stepped into the crosswalk, turning to tell Holly to get moving. Too quickly for my feet to respond, I realized the noise was wrong. Half a step later, there was a yank on my purse, slung across my body over my left shoulder.

I staggered backward, falling, unable to get my feet under me. I thought, "Thief!" at the same instant I understood the strange noise: a car was bearing down on me. Ten yards away, nine—accelerating? Eight, seven. Every cell in my body screamed to get out of the way, fast.

I was pulled backward again, by the back of my shirt this time. I fell hard onto my butt in the gutter, my lower back slamming into the curb. I curled my knees to my face. Pulled my feet in. Threw myself back, as far from the street as possible. The car swept by, still accelerating, missing me by inches. I tasted exhaust.

A clamor of voices. "Are you OK?"

"He was aiming at you!"

"Let's get you up."

"No, leave her a minute." That was Holly, who crouched next to me, murmuring, "You all right?"

I nodded, face buried in my knees, tailbone smarting. I tried to catch my breath from the kidney-punch against the curb. Tried to grab a coherent thought when my brain and body were jacked up on adrenaline and terror. "That you who pulled me back, Holly?"

"Yeah. Anything hurt?"

"I'm OK. Thanks."

"Then let's get you out of the gutter. It's unbecoming."

I laughed weakly as she helped me up.

Chapter Seventeen

I sat on the sidewalk for five minutes until the Atlanta police arrived, called by a helpful pedestrian. Unfortunately, no one could identify the car, let alone the driver. Four-door, black or dark gray. One person said a Ford, one said a Honda. The driver was alone, but shadowed. No one caught a license plate.

The officer took down notes about the death threats I'd received in e-mail—promising to contact the Sheboygan County Sheriff for more information and start an investigation into them. But he wasn't hopeful about finding the car and driver from this attempt. "At least we've got it on record if anything else happens," he said.

"Good Lord, let's hope not." Holly batted her eyelashes at the dimpled, muscled detective who smiled back at her.

I hated to break up the blooming love connection, but my adrenaline rush had worn off, and I felt cold and shaky. Holly and I walked slowly—and carefully—back to our hotel. Instead of the planned dinner out, she ordered room service while I took a hot shower. She ate on the couch, her chicken parmesan on the low table in front of her. I sat cross-legged on the bed with my food tray.

"Holly? I might be paranoid, but was that an accident?"

"I don't think so."

"Why is someone trying to kill me? It's bizarre to even say it. This doesn't happen in real life." I held up my hands, reading her look and remembering my narrow escape from a killer the previous year in Connecticut. "The guy last year was crazy."

"He's not the only crazy person in this big ole world—obviously, since someone killed Ellie."

"But who? Why? A fan because Miles got hurt? A redneck because I used the word as an insult? A runner-up spokeswoman because I got the Beauté sponsorship?"

"Someone angry at your success in racing?"

"Felix."

"I don't know."

I shook my head. "I still can't wrap my mind around the idea."

"Someone tried to kill you tonight. I'd say that makes it pretty clear Ellie died because someone doesn't like you. Stop with the denial and figure it out."

I opened my mouth, but she went on before I could speak. "And don't get wrapped up in guilt. It's not your fault, it's the killer's fault. The only thing you can do is make sure he's caught."

I shut my mouth and nodded. Accepted a few truths, straightened out my emotions. Holly ate her dinner while I worked it out.

"So we know someone's out to get me. One? Or more?"

"Good question." She put her knife and fork down on the plate. "On one hand, of course they're related, because how many people are out to kill you? On the other, you did piss off seventy-five million NASCAR fans by taking out Miles, so they could be different perpetrators."

"Not every NASCAR fan is a Miles Hanson fan." She looked at me and I sighed. "Right, only seventy-four million, nine hundred ninety-nine thousand are. No idea if we're talking one person or two. I'm going to assume one person, because the thought of multiple homicidal maniacs after me is terrifying. Which means it's someone who was at Siebkens last Sunday night and in downtown Atlanta tonight."

She picked up her tray of empty dishes and headed to the door to set it in the hallway. "I didn't do it."

"I'm glad to hear it." I followed her with my tray.

"We need a list of names of people at both places, then we cross-reference them."

"You'll help?"

"Of course." She handed me the hotel-provided notepad and pen. "Start writing."

Ten minutes later we'd come up with about fifty people we remembered seeing at Siebkens. We'd debated adding friends or people we only knew to have been outside the Tavern, not inside. In the end, we wrote every name down, including Stuart and Holly—at her insistence.

Then I started a new list for tonight in Atlanta, which was also long. I bunched pillows up against the headboard of my bed and settled back on them. "The problem is half of the ALMS paddock is already here for tomorrow's Series event. Everyone else could show up at any time to network."

Holly lay across her bed on her stomach, propped up on her elbows. "Plus, half of US racing is based between Atlanta and Charlotte. We need to include the Series people who live here. They're only forty minutes away."

I looked at the names and felt discouraged.

"Buck up, sugar," Holly said. "This is still easier than asking everyone if they hate you enough to kill you."

"I wish I could ask everyone in Miles' fan clubs."

"Or the Ringer."

"I'm staying away from him. I wonder—no, I'm not looking."

"I checked while you were in the shower." She shook her head at my hopeful expression. "He's got a transcript of your rant at Felix this evening."

"What kind of sources does this guy have? He's got to be someone in racing."

"That's the beauty of his process. It's all anonymous tips. Anyone can send anything in and maybe he'll cross-check with other tips or sources, or maybe he'll post it as unconfirmed rumor. Usually he's careful not to state it as fact, but as hearsay. Or he won't name the target specifically, but will describe him or her in a way that makes it clear who he's referring to."

"How do I make him stop?"

"Prove him wrong. I sent the audio file of Felix provoking you—which wasn't on the Ringer's blog—to your PR team. They'll counter his nonsense."

"Then what do I do with the people on both of these lists?" I looked at them side-by-side.

"Figure out who would benefit with you out of the way."

"Some driver who might take my seat at Sandham Swift. Some woman who might take my spot as a Beauté spokeswoman."

"Hmmm, those lovely, free products."

"Easy, killer. Someone who…wants to date Stuart? Who thinks I get too much attention in the paddock?"

"Money? They always say follow the money."

"No, I—oh. Something my father told me Monday." I'd shared the secret of my father with only Holly, Zeke, and Stuart. "I'm in the family will, and some members of the family aren't happy. Plus they'll all be at a private party sponsored by the bank on Friday. He wants me to meet everyone."

"That ought to be a hoot. How much money?"

"I didn't ask."

"Maybe some evil relation wants to rub you out so they get more inheritance? Is the money being distributed soon?"

"Not until my father dies, I think. It seems farfetched."

"Depends on the amount of money or the need. Maybe you should find out who isn't happy about you and where they've been the last week."

I looked at the clock: 7:30. Before I lost my nerve, I dialed my father, who had five minutes to spare before leaving for an engagement. He was initially angry I'd be suspicious of family members I'd never met, but when I explained the attempts on my life, he named two cousins, William Reilly-Stinson and Holden Sherain—also offering to verify their whereabouts on the two evenings in question. As an afterthought, I asked him the value of my supposed inheritance.

Holly raised her eyebrows when I told her. "That'd buy you a few racecars."

"I want to earn the racecars, not buy them. And talk about money with strings attached. Maybe I'll give it to the BCRF."

She shot me a look that very clearly said, "Are you nuts?"

"Topic over. I need a break. Let's watch a movie."

"Sure." She picked up the guide. "Perfect. We'll watch *Die Hard* now, and then you'll get up in the morning and go play with guns."

"Yippee kai yay."

Road Atlanta

Braselton, Georgia

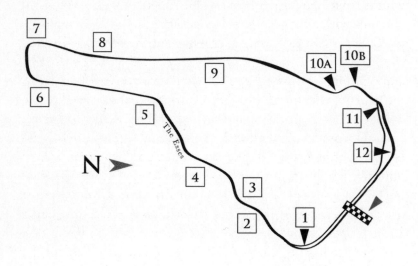

Chapter Eighteen

For our hunting trip the next morning, Mike, Jack, and I drove an hour out of Atlanta to meet six BW Goods executives, three winners of a "top hunter" contest the superstore sponsored, and two men with cameras. We walked around the woods of a private preserve for two hours, the hunters shooting at doves and me shooting at a tree stump, since I'd never fired a shotgun before and didn't have a hunting permit. Then we posed for photos with the wild boar the hunters bagged before we arrived. I tried not to dwell on how Benny the boar turned into my delicious bacon.

After a quick turnaround at my Atlanta hotel, where I showered the outdoors off, Holly and I headed north to the suburb of Suwanee, Holly driving while I checked in with the world. Racing's Ringer was at it again, beside himself with indignation over my doing what he'd berated me for lack of—stepping up, being a role model, and working for a greater cause. The hypocrite.

"The headline is 'Convenient News From Kate Violent,'" I told Holly. "He says I'm doing this only for the money, suggests I cooked this up to combat his challenges, and congratulates himself on prompting my 'better behavior.' Then he contradicts himself, claiming it's not better behavior because I can't truly be committed to the cause if I didn't do anything before now. Calls me 'self-aggrandizing' to be 'pulling this convenient stunt now when her public image is so tarnished, so in need of redemption.'

He ends by concluding I have no class to be grandstanding this way. Me?"

"I'd like to redeem my fist in his face, I tell you that much."

"He's got a post quoting an industry insider saying, 'Just because she's better looking than most drivers doesn't mean she can drive. Sexy doesn't mean talent—usually the opposite. That's just how it is.' And then—"

Holly interrupted. "Was that last bit a quote?" At my nod, she went on. "It's Felix—his tic is saying 'That's just how it is.'"

"That's what I need. Felix and the Ringer working together. Lastly, the Ringer makes fun of the beauty company—suggesting they scraped the bottom of the barrel by picking me for beauty."

"That's flat out unacceptable." She pounded the steering wheel with a fist.

"I can't take offense. It's what I thought."

"Talk about no class. A gentleman would never insult a lady like that."

"Maybe he's not from the South. He gets snippy about all the pink. 'Will poor Mike and the pit crew be forced into pink firesuits? Will Sandham Swift bear the indignity of a pink car? Will we all have pink stuffed down our throats and be unable to object because objecting means we like cancer? And how will BW Goods, the other key Sandham Swift sponsor, cope? Will Kate V. try to start a new trend in pink cammo?'"

I was out of breath, torn between indignation and laughter.

"He's got a bug up his butt about this. And you."

"The thought of the over-the-wall crew in pink suits and helmets is awesome. He sounds threatened. Defensive." I paused. "Could the Ringer be Felix?"

"They have a similar bias against you. I'm not sure the language is the same. Felix sneers privately. The Ringer likes scoring points off you publicly."

"But Felix is a journalist, used to spinning events a variety of ways. Have you ever heard rumors about the Ringer's identity?"

"Not a whisper." Her grapevine had no peer. If she hadn't heard anything, there wasn't anything to be heard.

"Have you tweeted today, Kate? You have to tweet regularly."

"@katereilly28: Join the #ALMS and Sandham Swift Racing at the Mall of Georgia this afternoon. Learn about racing, score giveaways, and meet drivers!"

After checking in to a hotel next to Highway 85 in Suwanee, Holly and I got back in my Jeep and headed eight miles further down the freeway to the Mall of Georgia, arriving half an hour before the official three o'clock start time.

The three-hour community event the ALMS was hosting took place in a square, cordoned-off section of parking lot, right in front of the open-air section of the mall, next to the Barnes & Noble store. Around the perimeter were tables under pop-up tents for the ALMS, key partners and sponsors—such as Michelin, Pirelli, Porsche, and Kreisel Timepieces—and a dozen regular ALMS competitors. At least half the teams, including Sandham Swift, had extra-wide tents housing a racecar along with crew and drivers. Two pop-ups in the center sheltered information tables and three Series-logoed street cars—a Porsche, a Corvette, and a track-package Mazda—used for taking VIP guests around the track before races.

Holly's team, Western Racing, wasn't involved in the event, so she wandered off to talk to other people, while I went straight to our setup. On one side of the large tent, Jack typed furiously into his phone and Mike helped Tom set out the team "hero" cards: summary information and full-color photos of cars and drivers, printed on eight-by-ten cardstock. At the other side, two crew members from the 29 car chatted with its drivers, Lars Pierson and Seth Donohue, while a third, cigarette dangling from his mouth, sprayed cleaner on the Corvette, rubbing away fingerprints and dust with a soft cloth.

A Series marketing person trotted over with a schedule of the afternoon's events and a request from Stuart that I find him for a quick word. The nerves jumping around in my stomach told me I was still conflicted about him—my feelings, his past, my friend. For a millisecond I considered avoidance as a strategy. That wasn't fair to anyone.

I walked to the Series tent slowly, studying the afternoon's schedule along the way. Activities were planned every twenty minutes, including pit stop demonstrations and tech talks about a driver's racing gear and tire technology. Sandham Swift was listed under "Other Giveaways" because Beauté would hand out information, makeup samples, and signup forms for the 5K next weekend.

Stuart met me a few steps away from his tent. "Kate, hi." He put a hand on my shoulder and ran it down my arm to the elbow.

I went still, flushing at the thought of our night together. I was uncomfortable being at my job and thinking about sex. "We're going to have to talk about how we handle this during races." I stepped back, causing his hand to fall. Enough of my life was fodder for public commentary. I didn't need to broadcast my romantic leanings also.

He stepped closer, but didn't touch me, and spoke in a quiet tone. "I wanted to see how you're doing. And ask if we could meet tomorrow night for coffee or dessert after a dinner I have to attend."

"I'm doing all right, I guess." I paused. *Did I want to see him? Of course I did, but I was afraid of making a mistake. Of being hurt.* "Sure, coffee's fine."

"Is this not what you want?" He didn't mean the beverage.

I paused, gathering my thoughts, trying to find the words. Aware every successive moment made the answer more "no" than "yes."

I opened my mouth, not sure what would come out. "Yes. I do. But I'm not ready to deal with a relationship."

"You want to date other people?" His voice sounded choked.

"What? Of course not. There's no one else. I like being with you. But…I've got a lot going on right now. I'm trying to build my career. I don't know if I have the time or the energy for a relationship."

"You shouldn't have to work at this, Kate. It should just be." His eyes searched my face. "We'll take it as it comes."

"OK." Part of the knot in my chest unraveled, but the rest of it was still there, uncomfortable. I eyed him. "If we're being honest here?"

"I hope we are."

"The thing with Ellie and you. That really rattled me."

Stuart raised an eyebrow. "Her death or the fact we were engaged?"

"Both." I closed my eyes for a moment. "I'm still in shock over her death, and the idea I was the target? I can't think about it or guilt will overwhelm me. Then learning you'd known her. Been in love with her. It's hard to deal with."

"You've had relationships before also. High profile ones."

Everyone always knew about Sam. "One. I don't expect you to have had no past. But I knew her. At least, I thought I did." I bit my lip, needing to get the next words out. "I thought I knew you, too."

"You do know me."

"Maybe? This—and with someone I knew—takes adjusting to. Making it fit the rest of the picture. I need time to get used to it."

He looked frustrated. "We'll start with coffee tomorrow."

I nodded and left, hoping to get my emotions straight before I saw him again.

Partway back to my team's tent, I ran into Felix, who stopped and put his hands on his hips, the chrome on his ALMS race-winner's watch catching the light. "If it isn't Princess Pink."

I waited silently, my arms crossed over my chest.

"What's the matter, Princess? The racing world too tough for you?"

I gritted my teeth. "No. It's irritating some people have bad manners, but it's nothing I can't handle. *You* are nothing I can't handle."

His face flushed, and he stepped closer. "You don't belong here and you don't deserve to be here. I have no problem making that clear."

I looked around for someone who might be a witness, and he understood.

"No one will believe you," he gloated. "I'm the nice guy, remember? Say something, and you'll look like the whiny bitch you are." He leaned closer, his smile a combination of satisfaction and meanness. "But I'm not the only one after you."

He whistled as he sauntered away.

Chapter Nineteen

He could try, but Felix Simon wouldn't intimidate or beat me—especially not when I had a recording of his threats he didn't know about. I kept walking.

Juliana stood in front of the Sandham Swift tent, typing something into her phone. She turned at the sound of my footsteps. "Kate, I want to apologize—for Felix—I don't…" She ended with a shrug.

"You couldn't have stopped him. Do you know how the tape got out?"

She looked embarrassed. "Someone back at corporate insisted. I tried to block it."

I made a mental note to have Matt and Lily send the full recording to SGTV and demand its airing. "It's OK, I did it to myself. So what are you here for today?"

Before she could respond, a big-haired mother and her gorgeous teenage daughter approached us. "Excuse us," the mother said.

Juliana and I both turned, and they zeroed in on her.

The daughter gushed. "Weren't you Miss Alabama?"

Juliana shifted her posture and smile, suddenly looking two inches taller and a couple molars more toothy. "I sure was, honey. What's your name?"

She was Annamarie Jordan, fifteen, from Alabama, and in town for a regional pageant. Her older brother was race-mad and insisted they stop at our event before a trip to the mall for pageant supplies. Confronted with an idol, the girl was torn between pageant-taught poise and outright hero-worship. I grinned, enjoying the show.

"What's the best advice anyone ever gave you?" Annamarie asked.

"That's hard. My mama—God rest her soul—molded me into a competitor by giving me the iron will to win, and the knowledge nothing would stand in my way if I worked hard. 'Be the best' she'd say, and if I didn't win she'd ask why I hadn't wanted it enough. If I was participating, I was 100 percent committed—finding and emphasizing whatever edge I had. Want it, and find a way to be on top."

Annamarie and her mother hung on every word. I was shocked by how life-or-death Juliana made pageant competition sound, as well as how her mother motivated her. But I kept my mouth shut, taking a photo of the once and future queens posing together with matching stances. After they departed, Juliana turned back to me, still glowing.

"You're a rock star, Jules!"

She dimmed the wattage. "I was once."

"I've always envied your presence. It's so effortless and magnetic."

I saw the sheen of tears in her eyes. "That's the nicest thing anyone's said to me in months, Kate. Now, it's your rock star turn today, and I think you've got fans looking for you." She gestured to people standing under the Sandham Swift tent a few yards away with posters and hero cards in their hands. I headed that direction.

We were busy for the next hour talking to fans, signing autographs, and answering questions about what it was like to drive a racecar. In front of the tent, two young women in khaki shorts and pink Beauté/BCRF polo shirts handed out makeup samples and signup forms for the upcoming 5K. In the background we heard the announcer directing people to different tents and activities.

The whirring wrenches of the pit stop demonstration thinned the crowd at Sandham Swift, though four fans stuck with us. A blond guy with a moustache chatted to our crew near the car, while his wife, who clearly believed in using makeup to hide the aging process, spent a long time with the Beauté representatives. Another was George Ryan, the fan from the Beauté event the day before, who stood at the edge of our tent taking photos of all four drivers.

The last was a short guy in his mid-thirties, with dark-brown, straight hair, thinning on top of his head. Like others I'd spoken with today, something about him was familiar. We interacted with so many people over the course of a racing season, I was forever asking if I'd met someone before. But I was pretty sure this guy was a repeater.

He surprised me by producing a press release from the Beauté event.

"Were you there? So was he." I pointed to George, who walked over.

"I think I saw you." George introduced himself.

The new guy shook hands with George, then with me. "Jeff Morgan. What you said yesterday was great, Kate. Obviously I don't buy makeup, but I'll encourage others to support you—and the non-profit."

I picked up flyers for the 5K. "Do you live in Atlanta? You can join us next Sunday to benefit the BCRF. You too, George." I handed one to each of them.

"All depends how tired I am after the race the day before," George responded.

The new guy bobbed his head. "Me too, but I want to support the people supporting my favorite driver. You'll be at the walk?"

"All of the spokeswomen will be, and a couple people from Sandham Swift or the Series. It'd be great to see you there."

"I'll do it! And can you sign the press release for me?" He and George moved away as other fans approached for autographs and the two of them stood nearby, talking and taking photos of our Corvette.

Holly hurried up, phone in hand. "The Ringer—I think he's here today."

I read the blog post from her phone. "'Seen and heard today in Georgia: Kate Violent making nice at an ALMS community event. Strangely, she's *not* wearing pink, but her two makeup minions are. Nice boost to Ms. Violent's oversized ego. She does seem to be taking her new role seriously, encouraging fans to sign up for a 5K next weekend in Atlanta to benefit the BCRF.'"

"It's got the eyeball logo," she said, pointing to the screen. "He could be here."

I looked around at hundreds of people in the ALMS area, then realized the futility of the gesture. I looked back at her phone and scrolled to the next item. "Did you see the next post? It's an open letter to Miles Hanson, asking if the rumors are true he'll make an appearance at Petit next weekend, and if so, suggesting he change his mind because, 'Who knows what Kate Violent might do to you this time for more media attention.'"

"For Pete's sake."

"I'm not sure if I'm more frustrated the Ringer is here, that he's snotty for the twenty-third time, or that Miles might show up next weekend."

"A photo of you and Miles would calm his fans down."

"Here's another post. He says, 'Trouble at Home for Kate Violent? Not only is trouble raining down on Kate V. from all sides, but I also hear she should look close to home for another possible source. Am I sure? No, but the connections are hard to ignore. Sometimes it's as simple as A-B-C-D...all the way to Z. Get some popcorn, Readers, this is getting good!'"

"That's weird. I wonder what he means?"

"And who."

She looked at her watch. "I owe the Porsche folks another hour of strapping kids into a racecar, but I'll help you figure it out after that." She hustled away again.

With fifteen minutes left before we could close up shop, the crowd dwindled and the light started to fade. Our crew was over at the transport trailer, parked against the freeway in the least-used corner of the mall lot, preparing to load the car back up. Three men swaggered through our event. They were large, round-cheeked and sunburned, wearing shorts, NASCAR t-shirts, and tan work boots. Friends on a construction crew, maybe. They stopped and stared when they reached our booth.

"Sheeeee-it, boys," one of them said.

"It's her," said another.

The first one spoke again. "Ain't it bad enough the Cup race was *ruined* for me today because Miles couldn't run? Now we gotta see the bitch caused the problem?"

"That kind of language is uncalled for." Mike appeared next to me and crossed his arms over his chest. "How about an apology?"

I felt heat rise in my neck and face. "Forget it," I murmured.

The three men stood silently, defiant. I returned their glares, refusing to back down. Jack moved to my other side and Tom stepped up behind me.

The third guy, who hadn't spoken yet, walked forward, coughed, and spit a wad of saliva, chew, and I didn't know what on the ground two feet from me. He curled his lip and returned to his friends. I wanted to gag, but didn't react.

The second one snickered, reaching a hand under his t-shirt to rub his chest, exposing boxer shorts bunched above low-riding shorts—more than I wanted to know about his clothing choices. "Don't know why they let her on the track anyway. My dog could drive better than her."

*At least there's **some** talent in his household.* I kept that to myself.

The impasse was finally broken by the appearance of Stuart and a huge, scowling security guard who looked capable of taking on all three fools at once and wiping the floor with them afterwards. I allowed myself the hint of a smile.

He approached them and spoke in a low tone. "Move along now. Show's over."

For a split second the trio looked like they might protest, but they settled for more sneers and dirty looks, then left in a hurry.

Mike and I exhaled at the same time. Jack looked grim and made Holly—who arrived a minute later, sorry to miss the excitement—promise to stick with me.

"You heard the man, Kate V. I'm with you. Ready to head back to the hotel?"

"Do you really have to call me that?"

"Yes, sugar, I really do."

Chapter Twenty

The only contact I had with the outside world that evening was a phone call from Zeke, who didn't bother with a greeting.

"What in *hell* is going on, Kate?"

"I'm not sure. Which problem are you referring to?"

"How many do you have? I'm talking about whatever you did to Felix."

"Are you kidding me?" My voice climbed two octaves. "Why would you say that?" *Felix was right, even my good friend thinks it's my fault we don't get along.*

"Felix likes everyone." He sounded confused.

"No, he doesn't. What did he say about me?"

Zeke paused, and I pictured him on the other end of the phone, habitually pushing against a piece of furniture with one foot to lean his chair back on two legs. He had the build of a fireplug and a smile made for toothpaste ads—straight, even, white teeth set off by his tan skin and white-blond hair. He didn't sound like he was smiling now. "He pointed me to recordings of you losing your cool."

"Minus the bits where he and a jackass fan provoked me," I put in.

"Ah. What happened with you and Felix, anyway?"

"Nothing. The first time I met him he didn't like me. I tried to be nice until he told me I'd wash out of racing and blame everyone else for my inadequacies. And he threw Sam Remington in my face."

"Why didn't you tell me? I'd have punched his bloody nose in!" Zeke's combination South African and Australian accent was stronger when he was emotional.

"It wouldn't have helped. I don't know why he doesn't like me."

"He's spreading bad news to anyone who will listen."

"As he told me today, everyone believes him, not me. He's got the Ringer listening—or *is* the Ringer. That's another one who doesn't like me." I filled him in on the efforts of my PR team.

"Maybe Juliana can ask Felix why the vendetta against you," he suggested.

"Good idea."

"It's good to see her back in racing. I knew she'd be top dog wherever she was, because she had more will to win than anyone I'd ever met. Not the talent you had, but if will was all it took, she'd be world champion."

"She seems happy. Eager to make her mark—she talked about wanting to be in the booth."

"She'll have to leapfrog Felix to do that—unless he cracks up and gets fired for inappropriate behavior. There's an idea."

"Don't tattle, Zeke. My big brother doesn't have to beat up the school bully."

"We'll see. I heard Felix's marriage broke up not long ago—or maybe it was some other family problem. Issues going on outside of work. Maybe he's taking it out on you. I'll ask around."

"Let me know if you figure out why he hates me."

He agreed and asked about Ellie's death, as the official media communications he'd heard contained few details. We had a long-standing agreement that everything between us was off-record, unless he was officially interviewing me, so I explained what I knew and told him about the possible hit-and-run. He got upset again and offered to drive me to and from the track every day.

I promised to contact him anytime I had a problem. "For now, tell me who you know was in downtown Atlanta yesterday."

He named a dozen drivers from the Star Mazda and World Challenge series. "We had a coaching meeting at a local go-kart track to prep for next weekend."

"You're here already? I thought you were home in Charlotte."

"We had a couple appointments, so we're here already, Rosalie and me."

"What about people at Siebkens last week, Zeke?"

He rattled off twenty names. Most were familiar, but I noted a few new ones. We were silent a moment, then he spoke again. "I still can't believe Ellie's gone. Ethan's doing what he can, but he's overwhelmed."

"You know Ellie's husband?"

"He's Rosalie's brother."

"I didn't know that."

He sighed. "They had a falling out a few years ago. She doesn't talk about him much. Short story, Ellie knew Ethan and Rosalie growing up. I dated Ellie a couple times, we stayed friends, and she introduced me to Rosalie."

"Wow, OK." I processed that for a moment. "Is Ethan—could I—"

"You want to talk to him?"

"To apologize, for maybe being the target."

"It's not your fault, Kate, and he'd say the same. Call him." He gave me the number.

We were saying goodbye when I thought of something. "Did you know Stuart and Ellie were engaged a while back?"

"Sure. Never thought Stuart was right for her."

"Why didn't you tell me?"

"Why would I? You didn't ask."

That was a man for you.

By the next morning, the Ringer posted "Standoff at the Sandham Swift Corral," which discussed how Kate Violent got herself and her team in trouble. I practiced letting his comments roll off my back. The constant, snarky live-blogging of my life was tiring, but he was so predictably nasty about the incidents he reported, I began to find him farcical. I wished the rest of the world felt the same.

I felt buoyant that morning because it was time to start preparing for the next race weekend. I ran five miles, pushed myself on the weight machines, and talked to my grandparents. I solved my daily Twitter dilemma by retweeting items from Beauté and BCRF about the new campaign. I also started my mental process of relearning the track by watching in-car video from Petit Le Mans last year and visualizing laps. I liked to get my head in the game before I set tire on pavement.

I had two other items on the day's agenda. The first was a follow-up test to ensure I had in no way been affected by concussion. All ALMS drivers were required to be baseline tested for neurocognitive functioning at the start of the season, and then we were required to be tested after any diagnosed—or suspected—concussions. To be allowed to race again, we had to pass at a level similar to our baseline capabilities to prove there were no lasting effects.

Strictly speaking, I didn't have to take and pass the test, because no one ever suggested I was concussed after the last race. But I wanted everyone to know I was at the top of my game, and it was easy enough to find a testing center. By the end of the thirty-minute session—during which a computer program tested my memory, reaction time, attention span, and problem-solving skills—I was exhausted. But I gladly paid that price to prove myself 100 percent fit for racing.

The second important activity was an educational appointment. Through the executive director of the BCRF, I'd arranged to meet with women currently undergoing treatment for breast cancer. I took Holly with me to a hospital near downtown Atlanta, where we learned about the disease, as well as the courage it took to meet the challenge head-on. The individuals we spoke with made it clear they were ordinary women with no other choice. Their stories were incredibly moving, and I was more grateful than ever to stand for them.

We exited the hospital and walked into a barrage of reporters and cameras. *Is someone famous in there?* I wondered. Then I heard the voices.

"Kate! Kate! Who were you meeting with? What can you tell us? Were you bringing comfort to ordinary women with cancer?

How did you entertain them?" There were only seven men, but they caused a lot of commotion.

My jaw dropped, and I stopped walking.

Holly tugged me forward, shouting, "No comment."

"Come on. You drag us all out here, give us something," one voice called from the pack. I ignored them.

We reached the car with two guys still following us, snapping pictures I hoped were useless. That's when I realized what I'd heard.

I turned around. "Wait. Will you tell me something off-record for a minute?"

The two photographers lowered their cameras, frowned at each other, and nodded.

"You said I called you?"

The short guy with curly hair and a moustache spoke. "I got a voicemail from you, saying you'd be at the hospital this afternoon with fresh details on your wreck with Miles Hanson and your efforts to atone by visiting women with cancer. So, do you—"

I waved a hand and cut him off, looking to the other guy. "Is that what you got?"

A brief nod accompanied the taller, balding redhead's skeptical look.

The first guy spoke again. "Now I'm pissed you called me out here. Gonna take me an extra hour to get home to my family for dinner."

I rubbed my temples, trying to stop the pounding in my head. "First of all—no, still off-record. I didn't call you. I'm sorry," I added, to counter their protests. "I didn't. I don't know who did, but I'll find out. Because this makes me look awful."

The redhead nodded. "Sure does. Looks like you're using us for publicity without giving us anything in return. Give and take, you know?"

I closed my eyes and took three deep breaths, striving for calm. I looked from one photographer to the other. "If I go on-record with you, will you report my whole story? That I didn't call you, but I believe I'm the victim of a bad joke?"

They both agreed, and I held an impromptu interview with them, both freelancers who focused on the sports world. I posed for photos, gave them my contact information for follow up, and promised them access at the track the next weekend. In return, I got their information and the promise of some good press, for once. They also said they'd look up the number "my" call came from.

Holly drove us back to our hotels while I made frantic calls to PR people at both Beauté and the BCRF to apologize and explain. Both reps took down the reporters' information, the BCRF woman promising to contact them herself.

After hanging up, I made notes on the men's business cards. "Colton Butler—he was the shorter guy with the moustache?"

"And the cowboy boots. Nice ones," she commented, merging into the next lane.

"Trust you to notice shoes. Jimmy O'Brien, he was taller, buzz-cut balding redhead, toothy grin."

"With a devilish glint in his eye."

"I'll remember them."

"You're avoiding the elephant in the car, Kate. Who called them pretending to be you?"

Chapter Twenty-one

Stuart had the same question when I saw him that night. He also asked the corollary. "Who knew you'd be at the hospital?"

"Holly. Everyone in the interview room, including the camera crew—who could have told Felix later. Or told the Ringer. Told anyone."

"Do you think the Ringer did this? He's not usually active."

I grabbed a stack of napkins and followed him to a bench outside the Bruster's Ice Cream on Peachtree Industrial Boulevard, three miles from my hotel. "I didn't find a Ringer post about it yet, but both the Ringer and Felix are out to get me. At least with Miles Hanson fans, like those yahoos yesterday, I know why—can even understand it."

"Obviously the Ringer has a habit of bullying—and no, I don't know who the Ringer is. As for Felix…."

"Do you think Felix could *be* the Ringer?"

Stuart looked blank, spoon poised over his hot fudge waffle bowl.

"I know, weird idea." I scooped up a bite of my peanut butter cup sundae. "Holly didn't think so either. I keep pairing them because they're both after me."

"It's an interesting thought. I don't think Felix knows how to interact with a woman as a peer—professionally or personally. I don't know why, but I've never seen it. Maybe Jack would know more. I think one of his brothers, or an uncle, raced at the same time as Felix."

"I'll ask Jack." I took another bite. "Good idea to get dessert."

He smiled sideways at me. "I thought I'd change things up with you. Coffee seemed too adult."

"You're calling me a child?" My tone was teasing, matching his.

"I have to be awfully serious all day at work. With you I like to lighten up, have a little fun. Try mine." He extended his spoon with chocolate ice cream and chocolate fudge, and I let him feed it to me.

I couldn't resist a playful, lighthearted Stuart, damn him. But mixed with the pleasure I felt in his company was a kernel of unreasonable anger at him and Ellie. I should have been able to enjoy a new lover, to be comfortable touching him, being with him. Instead I felt tense and prickly because of my questions and fears.

"Where did you go, Kate?" He ate more dessert, watching me.

"Sorry, lots on my mind."

"About that." He frowned. "Maybe you could stay with me for a couple days after this weekend. So we can talk. Stay in the guest room if you want, but give us a chance."

I felt relief out to my fingers and toes. *I can deal with racing first, him later.* "That would be good. I can't think straight now."

"You've got a few problems, don't you? People spreading stories about you spun the wrong way, plus making you look like a diva to the press."

Just before he picked me up at my hotel that night, I'd found articles online about my "duplicitous behavior" at the hospital. Most included quotes from a prominent women's activist group and a cancer-support organization taking me to task for a "blatant cry for attention at the expense of ordinary heroes trying to beat the odds." I'd also found a public statement from my BCRF contact refuting the stories, but it wasn't widely disseminated. Being unjustly accused still stung.

Stuart went on. "Also, someone tried to poison you."

"Don't forget trying to run me down."

Stuart looked at me, disbelief on his face. I realized he didn't know about the incident in downtown Atlanta, and I quickly explained. For a long time, he didn't speak.

"Are you all right?" I finally asked.

He got up to throw his empty cup in the trash, and when he sat back down, he ran both hands through his hair, stopping at one point and pulling on the roots. When he removed his hands, the curly bits I liked flopped down on his forehead.

"Don't get yourself killed, Kate."

"I'm trying not to."

"Try harder."

I went from mellow to annoyed in a heartbeat. "I'm handling everything as best I can. Don't get bossy on me. I know it's your natural tendency—"

"Give me a break," he cut in. "I'm saying this because I'm worried. Because I am panicked at the thought of you in serious danger."

Warning bells went off in my head. "If this is about racing—"

"This is not about your job." He sounded disgusted. "Do not confuse me with ignorant boys in your past who tried to prove their manhood by making you something less than you are. I would never stop you from racing."

"Holly told you stories."

He waved a hand in the air. "This is about you being run down on the street or poisoned in a bar. I'm not willing to lose you." He rested his hand on mine.

I nodded. "I don't want to be lost."

"Good. Then keep yourself out of harm's way."

"I also don't want to be told what to do."

"Your team tells—"

"By a boyfriend, Stuart."

"Then I'm asking."

I nodded and bent my head to finish my ice cream. A minute later, I threw my own cup away and pulled the two lists of names from my purse. "There's a way you can help. Tell me who else was at Siebkens or near Atlanta those nights."

He looked them over. "You have me down?"

"We were being thorough. Holly's there, too."

He mentioned a dozen people at Siebkens, including my father and someone else from the bank, plus some journalists whose names I recognized but didn't know by sight. He had no input for Atlanta, but conceded that anyone who lived in the area could have been there—if they'd known where I'd be.

That raised an interesting point. Maybe the hit-and-run attempt was opportunistic, not planned. Or even a simple, unrelated accident. I put the names away and held out a hand to him for the walk back to his car.

"It's still hard to believe someone tried to kill me," I said. "Trust me, I'm taking it seriously. I know there's an army raining everything from gossip to physical violence down on my head. I'm collecting names, but I have no clue—beyond members of Miles Hanson's fan club—about reason."

"Maybe you should shake things up—I can't believe I'm saying this." He stopped me next to the car, putting his hands on my shoulders. "I don't mean poke an alligator with a stick. But instead of being passive, at the mercy of whatever the bad guys do next, maybe you should take control. You'll be happier being active."

He was right—moreover, what he didn't say was also right. I'd been passive since the accident in the race, ducking or running away from the insults. Trying not to rock the boat, except when I'd held emotion in too much and lost my cool publicly.

I searched his face, the affection and support in his clear, green eyes making me gooey inside. "Shaking things up might make them worse."

"What's worse than feeling helpless and out of control?"

"Good point."

If I could only figure out what "take control" meant.

Chapter Twenty-two

I woke up the next morning, my head buzzing with Stuart, a killer, lists of names, angry fans, pranksters, a new sponsor to please, existing sponsors to please, tweets to send, a race to run, a season championship on the line, and deals to set up for the next racing year. Plus my father to deal with and new family to meet—if I went to his party. I needed a workout to clear my head.

I ran a mile down the road outside my hotel before I realized running alone on a deserted, public street wasn't a great idea. I returned quickly, watching all directions for a possible attack, and finished in the hotel gym.

After cleaning up, eating a late breakfast, and packing my race gear in my Jeep, I picked up three dozen doughnuts, a spread of cured and jerkied meats, and an assortment of bottled beer—a further thanks to the team for fixing the car I'd wrecked. Then I headed out to the racetrack, pulling in to Road Atlanta around eleven. I relaxed as I drove through the paddock to Sandham Swift. *Finally, I can focus on racing.*

I was opening the Jeep's back hatch when my phone rang with Lily and Matt Diaz on the other end, hoping I had a few minutes to talk. I sat down in the cargo area, legs hanging over the back bumper, and dug a notepad and pen out of my bag.

Lily sounded full of energy. "We've gone through your inbox."

"Our intern did the basic sorting, to be honest," Matt put in.

"Whatever, dude, don't interrupt," Lily continued. "We've got subfolders of messages in a couple categories: media, fans to respond to, crazies to ignore, and crazies to watch out for. It's the last group we want to give you a heads-up about, Kate."

It seemed to be time for me to speak. "All right."

"We'll be e-mailing you the summary with pertinent details," Matt said, "including which messages to respond to, and info on the media requests we're handling. We've noted some troublesome e-mails, since some of those are threats, as you discovered yourself. We'll help you keep an eye on those."

"Makes sense," I said.

"But there are a handful of oddballs," Lily said. "We want to talk about those."

"I'm ready."

"First," Matt shuffled papers as he spoke, "there are four people who want to give you things—homemade jam, a twelve-year-old's drawing of you and your car, an embroidered wall hanging of your car, and a framed photo of you in the Winner's Circle."

I was used to receiving drawings, photos, and other gifts—though the jam was new. "Sure, I'll respond to those."

Matt spoke again. "The second issue is five addresses that contacted you in non-threatening ways multiple times. They offered support, but since they e-mailed more than once, you might keep an eye out for references to those names."

"We use 'names' loosely," commented Lily, "given only one seems like a first and last name. The rest are nicknames, though one is pretty flattering."

"Flattering?" I was getting a sugar high from smelling the boxes of doughnuts next to me.

Matt shifted papers again. "One is 'racer28guy,' which could refer to you."

"Or his own racing number," I said.

"True." Matt clicked his pen a couple times. "The others are jimbo67, peterwheeler, mainstreet35, and mrguarddog."

I dutifully wrote down the e-mail names. "I see your point, Lily."

"They may be people you want to talk to. They seem harmless." She paused. "But there's one other sender that's a little odd."

I didn't like that buoyant Lily had turned subdued and serious. "Odd how?"

Matt spoke before Lily could. "Lily has her own opinion. The facts are his e-mail name is 'katefangmr' and he's e-mailed every couple days for the last two weeks."

I considered. "That's back to right before the Wisconsin race. Is he yelling at me about Miles?"

"The opposite," Matt said. "He's friendly, looking for your attention. He must have met you sometime, because he refers to that."

"I meet so many people at races, that doesn't narrow it down."

"And he doesn't give any clues to who he is. He says he admires you and wants to talk with you again. He grows increasingly attached as the e-mails go on. Tells you about his life and emotions."

I didn't see a problem. "That happens with fans. They follow my racing career, see me year after year, and all that good fan stuff."

Lily exhaled loudly. "That's usually great. But my gut's saying something different. You can't prove it from these e-mails, Kate, but if I had to place money? I'd bet you've got yourself a stalker."

I leaned forward and put my head between my knees. Focused on breathing. Thought of my new pal, George. *He's such a normal guy, it can't be him. Right?* I didn't look forward to watching everyone for signs of weird behavior.

Matt disagreed with Lily's opinion, and she admitted it wasn't clear my correspondent had entered stalker territory. So far he—or she?—was only very friendly, which Lily told me I could see for myself when they sent me their packet of information. Matt told me they'd keep handling my inbox for a while, which meant I was still getting hate mail. We said goodbye, Matt promising to keep Lily from scaring me again.

I shook off my concern and got up to haul the treats into the half-arranged garage area, smiling with pleasure at the music of clanking tent poles, banging mallets, and jangling metal tool chests being rolled around. This, the Tuesday before Petit

Le Mans, was setup day. Up and down the paddock, teams unfurled large awnings from the sides of transport trailers or snapped together sections of thick plastic mesh used as garage flooring. In pit lane, they erected popup tents over pit carts, tire racks, fueling rigs, huge plastic jugs of fuel, and person-sized bottles of compressed air trailing yards of hose. The racetrack looked and sounded like a circus had come to town, minus the elephant poop. It smelled like race fuel and cigarette smoke. It felt like home.

Over in the hospitality half of our team's setup, I saw Aunt Tee had set up two eight-foot tables, draped them with table-cloths, and placed sponsor and team information on one and snack food on the other. The two coolers were already stocked with sodas and bottled water. I saw her unfolding the hanging rack for firesuits and got my gear out of the Jeep.

"Good morning, Kate." She gave me a hug after I'd set down my bags. "Bringing food for the team was very thoughtful."

"I still feel bad about letting everyone down."

"You're a sweetheart. This is everything?"

I handed over my helmet in a soft-sided case, my team fire-suit, and a duffel containing my fireproof undergarments, my balaclava or head sock, radio cable with earplugs custom-molded to my ears, gloves, driving shoes, and Head And Neck Support or HANS device. Though the team had two other sets of my undergarment layer and two firesuits, I always traveled with my helmet and at least one set of gear, in case I was called on for promotional work or to drive when I wasn't with the team.

She got busy unpacking my bag, and I sat down in a chair to deal with a task I dreaded, calling Ellie's husband Ethan. He sounded tired as he picked up, but his tone warmed when I identified myself. I stumbled over condolences, and he thanked me, though he wouldn't hear my apologies.

"You're not responsible, Kate."

"I know that logically. My heart doesn't listen."

"I understand."

"How are you doing? Do you have help with your twins?"

"Ellie's parents live four miles away from us. They've been a big help the last couple years, stepping in when we needed them, and the kids are used to being at their grandparents' house—that's where they are now, in fact. I'm here trying to go through Ellie's things."

I felt a physical pain in my chest imagining Ellie's absence in his house. His life. "I shouldn't be interrupting."

"It's fine. I need the break."

I wasn't sure what to say. "I missed her all those years. I'm glad I got the chance to see how happy she was. I suppose I wanted to connect with you to say that."

"It helps keep her close. She missed you, too."

I blinked furiously to keep the tears at bay.

He chuckled, tired sounds. "Don't cry too much, Kate. You're at Road Atlanta this weekend, right? One of my favorite tracks."

"You're in the business, I heard?"

"With Dunlop Tires. I'll be back to my Grand-Am rounds next season. In the meantime, maybe you can go out there and win one for Ellie." His voice changed, as he choked up. "You know, so much was finally going well for her—the twins are strong and healthy, she'd turned a corner and found a goal, she had a new job to look forward to. It was all so positive. There was so much potential. It would mean something to her if you'd go fulfill *your* potential."

Tears streamed down my face, and I tried not to sniffle into the phone. "I will," I whispered. I spoke louder. "I'll do my best every time—for people like Ellie who won't have the chance. But this weekend's for her."

There wasn't much more I could say, and I'd taken enough of his time. We disconnected with thanks for the conversation on both sides.

Chapter Twenty-three

I spent five minutes thinking about determination before Mike arrived. He nosed his car up to mine at the rear of the paddock, bumping it, making it rock backward against the brake. I crossed my arms and glared at his laughing face through the windshield. Racecar drivers loved to play bumper-cars with rentals.

He got out, and I pointed to where his car still leaned on mine. "That's *my* car."

"A love tap." He smirked, retrieving his suit and helmet from the trunk.

We walked back under the awning, where he gave Aunt Tee a bear hug before turning over his gear. He pushed his sunglasses on top of his head. "Fancy-pants here?"

I laughed. "Fancy-pants" was the nickname he'd given Leon Browning, a brilliant, young, Scottish driver who'd joined us for the twelve-hour endurance race at Sebring in March and would race with us for the ten-hour Petit Le Mans. Back in January, we'd eyed the short, slight twenty-year-old with the flaming thicket of red hair, dressed to the nines in pointed shoes, artfully ripped jeans, and a fitted, wildly colorful button-down shirt. Mike had voiced the thought in my mind, "That's a hell of a lotta style for the US market."

"Run of the mill in civilized nations," Leon offered, smiling.

I shook his hand, eyeballing him and deciding we were equal in height, though I had five years and a different gender on him.

Mike crossed his arms, raised an eyebrow, and exaggerated his Southern drawl. "Ain't you sharper than a straight razor? Kate, this here's Fancy-pants."

Leon nodded at Mike, mimicking his stance. "Aye, then, ye great moose-boy."

A single beat, then Mike roared with laughter. They'd been pals ever since.

Aunt Tee clucked at Mike's question. "Leon has arrived. He's down at tech getting his gear inspected." She referred to the fact that all drivers and crew needed their firesuits, fire-retardant undergarments, shoes, helmets, and HANS devices inspected for compliance to safety and badging regulations at every race weekend. "He said he'd be back for lunch."

I looked at Mike. "Eat, then take a cart around the track?"

"Good plan."

An hour and a half later, the three of us commandeered one of the team's electric golf carts and headed down the paddock toward Pit In, to access the track.

"@katereilly28: With Mike Munroe and Leon Browning in a golf cart to tour the Road Atlanta track. Petit Le Mans in 4 days!"

Mike drove, I sat next to him, and Leon sprawled on the back bench seat. We'd welcomed Leon with hugs (me) and insults (Mike), both of which he responded to with vigor. In the months since we'd seen him, he'd taken the GP2 series—a support series to Formula 1, often racing on F1's qualifying day—by storm, winning a number of races. He'd never driven Road Atlanta, so he was eager for the reconnaissance lap we were making, as well as our advice. I'd driven the track the year before with the team, and Mike had been there many times.

We puttered down the main straight, and Mike spoke over his shoulder. "We'll talk you through it, all right, Fancy-pants?"

Leon settled his sunglasses more firmly on his face. "Take it away, old man."

Mike drove the racing line on the track as much as possible in the golf cart, moving at something less than one-tenth race speed.

"Up the hill from Turn 1, you're looking at sky," he began. "Blind hill, aim for that telephone pole. That'll set you up for Turn 2, which isn't much. Then you turn for the right-hander of 3."

We slowly crested the hill and followed the gentle sweep of Turn 2 to the left. Mike let the golf cart drift all the way to the left side of the track after 2, then angled right for Turn 3. He bumped us over the curbing of 3, the golf cart wobbling, and I spoke. "Use the low part of this curb—not the high part. It'll help keep you balanced, and you'll accelerate through it."

Mike stopped near the exit of three. An SUV went slowly past us, ALMS marketing staff hanging out the open back hatch, ready to place track signs for maximum television coverage. A driver also passed on a bicycle as we sat looking down at the valley that contained the Esses.

"Here," Mike pointed as he spoke, "set your hands for the sweeping left turn—don't get jerky. Find your arc and hold it. Feed throttle on."

We moved again, picking up speed as we curved through Turn 4 and the track fell away from us. Mike lifted his foot off the accelerator and the cart gave a jerk that sent Leon falling forward over the seat backs.

"Oy!" He shouted.

"You'll remember to lift here, won't you?" Mike pressed the pedal again and the cart moved faster downhill.

I turned to Leon. "This is my favorite part of the track. Great rhythm through here, no braking, accelerate through the curves. The runout of Turn 5 ahead is the other curb you want to use, but stay off the rest. None of them will help you."

We made it up the hill to 5, and Leon turned to look behind us as Mike went onto and beyond the exit curbing.

We cruised through 6 and 7 and turned onto the long back straight. The golf cart was slow on the gradual uphill of the first half, and just before we reached the top of the rise, a rental car went by. The racecar driver in the passenger seat nodded at us. The guy behind him, who I recognized as a prototype driver from a visiting European team, started to nod, then did a double-take at the sight of me, his nose wrinkled as if he'd tasted something vile.

"What the hell was that about?" Mike asked, after the car was gone.

I shrugged. "And who was it?"

"Dominic Lascuola." Leon leaned forward over the seats. "Races over in Europe, though he's a Yank."

The name was familiar. "Lascuola? Does he have a sister?"

"A younger sister," Leon confirmed. "Twenty-two, racing off and on with a Mazda team in Grand-Am."

"Colby, right?"

"She's here with a team in World Challenge this weekend." Mike raised an eyebrow at me. "I hear some call her the next Kate Reilly."

"God help her." I laughed.

We finally were headed downhill on the back straight, looking at Turns 10a and 10b, a quick left-right zig-zag.

Mike pointed ahead of us. "The most important turns on the track. Bottom line, you want to roll through 10a and square off 10b. Be fast out, because Turn 11 is nothing. You're accelerating from the exit of 10b to the end of the front straight."

Mike barely lifted off the accelerator as he swung through 10a to the left and turned hard right for 10b. Leon scooted to the inside of each turn, and the golf cart still leaned precariously. Mike kept his foot down going up the hill, but we'd slowed to a snail's pace by the time we reached the bridge across the peak of the hill.

I waved a hand at the sign on the bridge with "Road Atlanta" and three colored blocks in a row horizontally: black, yellow, and red. "Another blind crest, lots of speed. Aim for the yellow block and trust you're in the right place. Let the car settle back down on the wheels after getting light over the rise, then stand on the throttle."

Mike held the cart in a straight line as we swept down the hill, the track moving to the right. We touched the left side of the track partway down the hill, and he started to turn right.

"Bump!" Mike shouted, as we rolled over the bump on the racing line most of the way down the hill. "Happens every lap. Get used to it."

I turned to look at Leon again. "You'll hit about 130 through here, full throttle." I grinned. "They like to say it takes balls for this turn."

He winked at me. "Lucky all of us in the 28 car have them."

We rolled down the front straight again and entered the pits at Pit Out, driving the wrong way through pit lane to the paddock. Leon stretched his legs out again across the back seat, and I finger-combed tangles from my hair.

We parked the cart behind the garage and sat down in green molded-plastic chairs in the hospitality area next to Tom. Mike and Leon each took two of the cookies Aunt Tee offered around; I took one. Tom was occupied with the computer on his lap.

"You making media magic, Tom?" Mike asked between bites.

Tom looked up, more worried than amused. And he was looking at me.

The unsettled feeling returned to the pit of my stomach. "Now what?"

Chapter Twenty-four

"Good news and bad news," Tom said. "The good is fan voting closed for the ALMS Favorite Driver award. Informal polls show lots of support for you."

"Are you kidding me?"

Tom shook his head. "Most of the voting happened before the Miles incident."

"Oh, aye," Leon broke in, wiping his fingers on a paper towel. "I meant to ask about the last race. Wee bit of a mistake there, what?"

I pointed a finger at him. "Don't get cheeky, Fancy-pants." I turned back to Tom. "It's a nice vote of pre-wreck confidence. We'll get ready to congratulate someone else at the banquet." The favorite driver and "From the Fans" award were both voted on by ALMS fans via the Series website and announced at the championship banquet held Sunday evening, the day after Petit. The banquet was primarily for the distribution of season championship trophies, though there were other awards, tributes, and roasts presented as well.

Tom still looked grim.

"The bad news?" I asked.

"The Ringer's got a post addressed to the entire ALMS paddock titled, 'Brace Yourselves for Calamity Kate.'"

"What happened to Kate Violent?"

"He uses that, too."

I turned to Leon. "Have you heard any of this?"

"The Ringer's side, but I'm not witless enough to believe everything he says. Sorry about the loss of your friend."

"Thanks." I looked at Tom. "And?"

"He says, 'Attention ALMS paddock, fans, and race attendees. Series regular—but for how long?—Kate Reilly, aka Kate Violent, aka Calamity Kate, has arrived in Georgia. A walking, talking, driving disaster. Consider: in the past two weeks, she's wrecked a racing legend and herself, found a friend dead, lashed out at hardworking Southern folk, and pulled a bait-and-switch on innocent media representatives doing their jobs. Defying logic, she scored a plum sponsorship deal the likes of which the ALMS has never seen and is in the running for the fan-favorite driver award. Undeserved? Many think so. Frankly, readers, I can't wait to see what happens next...but I've got a Benjamin says we'll see more missteps than triumphs. For those of you in her orbit, watch your back!'"

Leon finally broke the appalled silence. "What's a Benjamin, again?"

I sighed. "Hundred-dollar bill."

"I always forget your currency. Also, good job on the makeup gig. Photos make you look fantastic." His voice was calm, even bored. He collected another two cookies, offering me one with a raised eyebrow.

I shook my head. "I'd give a lot to know who that guy is."

"Aye, they're wondering that throughout Europe as well. His range of sources is impressive."

"Are you all right, Kate?" Tom looked worried. "This is awful. Rude."

I felt frustrated, angry, scared about reactions from others— for a minute I thought I'd burst out crying. And then I moved beyond it. I let it all go. Felt free. Calm. "I'm really, truly bored of this. Time to focus on racing."

Mike nodded. "If your sponsor doesn't tell you to take a hike, and Jack has no problem with it, screw what the Ringer says. He's an anonymous bully."

I looked from Mike to Leon. "Thanks. I'll try to keep the drama away from you."

"There's one great thing to come out of this." Mike grinned.

Tom looked hopeful. "Yeah?"

"I'm absolutely calling her Calamity now."

So was the rest of the paddock—usually in jest. As I walked around with Leon, briefing him on different cars and drivers we'd compete against, I did my best to ignore speculative looks and disdainful repetitions of the Ringer's nicknames. For the first time, recognizing faces of people I didn't know disconcerted me—I imagined stalkers and poisoners at every turn. I needed to get a grip or I'd be a mess when 90,000 fans showed up over the weekend.

Leon and I stood chatting with Holly in front of Western Racing's paddock when sometimes-racer, sometimes-reporter Scott Brooklyn approached.

"Hi everyone, sorry to interrupt." He gave each of us a friendly nod and smile, greeting Holly by name and introducing himself to Leon. Then he held out a hand to me. "Kate, I'm Scott Brooklyn. I think we met last year."

I shook. "You're not driving this weekend?" He'd raced at Petit the year before, and I wondered if he'd made the transition from driver with fill-in reporting jobs to reporter with fill-in driving jobs. He was handsome enough for TV, with expressive brown eyes and an engaging smile.

"Not this year." He held up a small notebook. "Paying the bills with field reporting for a couple motorsports sites and a huge health and fitness portal. Would you have time for a short interview in the next couple days?"

I gave him Matt and Lily's information and explained I was routing all requests through them. "If you'll check in with them, I'll make sure it happens."

"Will do," he said, slipping his pen into the spirals of his notebook. "One good turn deserves another. Guy down in the Benchmark garage asked me and another reporter lots of questions about you. More hostile than friendly. You might steer clear."

I glanced at Leon, who nodded and said, "Dominic Lascoula?"

"That's the guy," Scott responded.

"Not much I can do, but I'll stay away." I thought for a moment. *Take control, Kate.* "Scott, did you know Ellie Prescott?"

"I met her once, and I know Ethan. Such a shame." He looked sad.

"You were in the Tavern that night, weren't you? Didn't I see you there?"

He nodded. "I was, but I left to meet a friend before anything happened."

"I guess you didn't see anything strange? No one near our table?"

"You were at the back of the main room?" He crinkled up his forehead. "I can't think of anything. I told the police that also. I sure hope they catch the guy."

"Me, too." I tried for more. "Were you in downtown Atlanta on Saturday night? I thought I saw you outside a restaurant."

To my surprise, he nodded. "I met someone for dinner. Was it Ray's in the City?"

"Near there," I said, wishing I had a good way to ask who his friend was.

"Must have been me. I'll talk to you in a day or two, thanks." He waved at the others and headed back down the lane. Leon and I said goodbye to Holly and finished our paddock tour.

The team activity that evening was a private party at the corporate offices of our longtime sponsor Active-Fit, a sportswear company Steve and Vicki Royal founded after Steve's pro-hockey career ended. We spent an hour mingling and taking photos with Active-Fit employees, then sat at long tables eating the best pork ribs I'd ever tasted.

Vicki and I talked about makeup while we ate. She was grounded, friendly, and funny—and as polished as you'd expect a former professional cheerleader to be. That meant intimidatingly gorgeous, with long, blonde hair and sky blue eyes. If her laughter was any indication, I entertained her as much as she tutored me in why and when I'd use different types of products.

"You think eyebrow gel is bad?" She wiped tears from her eyes from laughing so hard. "Has anyone told you about the tricks they use in pageants?"

I shook my head.

"Vaseline for teeth, tape so bathing suits stay put, hemorrhoid cream for the bags under our eyes."

"That's disgusting."

Another peal of laughter. "It's what you do to win."

"Were you in pageants?"

"Miss South Carolina, twenty years ago now."

I was astonished. "You don't look a day over thirty."

"You are now my best friend." She beamed at me.

"Would you know Juliana Parker? She was Miss Alabama at one point."

"I know of her, met her somewhere. She was ten or fifteen years after me. Beautiful girl." She finished eating her chicken and arranged her plastic utensils carefully on her plate. I was awash in barbecue sauce, but she'd stayed neat and clean. "Didn't I hear she's with SGTV? How did that come about?"

I explained Juliana's early focus on both racing and pageants and her change of career direction since her mother's death. "We bonded the one year we raced together—with Ellie also. Especially then, it was great to have other females around. I wasn't the only fish out of water."

"I realized as the only woman in the ALMS you have to do some things differently—not change in the main transporter space with the guys, for instance. But I never thought you might be lonely."

"Once in a while." I wiped sauce from my mouth and fingers. "I can't be 'one of the guys' all the time."

She put her arm around my shoulder. "Anytime you need a girlfriend around, you let me know. I can talk makeup and shoes and cute boys with the best of them. Now tell me," she leaned her head close to mine. "How is that new Beauté line?"

I laughed and promised her samples.

Near the end of the party she and I sat with Jack and Tom, discussing the idea of Jack taking the team to the 24 Hours of Le Mans.

My mind was on my current predicament, not future shots at glory—though I was eager for a crack at the famed race. I spoke into a lull in the conversation. "Who would you hire if I weren't driving for you, Jack?"

He turned to me, the look on his face a mixture of surprise and concern.

I held up my hands. "Just wondering who'd benefit if someone bumped me off."

"I did that last year, can we not go through that again?"

It hadn't been an easy time for me or for Jack when he hired me as a replacement after Wade Becker was killed. But I needed to know. "This is hypothetical. You must have ideas."

He sighed, seeming reluctant. Wary. "I keep my eye out. Might try to get Leon, if he'd run a full season. The Forbes kid running IMSA Lights this year looks good. Another kid over in World Challenge, that Colby girl, she's got some talent. Or I might give some guys with more experience a try, depending on what I needed…Scott Brooklyn comes to mind. Joe Jones. Evan McCoy. That enough for you, Kate?"

"Yes, only curious." I hadn't expected to hear Scott and Colby's names. I knew Scott had been at the Tavern, but I'd have to find out if Colby had been there, too. Or her brother. "One other question. Were you around when Felix was racing?"

"I think my brother was on a team with him at one point. Why?"

"I wanted to know if his bad attitude was about me or about all women. People who know him now don't know anything. I wondered if you knew him then."

Jack stared at me without speaking, long enough I became uncomfortable. Finally, he spoke. "My dad told me a story once about a season of go-kart racing back in the nineteen-sixties or seventies. A bunch of boys in the field, and one girl, who was really fantastic—later qualified and ran the Indy 500. You know how there are horrible fathers these days who get violent over their kids' little league?"

We nodded at him, and he continued. "There was one of those fathers that season who was so outraged at his son finishing behind a girl that he made his son wear skirts to the racetrack until the son beat her—berated him publicly, too. It was only three races, but we're talking ten-year-olds. Some parents tried to talk to the father, but he took it out on his son, so they stopped. But everyone pitied the poor kid."

Vicki lowered her hand from her mouth, shock clear on her face. "That's abuse."

"I won't argue. 'Motivation' has a lot of ugly faces." Jack turned to me. "That boy was Felix."

Chapter Twenty-five

After Jack swore us to secrecy, I spent a good portion of the night pondering the size of the chip on Felix's shoulder about female drivers, instead of sleeping. The next morning, I retained feelings of horror and sympathy for the young man, even if I despised the choices he made as an adult.

After a workout in the hotel gym, I met Juliana at a breakfast café. We hugged hello and went inside to be seated.

"I felt like a ghoul, doing that interview." She smoothed her napkin across her lap.

"It's your job. Besides, it was about Ellie more than me."

She looked up from the menu. "Until the end."

"That's why I called, to see if you could help me with something. How well do you know Felix?" Hearing Jack's story changed my approach only slightly.

"Not well. I shadowed him to learn the ropes at SGTV for five races."

"We don't get along—that's no surprise—and I don't know why, but I'd like to change that. I don't like someone being mad at me, and it does me no good for the outlet covering our races to hate me. I was hoping you'd talk to him, find out why he feels that way—possibly mediate a cease fire?" The idea of being conciliatory irked me, but for the sake of my career and my team, playing nice with the media was vital.

Juliana smiled and reached across the table to pat one of my hands. "I'm happy to see what I can do."

"Thanks. I also need to find out why the Racing's Ringer dislikes me so much—don't suppose you have pull there?"

We laughed as the waiter approached to take our order, and then we chatted about our plans for the off-season. She'd be covering events and developing features to use throughout the coming year's broadcasts, as well as finding a house in Charlotte, North Carolina, near SGTV headquarters. I'd be lining up rides for the next season, fulfilling commitments for Beauté, and going home to my grandparents.

"Where do you want to end up, Kate? I remember your dream was Formula 1."

"And you were going to be the first woman to win the Indy 500."

Her mouth twisted into a grimace. "That wasn't in the cards, apparently."

"You've had amazing experiences, though. And you're so good at what you do."

"That's sweet of you to say, Kate." Her face lightened, and she raised an eyebrow. "Did you know my mother used you to encourage me? If I was tired, didn't want to do another practice lap, didn't want to study my racing books, she'd tell me, 'If you don't, Kate Reilly will come right in and steal your wins. She'll take your victories. She'll get all the podium glory and press coverage.'"

My jaw dropped. "Good grief, Jules, I'd never—"

"It wasn't about you, silly. It was about my mother inspiring me to be better. She knew saying 'Be the best,' wouldn't be as effective as saying, 'Kate is better than you.'"

"Still. I'm sorry?"

She laughed. "You had to be true to yourself, and so did I. We were competitors. It didn't stop us being friends then, and it won't stop us being friends now. Deal?"

"Deal." I recognized Jules was the same victim of a relentless parent as Felix—fortunately, with less bitter consequences.

She smiled. "Good. We need to hold on to our friendship this time. For us and for Ellie."

"I can't get over the fact she's gone." I signaled to the waiter that I'd finished my omelet, and we both accepted coffee.

"Her poor kids—it's tragic. Have the police come up with any information?"

"I haven't heard. I've been meaning to call them again and ask."

"Have you received other threats?"

I nodded. "I'm not sure how many, since I turned my e-mail account over to my PR people after the first death threat."

"Kate, no!"

"NASCAR fans, I assume. The messages I opened referenced Miles. Otherwise, a car nearly ran me down after our interview the other day."

She gasped and reached for my hand. "Was it deliberate?"

"I was rattled from losing my temper at Felix, so I don't know—but the driver did run a red light."

"What did the police think?"

"We couldn't describe the car well. They can't do much."

"It's been a hell of a week for you, hasn't it, Kate?"

I huffed a laugh. "You could say that."

"Promise me you'll let me know if anything else happens or if there's something I can do, besides talking to Felix."

"You could tell me who was near the table at Siebkens while you were alone there. Or anyone you remember seeing that night."

"Aren't the police doing that?"

"I'm trying to cross-reference with people in Atlanta this weekend."

"I chatted a minute with Scott Brooklyn, also with Stuart. Felix blew past, looking surly as usual. Zeke Andrews and a tired-looking woman—his wife?—walked through the room but only paused a moment." She thought more. "A couple drivers and crew I could pick out of a lineup, but that's about it."

I jotted new names on the back of a receipt in my purse. "Thanks. I owe you one."

"For payment, tell me about you and Stuart."

I kept my groan to myself. "Not much to the story."

"Liar. I see the way you look at each other. There's something there."

"It's complicated, and the thing with Ellie is weird."

"That he found her?"

"That they'd been engaged." I saw the surprise on her face. "You didn't know either? I thought you and Ellie stayed in touch."

Juliana shook her head. "We'd only reconnected a week before the Road America race, when she called me out of the blue."

"Yes, Stuart and Ellie were engaged, and she broke it off. I'm not sure how I feel—and I don't have spare energy now for more drama."

"I understand. Forget I asked."

"What about you, Jules? Any husbands or boyfriends?"

Her expression turned mischievous. "I've been seeing someone recently who makes my heart go pitty-pat, but I'm still toying with him."

"Not sure you like him enough?"

"I like him plenty, but it's early days. I've got to be careful he's not just using me to get a job." She saw my frown and went on. "I'm teasing, though he is out in the cold this year with the change from SPEED to SGTV."

"Scott Brooklyn? I'm doing an interview with him tomorrow." I'd gotten word that Lily and Matt had set a time for us.

"I left the Tavern that night to meet him—though he was annoyed I waited to say goodbye to you two and didn't go with him."

That explained his glowering expression.

Juliana smiled. "Over wine some night, I'll tell you about the country singer and the NFL running back I dated. You won't believe the entourages, drama, and big hair."

I promised to take her up on that as we left the café. We were outside next to our cars when Juliana stopped me with a hand on my arm. "One other thing. Is your contract settled with Jack for next year?"

"Not yet, why?"

She hesitated. "I hate to add to your troubles, but I heard a rumor he might not want you to return."

I had to look down to verify there was still ground under my feet.

"It was only a whisper," she said. "No idea if it's true. But supposedly with your ideas of doing the 24 Hours of Daytona, Le Mans, some other races, maybe he's not happy. Wants you focused on his team?"

Because I wrecked? But I'm bringing money and exposure from Beauté. And Mike does other races. Was that why Jack looked so strange when I asked him about other drivers last night—because he's working on replacing me?

Juliana hugged me, her voice muffled. "I'm sorry. I figured you'd rather know."

I patted her back and extricated myself, focused on breathing, made myself smile. "You're right, thanks. I'll see you later at the track."

I got to my car as quickly as possible. Kept breathing. Waved at Juliana as she pulled out of the lot. Pounded my steering wheel a couple times. *Really? I needed one more thing to go wrong now?*

Fine. I'd deal with this, too.

Chapter Twenty-six

I arrived at Road Atlanta by eleven o'clock, refusing to let fears about job security take root in my imagination. We had a big day ahead, including our first practice session and a visit by a group of pink-clad VIPs. I was surprised when the "two representatives each from BCRF and Beauté" I'd been told to expect included the heads of both organizations—Beauté's CEO, Lindsay Eastwood, and BCRF's executive director, Jessica Whitmore, along with their heads of marketing.

"@katereilly28: Ready to give Beauté and BCRF reps a tour of my #racing world. The #ALMS paddock goes pink for breast cancer awareness!"

I introduced everyone to Tom, who was driving the six-seater golf cart I'd borrowed from the Series, and we headed back down the hill from the parking area. Once on flat ground, he rolled slowly through the paddock, dodging race fans whose attention was focused on racecars, not golf carts.

Our team space sat in the middle of the front row of garages facing the pits, halfway between Pit Out at one end and Pit In, the Winner's Circle, and Series trailers at the other. I stood out front with the four women to explain the physical setup of pits and paddock, as well as what happened in each space. I also covered the structure of the race and the weekend itself: different classes of cars competing on the same track for overall and class wins, multiple drivers sharing a racecar, technical inspections, practice and qualifying sessions, and the race itself.

The Beauté marketing director looked up from a small note-pad. "What makes this race so special, Kate?"

"Petit Le Mans is based on the granddaddy endurance race of them all, the 24 Hours of Le Mans, in France. More than a decade ago, Don Panoz decided to run this race, and then he turned it into a series."

"Of course, Petit or *little* Le Mans," Lindsay said.

I nodded. "It's ten hours or a thousand miles, whichever comes first, and it's one of the major endurance races worldwide. Winning your class guarantees you an invitation to race at Le Mans. We want to win Petit for a lot of reasons."

Lindsay cast an eye down the paddock, then looked from Tom to me. "Can you?"

"Anything can happen on any day," I said. "We're not always the fastest in our class, but the Corvette racecar is solid and reliable. Our team works incredibly hard. Simply finishing is a big deal—that's a marathon in itself. Any spot on the podium would be a major accomplishment."

"Would you go to Le Mans if you won?" That was Jessica, the BCRF director.

Tom spoke up. "Jack's considered it. We've been eligible in the past, but he's never gone—it's quite an expense and under-taking. He hasn't said no for next year. Like Kate said, anything can happen."

"Who's ready to get in the car?" I led them to the garage side of our setup and introduced them to Jack and Mike. The rest of the crew kept to the background, looking amused at the influx of femininity.

The door was off the car, offering an unobstructed view of the tube-frame, molded seat, and interior. I explained how to climb in, demonstrating once, and Lindsay got in first. I leaned across her to take the steering wheel from its ceiling hook and snap it into place on the column, as well as explain the functions of the buttons and switches she saw. Then we took photos of her before she climbed out.

Tom went to fetch my helmet and HANS, at my request. After he helped Lindsay put them on, he spoke quietly to me. "Check the chinstraps. One seemed loose."

I nodded and continued my explanation. "Your helmet is tethered to the bit of the HANS standing up like a collar behind your neck, so your neck can't move beyond a limited range. Instead, the HANS transfers the force of any impact—that might otherwise give you whiplash or worse—to the braces on your shoulders and the rest of your torso. The seatbelts also go on top of the HANS on your shoulders, which minimizes violent movement even further."

I helped the last woman take the helmet off and pulled the HANS away with it. As Jack stepped forward with team hats for each of them, I felt for my chinstrap. Tom was right, the webbed strap on the right moved too much. I turned the helmet over and found the material almost severed.

"Kate, joining us?" Jack gestured at the four women entering the team's transport trailer.

"Right there." I crossed to Aunt Tee, who sat near the motorhome. "My chinstrap's split. Can you run down to the helmet guys and get them to fix it before practice today?" Stand 21, one of the two main suppliers of safety gear to Series participants, operated a combination storefront and repair shop in the paddock.

"Of course, I'll do it right now."

I hesitated before putting it in her hands. "Don't give it to anyone else. And keep the strap."

"What—"

"I'd like to see it. I owe you one." I scooted into the transport trailer.

For the next two hours, the women in pink and I met with Sandham Swift (Jack and Tom) and the ALMS (Stuart and two marketing minions) to discuss how the team and Series could support BCRF and Beauté. Jack's talk of possible promotions next year gave me hope Juliana's rumor was incorrect. In the end, all parties were excited about opportunities to reach new audiences for their products—whether makeup, racing, or cancer awareness.

All four women thanked me lavishly as Tom prepared to whisk them back to their cars. Before she got in the golf cart, Lindsay made a point of telling me her door, or phone line, was always open if I needed advice—from one woman in a man's world to another.

"But..." I looked past her to the other women.

"Even in a beauty products company, the business side of things—like our board of directors—is primarily male. I have an idea what you're dealing with. But you've got the goods." She gave my hand a quick squeeze and left with the others.

As I watched the golf cart set off down the paddock, I noticed a young woman on the other side of the lane looking from the retreating golf cart to me. She nodded at me and crossed through the moving crowd.

She approached, a hand extended. "Kate, I wanted to introduce myself. I'm Colby Lascuola. I'm running World Challenge this year."

"Great to meet you, Colby. I've heard good things."

We shook hands, sizing each other up. She was a couple years younger than me, an inch shorter, slim, and fit. A sunshine blonde with long, straight hair pulled back in a simple ponytail. She looked like she meant business, and her handshake confirmed it. We smiled at the same time, breaking the tension we both must have felt. I liked her.

"I hear they insult you and call you the new me." I put my hands to my hips. "I hope you tell them I'm the old you."

"Something like that." She laughed. "I've heard worse, you know?"

"Me, too."

She gestured in the direction of the golf cart. "Was that a group from Beauté?"

"And the Breast Cancer Research Foundation, yes. They were here for a tour."

"Thought so. Congratulations on getting that. I hoped they'd pick me."

"You knew about it? The first I heard was when they offered it to me."

"My management company told me Beauté was asking about me." She shrugged. "I wasn't supposed to know."

"Sorry you didn't get it."

She laughed again. "No, you're not. I'm not worried. Something else will come along."

I didn't doubt her, because she was pretty, engaging, and well-spoken, besides being a good driver. With a management company. I might look into one of those.

"Colby, were you in Atlanta Saturday night? Did I see you outside Ray's in the City?"

"Yes, but that couldn't have been me. Dom—my brother, Dominic—dragged me to a place called Sweet Georgia's Juke Joint. Good food."

"I'll check it out." I'd have to look up where that was, to see how close she and her brother had been to me.

We chatted another minute about our races this weekend, wishing each other well, then exchanged contact information before she took off down the paddock. I was glad I'd met her.

I looked at my watch: 2:20. More than an hour until practice. I found Mike, Tom, Leon, Aunt Tee, sandwiches, and fruit inside the motorhome.

Aunt Tee pointed to my helmet, sitting on the kitchenette's table. "They fixed the strap, checked it over. I haven't let it out of my sight."

I let out a breath, releasing tension I hadn't been aware of. "Thank you."

"But Kate…" She glanced at the others.

"You boys," I addressed them. "Don't go running to the Ringer with this."

Tom shook his head, his mouth full of sandwich.

"You always ruin our fun, mom," Mike whined.

Aunt Tee drew the strap from her pocket and showed me the clean edges of the split in the webbing. "They said it was cut."

I sagged down onto a couch next to Tom. "And no telling who did it." During daylight hours, my helmet sat on a table at the rear of the hospitality space—not out of sight, but out of focus. Anyone with a legitimate reason to be in our area could have gotten to it.

Aunt Tee nodded. "Every time I turned around the last two days, there was someone new here—and the crew didn't notice anything, unfortunately."

"Who do you remember seeing?"

She handed me a tuna sandwich and rattled off names that included Stuart, Holly, Leon's father, Zeke and his wife, an SGTV camera crew, Scott Brooklyn, Felix, Juliana, a couple fans she recognized as such but didn't know the names of, and "that bank representative and another young man in a suit," which had to be my father and a colleague. No way to know who did the deed—though Felix's name stood out.

"I'll store everything in here this weekend," she decided.

"Sure. Though I think the target was me alone."

Tom stood up, capping his water bottle. "I'll help bring stuff in. But isn't cutting a strap a pointless thing to do? You'd be sure to notice it. It seems petty. Flailing."

"Kid's got a point." Mike pointed at Tom with his half-eaten banana.

I shrugged and kept eating my sandwich as Mike and Leon talked about the car and the track. I was eager to think about driving, to prepare for practice.

Tom and Aunt Tee returned, their arms full of helmets and firesuits from the racks outside. Jack followed, carrying a single suit. Mine. With slashes down the front and stuffing spilling out.

"This has gone far enough," he growled.

I felt sick.

Chapter Twenty-seven

Tom shook his head. "That's more than flailing. That's pure spite."

"Or temper tantrum," said Leon.

I nodded, numb.

"I've got the other suits, Kate, don't worry," Aunt Tee said. "And I'll watch your gear personally from now on."

"You could help keep an eye on my food and drink, too." I filled them all in on the possibility I was the target of Ellie's fatal drink.

"Kate, don't go anywhere alone." Jack pointed at the others. "Mike, stick with her. Tee, watch her gear and her food. No one's messing with my driver, dammit."

He dropped my ruined suit on the driver's seat, telling us not to touch it, and stomped out of the coach, grumbling about extra security.

Mike smiled as I looked at him. "Big, ugly bodyguard, right here."

"Short, scrappy one here," Leon added.

"Thanks. I just want to get in the car and show the jerks they can't win."

We changed into our racing gear, and I took an extra minute in the back bedroom alone, sitting on the bed. I closed my eyes and concentrated on breathing and pushing every problem out of my head. Drama did not get in the racecar with me. It wouldn't run, or ruin, my life. Wouldn't affect my ability to kick butt on track.

Amazingly enough, practice went well, because the car was a rocket. At some races, the setup based on last year's data—minute adjustments of suspension, downforce, brake bias, and more—was no good at all, and we spent hours in practice chasing the right feel and grip. Almost never were we blindly lucky that the first whack at adjustments was perfect. But it happened this race.

I went out first, for the preliminary shakedown, but handed the car over to Leon quickly, because there wasn't much wrong, and he needed laps more than I did.

As he pulled out of the pits, I took off my helmet and turned to Mike, Jack, and Bruce. "The car feels like hour two of last year's race: smooth and fast. Maybe Mike will find something. But...wow."

Mike took the lead in fine-tuning the car's setup, since he had more experience. I was learning from him and beginning to offer the kind of precise feedback that helped the crew make adjustments. But even Mike had no suggestions. We kept our smiles small and our responses to questions subdued. No need to tip our hand yet.

Gramps said the same thing when I talked to him later that night, after a team dinner that was Jack's thank you to key suppliers for the season of support.

"Don't broadcast what you've got," he commented. "Strategy is key."

Hearing his voice never failed to make me smile. "Busy in the shop, Gramps?"

"I've got a few things cooking. Some orders for your competition next year." He chuckled. Gramps was one of the most sought-after makers of racecar wiring harnesses—the complete set of wires needed to supply power and communication throughout the car—which he produced from his shop, a small structure in the backyard of my grandparents' split-level 1970s home in Albuquerque. He loved the thrill of all kinds of racing, from pro to amateur, dirt track to drags.

"But Katie," he continued. "We're worried about you."

"I'm doing fine, being careful." I'd come clean to my grand-parents about Ellie's death and my being the target. I hadn't mentioned the possible hit-and-run or my slashed equipment. But Gramps had sources.

"We heard about your helmet and suit today, Katie. We don't like the sound of that. And that horse's ass Felix Simon—well, I'm sorry, Vivien, but that's what he is." That was directed to my grandmother, whose voice I heard in the background.

Gramps again. "Occasionally a strong word is appropriate. Anyway, Kate, this Felix Simon. Someone told me he's a real charmer, except for a vindictive streak."

"No kidding. I didn't do anything to him, but he hates me. I heard a story he had issues with female drivers in his youth, but I'm trying to get past that. Juliana's helping me broker a truce."

I heard indistinct voices on the other end of the line again, and then my grandmother's voice. "Katherine."

I closed my eyes. "Hi, Grandmother. I miss you." As regimented and rigid as she was, I loved her dearly. The regularity of her habits—the weekly menu that never varied, the day of the week assigned to cleaning and the one for laundry, her evening ritual of a sparkling clean countertop, tea, one cookie, and a book—stifled me until I was out of the house. Then I understood them as comfort and defense against a chaotic world.

She cleared her throat. "I miss you, too, Katherine." Both of us referred to more than our physical separation. "Now then. I've never trusted some of those people in your business, but we raised you to have a good head on your shoulders. Keep your wits about you, and remember a handsome face or pretty manners can hide a viper's nest. You've discovered as much before with some of those people you call friends."

"Sometimes it's hard to know people," I muttered.

"You're too trusting, Katherine. Billy in high school, those girls in the formula series—"

I broke in, thinking of the silly jealousies that affected the friendship between me, Juliana, and Ellie. "That was a stupid thing between kids. It's different now, with Ellie gone. I'm glad to have Juliana around."

"Also Sam Remington and that family—" she broke off and took a shaky breath. "I don't want you getting hurt."

It was the closest she'd ever come to the topic of my father.

"I'm being careful, Grandmother. I promise you, I won't let him hurt me."

I felt her withdraw again. "Good. That'll be fine." A pause. "All *right*, Horace, you can have the telephone back. Good bye, Katherine, I'll speak with you soon."

"I love you, Grandmother."

"Yes, dear, I love you, too."

A rustling, and Gramps was back on the phone. "That was clear as mud."

"She's saying don't get hurt. Make sure my friends are really my friends by looking below the surface. You know, like you need to look under things for your keys?"

He let out a loud breath. "Forty-eight years of marriage. I know she hides them on purpose now. There's a reason she always finds them when I can't."

"The reason is your lack of diligence in looking for them."

"That's terrible. You sounded exactly like her."

"Now you're being mean, Gramps."

I rode to the track the next morning with Mike and Leon, since we'd all start with the same team meeting before our ten o'clock practice and end with night practice from seven to nine. It would be a long day, but all three of us were excited to see how the car held up over more running time and different track conditions. A hum of excitement now accompanied the current of fear I'd lived with for a week and a half.

Jack ran the morning meeting, in which our crew chiefs— Bruce Kunze for the 28 car and Walter Bryant for the 29—talked setup and adjustments with the three drivers from each car. Sam Nichols, who was Aunt Tee's husband as well as the chief engineer for both cars, discussed track conditions. Jack chimed in about strategy for the three practice sessions we'd have that day.

Jack also informed everyone about the incident with my helmet and firesuit, telling them to be careful with equipment and watch for people who didn't belong in the team paddock. Sam assured us the crew checked every bit of safety equipment in the cars, verifying all was in perfect working order. We'd also had a security guard posted overnight to ensure no further damage.

The drivers stuck around when the others left to get cars to the pits and ready for practice in half an hour. The 29 car drivers—Lars, Seth, and their third driver, Paolo Ramalho, a Brazilian from the Indy Lights open-wheel series—wanted to know the current status of public opinion about me and the wreck at the last race.

"We know what's been out there on the Ringer's site," Lars said, his Danish-accented English sounding stilted and choppy to ears used to a Southern drawl. "I expect ill-will from the NASCAR side, but the idea of someone acting on their anger, not only spouting bad words, is not good."

"Maybe it's jealousy," suggested Mike.

I looked at him in surprise. "Pretty extreme for jealousy."

"You've gotten a lot of air time—more than some drivers get in their lifetimes. That *People* article last year, media wanting comment at every race, this sponsorship deal now taking you way beyond the racing world...some people could be angry you're getting all the attention. Especially if they've worked for years with little recognition. I mean drivers, but a team owner could feel the same way."

The other drivers nodded, and Leon spoke. "I can see that."

I was dumbfounded. Defensive. "I don't *ask* for it."

"*We* know that," Lars said. "You're the novelty, what sells—and you're good, so at least you back up the flash." He winked, to soften the blow. "Plus you look lovely in the photos."

"What do I do? Turn the media down, point them to 'more worthy' drivers? Besides, Mike, you don't..." It was hard to finish the question.

He waved his hands and grinned. "I'm happier in the background. You bring attention to the team and handle media better than me. I'm on Team Calamity over here."

Paolo leaned over to Mike. "Wasn't it Team Violent?"

Seth, a gentleman driver with a day job running luxury hotels, spoke up. "No one here has concerns, but I expect some out there do. You get a lot of exposure, and jealousy is a fact of life, especially in a small environment with many outsized egos. Is there enough jealousy in this paddock to lash out? I'm not sure."

Paolo stood, all five-foot-one of him, fists to hips. "There are two expressions, I believe." Paolo was infamous for trying to master—and always mangling—English idioms. "The first is, 'The cream, she will be on top.' The other is the attitude you take to those jealous ones, 'If you can't take the heat, get the kettle off the stove!'"

I patted him on the shoulder as we got up to head to the pits. "Close, Paolo, and thanks."

Chapter Twenty-eight

The schedule for Thursday gave us an hour on-track from 10:00 to 11:00 that morning, an hour starting at 2:30, and two hours at night to prep for the racing we'd do in the dark. I offered my morning practice time to Leon to give him more laps. So while Mike went out for the first few minutes of the session, I sat in my street clothes on top of the pit cart next to our crew chiefs.

I kept an eye on Mike's times, ignored fans and other teams around me, and browsed the Web on one of the team laptops. The Ringer offered sarcastic comments about the combination of my new beauty company sponsor and the team's hunting superstore sponsor, as well as my suitability to be a representative of either one. *The same questions I ask myself, he's just public and rude.* I shrugged and navigated to other motorsports news pages.

The pit crew started moving around, pulling on gloves and uncurling hoses, in preparation for Mike to bring the car in. No one in a hurry, since Jack decreed we wouldn't work on driver changes until later that afternoon. Mike turned the car off and got out, stopping to say a few words to Leon at the front of the Corvette before patting the top of Leon's helmet and climbing over the low pit wall. While the crew inspected tires and topped off the fuel, Leon settled in.

I saw more than heard Bruce next to me do a radio check with Leon—Bruce wore a radio headset combining ear muffs and a microphone, while I only wore earplugs—and tell him to start it up when ready. A minute later, Leon was gone, forty minutes in hand to get comfortable with the car and track.

I turned my attention back to the website for *Racer* magazine, where I found an article by my old friend Mitch Fletcher, titled "The Yin and Yang of Being Kate Reilly." I was apprehensive about the content, but shouldn't have worried. While the Ringer spouted gossip and innuendo—with occasional kernels of truth—Mitch and *Racer* had always been fair. Real journalists. While this editorial capitalized on the recent popularity of Kate Reilly stories and rehashed some of the worst rumors, it also linked to a full transcript of Felix provoking me into an outburst—the only media outlet I'd seen do so. The article was an objective discussion about why I'd become such a story. I was curious, too.

Mitch examined the recent highs and lows of my popularity and speculated about the impact of bloggers on the story—those who were influential, as well as those actually knowledgeable about racing. In today's Internet age, he suggested, any individual with a loud enough voice or a big enough platform, credible or not, could influence the story—as might be expected in a culture where people were famous for being famous. He concluded hating me was a trend on its way out.

His last words were, "I won't claim Kate Reilly is a perfect driver, because no one is. But she has considerable talent. I've read much that's been written about her and have spoken with and observed her myself. I've seen a young woman building a career and simultaneously coping with a lightning-strike of popularity and attention. She's earned her place through hard work, but she's also been lucky, and I don't think she'd disagree. My own hope in any endeavor is to be judged by my work and my character, not by what other people say about me. So, however jealous, astonished, or skeptical I may be of her good fortune, I owe her no less."

I dropped my head in my hands, nearly weeping with relief. Boy or girl, I'd have to name my firstborn "Mitch." I was glad he felt negative sentiment against me was lessening, because I didn't yet see it in this paddock. His article was a good start.

After a quick glance to check Leon's lap times, which dropped steadily as he got more comfortable, I tweeted a link to the article, then sent it to Matt and Lily, asking if they thought things were looking up. Five minutes later, I got a response from Lily who agreed my image was improving slowly, but was concerned over the helmet incident I'd mentioned to her. She asked me to call later that afternoon.

The essay in *Racer* made me feel confident enough to look at the communications from my strange fan. Though I didn't have the first two e-mails in the chain, I could deduce their contents. The initial contact would have praised my driving and expressed hope of meeting me some day. To eight or ten messages like that each week, I responded, "Thank you for your kind words. I hope to see you soon at a race, and I appreciate you cheering us on!"

I made those guesses because the e-mails from "katefangmr" started off by telling me I was welcome and he—*had to be "he,"right?*—would definitely see me at the Road America race in Elkhart Lake. Another e-mail before the race weekend reiterated how much he looked forward to meeting me. One from Saturday night told me he saw me in the paddock but couldn't get close enough to say hello, but he'd see me race day at the autograph session. Everything signed "Your #1 fan."

The fourth e-mail from him in this collection expressed his condolences for the accident I'd had in the race, as well as his delight at talking to me twice that day. He added, "Please don't worry about your PR person cutting our conversation short. You're so busy, and you had to go do something else. We'll have other opportunities!"

We would?

I thought back to the autograph session at the last race and remembered Tom moving talkative, lingering fans along. I always made a point to stay until everyone had the autograph he or she wanted, but these people had their signatures and wanted me to listen to them—which I didn't have time for on race day. I struggled to picture who'd been there, but only came up with two women and a blond, goateed man, who wore a red shirt tight over his pot belly.

The last e-mails were more familiar in tone, as if we were close friends. One was short, saying he'd had a bad day, but thoughts of the last race of the season had kept him cheerful. "I can't wait to see you in Atlanta," he wrote.

In another very long e-mail, he told me his life story—without any town or company names to identify him. I didn't read it all, because my skin was crawling partway through. "Katefangmr" freaked me out, and I sent a message to Lily asking what I should do about him. Then I closed my eyes and took three deep breaths, listened to the cars in the pits and on the front straight, and centered myself on my job. I opened my eyes to see Leon clocking a lap time two tenths of a second off mine from the previous year. I turned to Jack with raised eyebrows.

He grinned. "Yeah, you'll have to up your game."

I gave Jack a thumbs-up and returned to e-mail for one last action I'd been putting off. I pulled up Tom's message from the previous weekend and opened the two photos he'd taken of me, Juliana, and Ellie.

One was a wide-angle shot of the whole Siebkens room, taken while we were moving into position. The other was a close-up, an exquisite photo of all three of us. Juliana outshone us with her pageant-perfect posture and smile, Ellie looked heartbreakingly happy, and I grinned like a school kid. I relived the emotions I'd felt that night: love and excitement, then sadness. I wondered how Ethan was coping.

The Porsche next to us came in, and I turned my attention to it with relief. I evaluated how they pulled in, how their team maneuvered around the car, and how I'd avoid them if I had to enter my pit stall with their car in place—all topics we discussed at a meeting with our car chiefs after practice.

We'd just finished that debrief when Stuart arrived in the paddock with eight VIP guests from Kreisel Timepieces, the biggest Series sponsor, hoping Mike and I were available. We stood with them near the cars and talked for ten minutes about what it was like inside the Corvette and how to drive the Road Atlanta track—attracting a small crowd at the barrier to the garage area who were also able to hear us. Then we took questions from the VIPs.

The fourth man to speak was in his sixties with a full head of white hair and a Tommy Bahama shirt. "How do you deal with two sponsors that conflict so much as BW Goods and the makeup company? I heard the combination is the joke of the paddock."

"I didn't hear that," I said. "But I did hear something about pink cammo."

Mike raised a finger. "I know women who hunt and wear lipstick."

"And men get breast cancer or are affected by it," I said. "I'm proud to partner with an organization that helps people fight a terrible disease. Sure the two sponsors are pretty different, but we treat all companies generous enough to support our racing with respect and gratitude, whether we're talking motor oil, snack cakes, or deodorant. We take all the support we can get."

"Amen to that," Mike said.

We posed for photos with the Kreisel guests, and then walked to the rope line to sign autographs for the fans there.

We'd signed the last hero card when a passing golf cart swerved to a stop in front of us. Dave Hacker, who was driving a Porsche for Holly's team this year, was at the wheel, Holly beside him.

"You can't drive that any better than you drive your racecar," Mike shouted.

Dave grinned at us. "Bring it on, big man."

"Glad we saw you," Holly said to me. "Dave, tell her."

"Felix Simon is suggesting the biggest risk to safety in the race is you and implying we'd all be safer if someone took you out."

I stared at him, my stomach churning.

Mike recovered first. "He's officially gone round the bend."

Dave assured me no one listening—and no one he knew— would take Felix seriously or act on the suggestion. I hoped not. I was grateful Felix wouldn't be behind the wheel of a racecar. Felix in the pits was bad enough.

Chapter Twenty-nine

Though Mike and Leon assured me no one would mete out vigilante justice, Jack was unconvinced and made a point of notifying the Series. The rest of us prepared for the next practice session, hoping the Corvette was still fast.

The first step was driver-change practice, which we did in the pits while the Star Mazda series qualified on track. Lars and I strapped into our respective cars, and the other drivers waited behind pit wall with the crew, who wouldn't practice fueling and tire-changing with us this time.

At the wave of a red shop rag, two drivers and a crew member leapt into action at each car. Inside, I removed the steering wheel and hung it on the ceiling hook. I also twisted the lever to release my seatbelts and flipped the two lap belts over the left and right edges of the seat so the next person wouldn't sit on them. I hadn't tightened the shoulder belts—I would have loosened them as I rolled down pit lane for a stop—and they retracted toward the ceiling on their bungee cords, out of the next driver's way.

Bubs, the crew member who acted as our driver change assistant, had the door open and the window net down in the seconds it took me to remove the belts and wheel, and I pointed my helmet toward the opening, twisting my shoulders so I faced the sky. I reached up, grabbed the car's tube frame above the window opening, and pulled myself through it, pausing with my torso out and butt on the frame rails protecting the cockpit.

I pulled my left leg out and stood on it, hopping backward and pulling my right leg out. I dipped back in for my seat insert. As soon as I got out of the way, Leon dashed in with his insert and Bubs helped him get belted and fastened.

Behind our 28 car, Lars and Paolo went through the same drill. They slammed their door closed a fraction of a second before Bubs shut the door on Leon.

Jack looked at his stopwatch. "Could be worse. Next set."

I heard crew chiefs behind me radio drivers to unhook their helmet's air conditioning hose, drink tube, and radio cable and loosen their belts—tasks they'd perform on the way to the pit stall.

"Go!" Jack said the word and a crew member waved the red "flag." Seth and Mike jumped over the pit wall with the crew. Another short break, and it was my turn to get back in as Mike got out.

Once there, I heard Bruce over the radio. "Kate, five minutes to the start of practice. Time on the change was good. Stay there, since you're out first. You set?"

"Copy that, Bruce." I spent the time resolutely pushing the thought of other drivers gunning for me out of my mind. I focused on the car and the track, envisioning its turns, one after the other.

I roared out of the pits and discovered the car was every bit as good as it had been yesterday. I quelled my bubbling spirits with the thought that track conditions had been similar in every session. The real test would be how setup and tire compounds reacted to cooler temps during night practice later. And possible rain.

Still, I had a fantastic twenty minutes on the track, finding a rhythm and getting comfortable with the flow of the turns and straights. I remembered where on track I liked to pass, how to vary my entry and exit of corners, and where to watch for my own mistakes. My share of practice flew by.

Coming down the back straight on my last lap, I unplugged my air and drink tubes. Left-right through Turns 10a and 10b, and then slow, hugging the right line up the hill into Turn 11, making it clear to other cars on track I was pitting. Just over the crest of the hill, I pulled into pit lane, braking hard and downshifting as I wound down the slope.

I turned right at the bottom and hit the speed limiter button as I crossed the commit line. Loosened my belts and unplugged the radio cable, the car making angry, flatulent sounds as the limiter shut down cylinders in the car's V-8, restricting me to thirty-seven and a half miles per hour. I veered into our pit stall, pushed the button to turn the car's engine off, and stopped.

I was out well before the fueling was done—though for this stop, the crew only pretended to fuel the car for twenty-five seconds. Another signal and two tire-changers on each side of the car lunged forward, wielding air guns on the first wheel nuts as the air jacks lifted the car up. Bubs slammed the door shut and was over the wall as the tire-changers moved to their second wheel. Hands in the air from the driver's side crew. Hands in the air from the other side. The air hose yanked from the air-jack plug, Leon starting the engine even as it bounced down on four wheels. The crew member who'd held up a hand indicating "stop" waved the driver on. I imagined Bruce on the radio shouting "Go, go, go!"

Then Leon stalled it.

I pulled my helmet and HANS off with Aunt Tee's help. "Oops," I said to Jack.

"He'll learn the lesson this way. You did."

Leon stalled because I'd deliberately left the car in fourth gear at Jack's request. My job exiting the car was to leave it in first gear—the gear required for the speed limiter. His job entering was to check the gear, so he didn't lose precious seconds stalling or speed out of pit lane. A year ago, I'd learned my lesson, starting and stalling three times before noticing gear selection. I'd never forgotten again.

I apologized to Leon later, as we stood in the garage watching the crew inspect our suspension. He grinned and shook his head. "Like you, I'll no' forget again."

Holly walked up, looking like a five-foot-tall movie star with big, black sunglasses and red lipstick. "How's the car?"

"Good." I winked at Leon.

Holly studied our faces. "That's it?"

We smiled at her.

"Glad you got some good news, because the Ringer's at it again. He's calling you a sponsorship-whore."

"Where did that come from?"

Holly took off her sunglasses as she and I moved to the motorhome side of the setup. "You spoke to a group and said you'd hawk anything a sponsor threw at you."

"It's not what I said, but it was here, to guests in the paddock."

"Someone tipped off the Ringer. Who'd you see?"

I sat down in a plastic chair. "No one I recognized. Kreisel VIPs, guests. Regular paddock people. Mike. I think the Michelin Man walked by."

"Could be him. Bib is a sneaky guy."

I nodded. "You know Colby Lascuola? I met her today."

"Girl in World Challenge? Brother racing in Europe but here this weekend?"

"That's her. Get this, she was up for the Beauté sponsorship." I nodded at her surprised expression. "She said she wasn't upset. She's also one of the drivers Jack said he'd hire if I wasn't here." I related other names he'd mentioned.

"World Challenge ran with the ALMS in Wisconsin, so she could have been in Siebkens. Was she smarmy, aggressive?"

"I liked her, but her brother gave me a hard look."

"Dreamy Dominic?"

I laughed. "I should find out if they were at Road America and the Tavern that night, since they were in Atlanta on Saturday."

"I'll ask around."

"You have a minute?" I updated her on who'd been in which locations.

She tapped her finger against her cheek. "In both places we have me, Stuart, Juliana, Tom, Felix, Scott, Zeke and Rosalie, and a couple dozen Series and team crew."

"Plus George Ryan, super-fan guy."

"Swimming in motive in Wisconsin, but the people also in Atlanta? Not so much. The only one with any motive so far in both places is Felix."

"I'm sure there are more people—and motives. I'll keep on it."

We were silent a moment, then I spoke again. "Colby has a management company. Should I have one?"

"What would it get you? You've got a job and a great sponsor."

"About that." I looked around before whispering. "Do you think Jack will hire me back next year?"

"He'd be a fool not to, why?"

"Juliana heard a rumor he wouldn't."

"I don't see it—and I haven't heard anything. I think you're safe." Knowing her sources, I almost believed her.

Holly had been gone only two minutes when Zeke appeared, Rosalie following him, looking tense. But she smiled when she saw me, throwing her arms open for a hug. Zeke and I took care of a quick interview for SPEED's daily report, then we all sat down.

"I can't believe it's been so long," I said to Rosalie. "What have you been doing?"

"Still freelance public relations work for the racing world. Teams, mostly, a couple drivers here and there. Working from home. Playing with the dogs." She and Zeke had two Corgis they treated like children.

Zeke put his hand over hers. "Word of mouth brings her new clients all the time, because she's so good."

"Been doing it a lot of years now." She gave a wan smile. I thought she looked more tired than I'd ever seen her. She still didn't look her age, which was nine years more than Zeke and twenty more than me, because her Italian background had gifted her with nearly unlined olive skin and shiny, thick black hair. But she didn't look healthy.

"Are you doing well otherwise?" I asked.

She nodded. "I'm fine. And how about you this weekend? I'm sorry it's been a rough time for you."

"Car's good, everything else is crazy. I could go on, but that's the bottom line. Zeke, what do you know about Scott Brooklyn?"

"We've known him for ages, but not well." He glanced at Rosalie, and when she shrugged, he went on. "I worked with him a few times at SPEED when he did pit work. He's still racing when he can. Quiet, smart, thorough. Good guy. Why?"

"Curious. Juliana's seeing him, plus I've got an interview with him in a few minutes. He's still pretty young, right? Why isn't he racing more?"

Zeke scratched his head with the end of his pen. "Early thirties? Good enough driver, but never scored a big-deal drive. He's almost too nice to make it in racing—no killer instinct for making deals. Decent talent on the mic. Speaking of talent, you're staying out of Felix's way?"

"Sure, but rumor is he's trying to get everyone to run me off the track."

Zeke flushed bright red, his eyes furious. "That's enough. He makes every journalist in the business look bad, and has no call to threaten you. I'll get to the bottom of this." He left abruptly, Rosalie following after a quick hug for me.

I wondered what I'd unleashed on Felix.

Chapter Thirty

The interview with Scott Brooklyn went smoothly, and I thought I'd tell Juliana I liked her choice in companions. However, the sight of her in the paddock lane a few minutes later drove the thought from my mind. Juliana looked disheveled. Unsteady. I jogged toward her, shocked to see grass and dirt stains on both knees of her khaki pants. I got closer and saw blood on her hands.

"Jules, are you all right?"

She looked up from her examination of her broken purse strap, her eyes wide, shocked. "There you are." She looked at her purse again, then back to me. "Can you believe, they broke my purse?"

"What happened to you?" I took her arm and led her to the Sandham Swift paddock.

"Car came at me in the lot up the hill."

"What?"

She nodded. "Big, dark car. Didn't see it. But suddenly it was on top of me. I jumped. Fell. Broke my purse."

She seemed jittery, and I sat her down in our hospitality area. "Hang on." I dashed into the motorhome and returned with Aunt Tee and a first aid kit. I took Juliana's purse from her and set it aside, while Aunt Tee went to work cleaning Jules' hands and knees. The blood was mostly from a cut on the outside of her wrist. Otherwise, her hands and knees were dirty, she had a tear in one knee of her khakis corresponding to scraped skin, and her shins looked to be bruised.

I went back inside at Aunt Tee's direction for a glass of sweet tea, my mind racing at the implications of an attack on Juliana. *Who would be after me **and** her? Why?*

Juliana drank down the tea and seemed less shaky. I looked her in the eye. "Are you sure you're all right?"

"Better now, and no permanent damage. Thanks to both of you for the care."

Aunt Tee collected her supplies. "You sit here until you feel all right. I'll bring more tea and some cookies in a minute." She disappeared into the motorhome.

I looked at Jules again. "I don't know how or why, but this has to be connected to the person who tried to run me down. We should tell the police."

"I suppose." She frowned. "But they won't be able to do anything. It's been half an hour now. Even if the car's still at the track, we'd be looking for one of a hundred thousand cars here."

"At least tell track security, and maybe they can relay the information to the police?"

She nodded and got to her feet, steady this time. In command, but frowning down at the stains on her knees. "I have to get to the media center, because the show must go on. Thank goodness I have a change of clothes there. But I promise I'll talk to security right away. Thank you for this." She hugged me, then pulled back. "Oh, I spoke with Felix."

"And?"

"It's so dumb. He doesn't think females should be racecar drivers. 'Girls don't have the temperament for it,' he said. He won't let up on you because he doesn't think he's treating you any different than the men. He gave me a song and dance about handling all of our subjects fairly—as if I need a lecture on journalism from him."

"I can't believe you didn't kick his butt six ways to Sunday."

She laughed. "It took some restraint—but at least I could vent to Scott, since he understands. Mark my words, Kate, I won't be stuck with Felix forever. I'll beat that chauvinist to the top."

"I look forward to that. So there's nothing I can do about him?"

"Tough it out. Avoid him as much as possible and do all your interviews with me. I'll explain to the bosses there's a conflict and see what we can do."

"I wish it was something I could fix. But at least we tried. Thanks."

She pointed her forefinger at me. "Drive smart, Kate."

"Drive smart, Jules," I said, returning the gesture and repeating the girls-only mantra, blessing, pep-talk, and cheer we used when we raced together. With Ellie. I felt a tug in my chest at the memory as we parted.

"@katereilly28: A 'Drive Smart' shout-out to memories shared by Jules and Ellie. Miss you, E."

I suited up by 6:30, half an hour before night practice, and sat in in the motorhome listening to Seth, Tom, and Mike talk about wine.

I turned to Seth. "How do you deal with the people who do nothing but get in your way?"

"In the business world, you mean?" At my nod, he went on. "I know I'm good at what I do, and I give my work my full attention. Beyond that, I ignore the haters. There will always be haters. Don't let them shake you."

His words made me realize what a blow my confidence had taken the last two weeks. I'd had positive messages streaming at me from all angles—my new sponsorship deal, personal support from Beauté's CEO, fans eager to interact with me, my teammates rallying beside me—but I'd been caught up in the negative. *From now on, to hell with anyone trying to bring me down.*

Jack and the others arrived for the meeting, and I asked for a minute first. "I wanted to thank you all for your support and tell you I'm through worrying and cowering and feeling like my life is out of control. I'm here to drive, and if jerks out there don't know that's my goal, I can't help them."

Everyone applauded, and Jack spoke. "About time. Now, let's focus on racing."

We left the motorhome for the pits and I realized I was happier than I'd been in days. *What did they say? You can't change how others behave, only how you react.* Finally, I'd taken control of my emotions. I looked at the stars appearing in the twilight, saw lights in pit boxes making tented awnings glow, and felt centered again.

"@katereilly28: I wear lipstick, can shoot a gun, and kick ass on track. If you have a problem with me, have the guts to say it to my face. I'm over it."

We had two hours of practice ahead of us, during which each driver had to put in at least three laps as a prerequisite to driving in the race, which would end in the dark. At seven o'clock there was still enough daylight to identify specific cars behind the glare of their white (prototypes) or yellow (GTs) headlights. But when you raced in the dark, on a track like Road Atlanta that wasn't fully illuminated, you operated with a lot less information about the cars around you than you did during daylight hours.

On the other hand, cool air and pavement made the car faster, and less external stimulus made a driver's focus more complete. Stints last year at Petit and this year at Sebring gave me my first taste of night racing, and I'd enjoyed the quiet bubble of the car. More than once Bruce startled me, calling me in to the pits after an hour's run that seemed only ten minutes long.

Mike put in twenty-five minutes, and then Leon strapped in, getting comfortable quickly and inching closer to Mike's times as he clicked off laps. Jack left Leon in there for forty minutes, with one stop midway through for Leon to get out and resettle his seat insert, which was hitting a pressure point and making his left leg go numb. Drivers were strapped down and subject to so many forces that the slightest discomfort could quickly morph into something much worse. Seat position was a tricky thing.

Finally, it was my turn in the car. I took my time getting in as the over-the-wall crew added some fuel and looked over my tires. They also raised the engine cover and gathered around the engine, tools in hand. Jack had prepped me for this.

"We're going to take a look. Wave tools around, look concerned. Think of it as misdirection." He'd winked.

The car was still a rocket, I'd translated.

The clustered crew members dispersed, latching the hood. I got a thumbs-up from Bubs and a radioed command from Bruce. "All yours, Kate. Fire 'er on up."

My laps passed in the blink of an eye. The Corvette felt as solid and fast as I'd ever experienced, and I got out of the car excited about our chances in the race. Then I calmed myself. A thousand miles was a long distance, and anything could and would happen—from weather to breakage to accidents. But on speed alone, we had a contender.

Near nine o'clock, at the end of practice, pit lane operated at half its typical activity and energy levels. I climbed back over the wall, unstrapping my helmet, taking deep breaths, and feeling my heart rate slow from the typical 150 beats per minute I experienced on-track. Helmet and balaclava off. Wet towel from Aunt Tee on my sopping-wet head. I rubbed the towel over my face and used it to push back my hair. Then I gulped down a bottle of water. My firesuit and undergarments were soaked through, as usual.

Jack climbed down from his perch at the control center. "Looked good, Kate. We'll talk back at the motorhome in five."

All six drivers filed out of the pits, me bringing up the rear. When I stepped into the paddock lane, I nearly collided with Felix. Predictably, he snarled at me. My head was full of the performance of our car, and I was in no mood to waste time or energy on whatever bile he offered.

I spoke before he could. "How about you stay out of my way?"

If looks could kill, I'd have been bleeding on the ground. He leaned close, his minty breath belying the hateful words spilling from his mouth. "Now you're looking for special treatment? You think you're God's gift to racing *and* God's gift to beauty—I'm not helping you shove that down anyone's throat."

I didn't speak, but made a big show of looking around and behind both of us. Team members and drivers passed us as they left the pits. Fans watched the action.

"What are you doing?" he asked.

"Looking for the camera or microphone. Isn't that your trick?"

"Listen, you bitch—"

"Listen to *me*, you misogynistic piece of garbage, before you say something I'll make you regret. I don't care if you think women don't belong on the track—it's time to get over whatever hang-up you have. Welcome to the twenty-first century. I'm a racecar driver, and you can't stop me."

Felix's face went white, then flushed red. He shook a finger under my nose, his Kreisel watch flopping around with the motion. "None of you females belong in racing. Not your friends—stupid idea, calling them 'pit princesses.' That won't work now." His short laugh twisted his face into something even uglier. "None of you belong. Especially not you. Think you're better than the others—"

I drowned him out, shouting, "I don't care. I don't want special treatment. You won't believe it. So we're done. I don't care what you think. Just stay away from me."

By the time I reached the motorhome, I was cheerful, happy with the pace of the Corvette, and glad to have finally stood up for myself.

Plenty of drivers are hated. If that's my destiny, so be it. I whistled a few bars of "I Will Survive."

Chapter Thirty-one

We were back at the racetrack the next morning by eight. In contrast to the workmanlike atmosphere of the past two days, by Friday we felt a buzz in the air. We were close enough to the main event to taste it. The weather was cool and overcast, in contrast to the sunny skies of Thursday, but the experts forecast no rain. I hoped they were right.

I sipped a cup of coffee and leaned against a pole supporting our garage awning. The 29 car's crew had a rear brake assembly in pieces on the shop floor and our brake whiz, Alex Hanley, was in the thick of the rebuilding effort. The crew of our 28 car polished already gleaming bodywork.

"Kate?" I turned to see an SGTV cameraman and Juliana, looking frazzled. "Could we have a quick word?" she asked.

I set down my cup and crossed to her. "Sure. How are you feeling today?"

"I'm fine. Damn him!" She fumbled through a sheaf of papers. Not her typical behavior.

"Hold on, Bernie." That was to her cameraman. Crouching down, she dropped the papers on the ground and flipped through them to extract a single sheet. Then she straightened, planted her foot on the pile, smoothed her hair back, and with one deep breath, transformed into the polished belle I knew.

"What's going on, Jules?"

Now she was all business. "Can't find Felix, doing it without him. Topics: how your car feels for the race and the idea of racing with all the European imports who've come over for the event. Ready?"

Typical stuff. I nodded and straightened my shoulders.

Two minutes later, she had her sound bites. "Our car's responding well to our testing and adjustments so far, and we're optimistic for the race—but you know there's a lot of racing to do, and anything can happen," and "I'm excited to race with the drivers and teams who've come over from Europe to compete with us. Not knowing their styles and habits will make it harder to predict how they'll move, but it's great for the Series and fans to see new competition and faces."

I squatted to help her assemble her documents, and she put a hand on my forearm, speaking in a low tone. "I heard you and Felix had words. I'm sorry if what I told you made it worse."

"Don't worry about it. I'm tired of his crap, and I let him know I wouldn't stand for it anymore. Something he said made it sound like he's after you, too—like it could have been him trying to run us both down."

"Trust me, I'm watching my back. You do the same. But the Ringer's got your argument last night."

"That figures." As she left, I stepped back into our paddock and pulled out my cell phone to fess up to my PR team. Lily and Matt were as annoyed with me as people I was paying could get. It didn't help they were only on their first cups of coffee.

Lily was the most exasperated. "Ix-nay on the antrum-tay, all right?"

"Now, Lily," Matt soothed, "Kate's letting off a little steam. Though we'd prefer you pick a more private forum, Kate. Somewhere the Ringer's tentacles don't reach."

"Tough to know where that is. Look, I reached my limit of verbal abuse from him—member of the media or not. He's got serious issues with women, and I refuse to be the focal point for them. But I'm sorry for saying so in public."

Lily's voice rang down the line. "You need to rise above! Smile graciously, and decline to comment. Go all Oprah on their petty-minded asses!"

Petty-minded…never mind. "Oprah?"

"Oprah, the Queen of England, whoever. Ignore the name-calling and do your thing. Be confident, true to yourself—like Oprah. Don't give the riff-raff the power to tear you down."

"Rise above." It worked as a pep talk.

"And keep your mouth shut—no, you can't do that. Don't say anything about threats or the Ringer or being under attack. Smile and say you're grateful for the support of your loyal fans."

"And keep referring media inquiries to us when appropriate," added Matt. "Not the quick quotes or car-related stuff, but anything more than that, we'll field first."

I nodded, though they couldn't see me. "Thank you for everything you're doing. I'll try not to make your jobs harder again."

As much as yelling at Felix might have been a mistake, I continued to feel better about my situation. More in control of my life, which made it easier to turn off the rest of my brain and focus on the car.

I headed into the motorhome, changed into my driving suit, and sat down on a sofa with the official list of race competitors. I knew the ALMS regulars: who drove what car and how each driver behaved in his car. But for Petit, regular teams added third drivers I was unfamiliar with, plus a dozen cars I'd never raced against were piloted by trios I'd never seen. Jack wanted us to pool information about the behavior of competitors, so I used the list to match driver names and car numbers with a mental picture of the car on the track.

Jack reinforced the need for observation and collaboration twenty minutes later when he gathered us on the sofas. "Time for some recon work this morning, boys and girl. Leon, you're comfortable in the car?"

"Right as rain."

Jack nodded. "You three," he pointed to Leon, Mike, and me. "Everyone watching the feeds, paying close attention to the others in class. How they look, where they're fast or slow."

At our nods, Jack pointed to Seth, Lars, and Paolo. "Your car setup's close, and hopefully we've licked the understeer issue we've been working on. Your first priority is setup. All of you, any information on drivers in other classes to watch out for, give room, or whatever, we'll take it. We'll compare notes after." He checked his watch. "Practice starts in fifteen, so let's get over to the pits. And keep it clean. Don't hit shit."

Jack decreed each of us driving the 28 car would get fifteen minutes of track time, give or take, during the hour-long practice session. I'd go first again. The six drivers trooped to the pits together, and I got busy putting my earplugs in and securing them with a square of red tape over my ear. As had become my habit, I checked all straps on my helmet and HANS—still solid—then put them on. I grabbed my gloves, and I was ready to go.

The car still felt fantastic. Fast, balanced, and a whole lot of fun to drive. My laps were a joyride, a chance to find my balance for the day in the car and on the track. Then a blue-and-white-striped European prototype went up the hill into Turn 2 behind me.

Coming out of Turn 4, heading for the Esses, the driver from Benchmark Racing popped up on my left side and swept around me as we went through the downhill right-hander. But I needed to use all of the track to carry my speed, including the outside line he was on. My choices were hit him or brake hard and go for a ride. I chose curtain number two, which sent my car fishtailing and bouncing over curbing—undertray slamming onto the raised ridges—then speeding down the hill on the grass and up over the curbing again onto the track at Turn 5. By the time I got four wheels under control and on pavement, the other guy was through Turn 6.

From the moment of near-impact, I cursed his name, team, country of origin, and the boat they'd all come in on. Silently. Because I strained to hear the sounds of the car over the noise of my pounding heart. Something was off. But not horribly. Yet.

"How's the car, Kate?" Bruce's voice was calm on the radio.

"Something's wrong. A little. Coming in." I heard traces of panic in my own voice. I keyed the mic again. "What the hell was that guy thinking? This is *practice!*"

"Stay calm, Kate. Jack's gonna find out. Roger you coming in."

I finished the lap at half to two-thirds speed, focusing on how the car felt in a straight line, under braking and acceleration, in right and left turns. Relaying that to the team.

"Racing change," Bruce reminded me, as I headed up the final hill, hugging the right side of the track as preparation for entering pit lane.

I was angry my practice time was cut in half by an arrogant jerk who didn't know the track and mad also I'd forgotten the plan for a full-speed driver change. I reached back to unhook my air conditioning hose and radio cable and yanked on my drink tube as I cruised down the hill.

I continued muttering obscenities about the other driver as I stopped the car and hauled myself out. Leon jumped in after me, finishing the driver change in acceptable time. Then he sat there waiting as the crew examined the car. I watched with Jack and Mike from the pit wall, my seat insert still in hand, helmet still on.

After an agonizingly long couple of minutes, I saw the lead over-the-wall mechanic key his radio and speak. The speed of the crew slowed. Jack nodded.

"What?" I shouted through my helmet as I tossed my seat insert down on a chair. I hurriedly unbuckled my chin strap and yanked helmet, HANS, and balaclava off.

Jack held up a hand to calm me. "We're taking it back to the paddock."

I bolted from the pits before he could say another word, planning to kick some visiting-driver butt.

Jack caught up to me two steps later and held me there, though I struggled briefly. "Kate, it's not major, but there's no need to rush. We'll take our time and get it right again."

I turned to see Leon climbing out of the car, and a wave of guilt and anger hit me. Leon and Mike wouldn't get any laps in this practice session. *Had I wrecked us again? No, this was absolutely the other guy's fault.*

"Fine," I bit out. "But someone needs to have *major* words with the jackass who caused it." I was on the balls of my feet, still considering a trip down pit lane.

Jack straightened and crossed his arms over his chest. His glare pinned me in place more effectively than his hands had. "Cool it."

"It was his fault."

"Trust me, I delivered the message. Cool off. Don't get yourself in trouble."

I struggled with my anger. I took some deep breaths. "Fine. You're sure you—" I saw the expression on his face. "You gave them hell. Good."

"Come on, let's get back to the paddock."

"Who was it anyway?"

"Dominic Lascuola, Benchmark Racing."

Chapter Thirty-two

Though Jack and Bruce assured me the fix was minor, our crew took the precaution of tearing back and rebuilding the suspension on the car, in case something that wasn't obvious had been damaged. I fumed silently, watching them work. Wondering if Dominic Lascuola had made a mistake. If he'd been following Felix's advice to take me out. Or trying to advance his sister's interests.

"@katereilly28: Frustrating to watch team working on a car damaged by other team's stupid move. Can't drive our GTs like your LMPs!!!!! #idiotmove"

Shortly after the practice session ended for the rest of the cars in the ALMS, the drivers, crew chiefs, and Tom gathered again in the motorhome for a team meeting. Leon and Mike waved off my apologies for their lack of morning practice time.

"It's the fault of that stupid git Dominic." Leon made his point with a finger jabbed in the direction of the Benchmark team paddock.

Paolo shook his head. "He is not so bad, really. I think he just put his foot in the sea and take too big a bite."

I met Seth Donohue's blank look with one of my own. Then I saw comprehension, and Seth translated. "Dipped his toe in the water, but bit off more than he could chew."

I hoped Paolo was right, that Dominic had made a simple mistake through being new to the track and the Series. Time would tell.

Jack banged the door shut behind him and clomped up the stairs, sitting at the front edge of the driver's seat turned to face the center of the room. He leaned forward, propped his elbows on his knees, and rubbed his hands together.

"Autograph session at 12:30, qualifying at 3:15. That'll be Kate and Lars."

I was surprised. I'd only qualified once that year, at Mid-Ohio, the race prior to my accident at Road America. Plus I'd wrecked the car the last time I drove it in the heat of battle. Maybe this was Jack's way of building confidence. I nodded at him. "Great."

"That session is twenty-five minutes, long enough to take a couple laps to test setup—especially the 28 car now—make an adjustment, and still qualify. We'll need to be quick. But again, start position doesn't help much for a ten-hour race."

Mike raised a hand. "Assuming the car's steady, she goes all out?"

Jack shrugged. "Sure, give 'em whatever you've got."

Excitement fizzed in my chest.

"If the car's still great," Mike said, "they'll claim we were sandbagging."

"Aye, and we were," Leon put in.

Jack grinned at him. "Damn right. Now, let's talk about the other cars and drivers out there. What have you learned?"

For the next fifteen minutes we shared observations on the driving style and tendencies of other cars we'd encountered—though I let my eye-rolling speak for me when it came to Dominic Lascuola in his prototype. After that, Jack went through our code words: innocuous phrases we'd use over the radio to tell our teams something we didn't want others to understand. For instance, "make sure you're drinking plenty of water" meant "ease up a little and save some fuel," and "nice and smooth" meant "slow down."

Jack finished the meeting by making sure we knew where to be and when, and we left the motorhome to the sound of the track announcer calling a GT3 support race. I saw two familiar faces among the fans at our rope line, and I crossed to them.

"Colton Butler and Jimmy O'Brien." The photographers had adhered to the bargain we made outside the hospital on Monday by not slamming me in print—unlike the other journalists who'd been there. I was grateful they'd gotten over their anger and helped me out. Time for some payback. "You guys want in?" I unhooked the rope and escorted them over to the cars.

Tom raised an eyebrow as we approached, and I spoke in his ear. "The good guys at the hospital Monday. I owe them."

"Fair enough." Tom introduced himself, and, once he discovered they didn't usually cover racing, helped me give them the full tour of the garage, complete with car specifications, Series structure, and race weekend schedule. They took tons of photos. I dragged Mike and Leon out of the transport trailer to join me for group shots with the car.

It was unusual for me or the team to lavish attention on two photographers with not much racing background and no ties to big-name media. But Butler and O'Brien had resisted the rush to judgment about me. They'd been kind. *If I have to rebuild my reputation one journalist at a time, so be it. I did it once, I can do it again.*

I walked them to the paddock lane a few minutes later and thanked them again for their interest.

O'Brien, the taller, once-redhead, was about to follow his shorter pal into the crowd when he snapped his fingers. "Almost forgot." He dug a business card out of his shirt pocket and handed it to me, his contact information printed on one side, a phone number handwritten on the other. "That's the number called us about your hospital visit. Good luck."

They were gone before I could thank him. I hurried to a quieter spot at the back of the garage and dialed the number on my cell phone. I didn't stop to question if calling was a good idea, but five rings gave me enough time to panic.

Voicemail: "Hi, you've reached Felix Simon of SGTV. Leave me a message, and I'll call you back."

By the end of the beep, I was at full boil. "You set me up! I can't believe you. Don't ever bother me again, you son of a bitch, or you'll live to regret it." I jabbed at the off button on my phone and resisted the urge to throw it across the garage.

I held my breath and marched into the office of the transport trailer, making Tom the only witness to my fit of couch-kicking and swearing. Only when I'd calmed down and collapsed into a chair did he speak.

"Can I help with something, Kate?"

"Rearrange Felix Simon's face?"

"Uh oh."

"He called reporters with my name saying I wanted publicity for my visit to the cancer ward—to get me in trouble with every-one. All because he doesn't think women ought to be in racing."

"But he's such a nice guy."

"That's what everyone says. But I can prove he set me up for Monday. I bet he's behind everything else, too."

"I wonder why he'd do that. Maybe he's worried for his job because he's got a new, young partner? But to take that out on you?"

"From what Juliana said, he doesn't like any woman in racing."

"Then her being his partner must really make him mad."

"I hadn't thought about that." I looked at him in surprise. "I wonder how rough he's been on her?"

I tested the idea of Felix behind everything that had gone wrong for me lately. I knew he'd planted stories with the Ringer—or was the Ringer. I couldn't lay blame for NASCAR fans hating me at his door, but I was convinced he'd stoked the flames.

He'd been on the spot in Atlanta and could easily have tried to run me down. And done the same to Jules here at the track. Could he have killed Ellie while trying to stop me from racing? If so, any female around might be in danger, as Tom suggested. Should I warn Juliana there could be other attempts? Warn Colby?

"With an imagination like this, I should write for soap operas," I muttered.

"Aunt Tee's got lunch outside. You coming?"

I waved Tom on and made quick calls to the Wisconsin sheriff and the Atlanta police officer we'd spoken to, relating my suspicions about Felix. Both men agreed to add the information to their files and follow up, but I realized how little detail or proof I was offering. I hung up convinced they didn't believe me. I remembered that last year in Connecticut Detective Jolley hadn't believed me either. Must be a cop thing.

I sat still for a time, eyes closed, breathing deeply. Trying to center myself and let go of the tension and anger I'd been feeling. But the heavy sensation in the pit of my stomach didn't go away, and I began to regret leaving that message for Felix. Not because I yelled at him—that felt as liberating as when I'd done so the night before. But I wondered if I'd put him on alert, by making it clear I knew what he was doing.

Even if the police didn't think so, I was convinced Felix was behind the negative campaign against me—if not also Ellie's death. I just needed to prove it.

Chapter Thirty-three

"Girls kick ass, Kate!" screamed a female voice at the back of the crowd.

"Damn right." I looked up with a smile, my response eliciting chuckles from those in earshot.

We were halfway through the driver autograph session mandated by the American Le Mans Series as a way of giving fans access to its cars and stars. Mike, Leon, and I sat together at an eight-foot folding table—Seth, Lars, and Paolo to our right at another—in front of our garage setup, facing the paddock lane and a line of people I couldn't see the end of. The racetrack air tasted unusually earthy and wet with Georgia humidity, and we were grateful for the pop-up tents shading us.

The thirty-something male fan in front of me chuckled as I flapped the collar of my shirt to cool off. "It's a balmy Georgia day! Y'all take care in that car tomorrow."

"Thanks very much. Enjoy the race from somewhere cool." I handed him one of Sandham Swift's hero cards, with six driver signatures across a photo of both Corvettes.

I turned to the next person in line and had to drop my gaze to the edge of the table to find brown pigtails above an adorable, round face and serious blue eyes. "Hi, what's your name?"

"Mandy," said the adult man holding her hand, as Mandy dimpled up.

"What do you have for her, Mandy?" He reached under the table to help her reveal a worn photo: a years-old shot of me from my rookie year in Star Mazda.

"Where did you get that?"

"I'm John Wheelen, her father." He released Mandy to shake my hand. Mandy gripped the edge of the table and pulled herself up, revealing a toothy smile and a smudge of dirt on her chin.

Her dad spoke again. "We've been fans of yours for years, Kate. My wife and I love going to races—and Mandy does, too. We got your photo a couple years ago, and she hasn't let it go since. She says she's going to be a racecar driver like you."

I choked up. The world wasn't all bad—and the Ringer wasn't always right—if I could inspire little girls to dream about racing. I leaned forward, as close to Mandy as possible. "You must be my biggest fan, Mandy. What do you think about that?"

I saw the dimples again before she dipped her head under the table.

I reached over and tapped the back of her right hand. "Mandy?" Her head popped up. "Would you take a picture with me?" She nodded, and as she walked around to the side of the table, I looked behind me. "Tom, would you get a shot also?"

Photos taken, I turned to Mandy. "I won't forget you. Will you and your dad promise to tell me when you start racing?"

She nodded soberly at me. "Promise."

I signed Mandy's photo—"To Mandy, my biggest little fan, Love, Kate Reilly"—and wrote my e-mail address on another piece of paper for her father. "Please write. I'd love to hear what she's doing."

He beamed and waved goodbye. I was high for the next fifteen minutes, until, over the chatter of the people in front of us, I heard a disdainful voice. "Bobby, girls can't drive. Why y'all gon bother with her?"

The crowd quieted, and many of us looked to my left where Bobby's father, I assumed, stood with his son, an enthusiastic twelve-year-old whose race poster Mike and I had just signed.

"Dad!" Bobby looked anxiously from his father, to me, to others staring at them.

Dad took a big swig of his extra-large beer, glanced at Bobby, and turned to me. "I don't care who hears me. It's a free country, innit? I got a right to my own opinion."

He raised his voice. "And I say girls cain't drive. 'Specially that one. Hear she only wrecks 'em." He kept staring at me, his eyes narrowed.

Rise above. I shrugged and turned away.

Triumph rang through his voice. "That's what I thought. Let's go, Bobby."

I smiled at the boy in front of me, a tall, skinny teenager with bad acne. "Here's a tip for you: don't waste time on people who want to tear you down."

He gulped, leaned forward. "Don't listen to him. You'll show them tomorrow."

"That I will." I kept signing, smiling, and thanking our supporters.

Thirty minutes later, as I changed into my firesuit in the motorhome's back room, I realized Bobby's father had been the only negative voice in the autograph session—undoubtedly because Felix Simon hadn't wandered by. *Thank heaven for minor miracles.* I grabbed my phone and checked the Ringer's site, finding nothing but the story about my outburst at Felix last night and a short item scoffing at my angry tweet this morning. Maybe Kate-hating really was on the wane.

I followed our cars out of the paddock, everyone heading for qualifying, and saw Zeke standing near the entry to pit lane, writing something in a small notebook. He looked up at my approach and smiled wide.

"Katie-Q, how are you?"

"Doing fine, qualifying in a few minutes."

"Give 'em what-for. Show everyone these bloggers are full of shite."

"Will do." I paused. "How's Rosalie doing? She didn't seem well."

"She's OK. She's been stressed lately. But she was glad to see you."

"I hope I can see her again before the weekend's out. What happened with Felix?"

"Never saw him."

"What's he like when he's not after me?"

"Before this, I'd have said nice guy, salt of the earth, knows bucketloads about racing. Now, I'm torn." Zeke nodded a hello to someone behind me.

I turned to see Duncan Forsyth, one of the factory Corvette drivers, entering pit lane. I looked back at Zeke. "You were ready to rearrange his face."

Zeke shrugged. "I calmed down, got some facts. Felix had a crappy home life growing up—pots of money, but his father was abusive and his mother a drunk. These days, he doesn't deal with women much—not hard in the racing world. Three marriages to trophy-girl types, all fell apart fast."

I added this information to the story Jack told us, and marveled Felix had ever been sane. "We've all got problems, Zeke. That doesn't excuse his behavior."

"I've always thought if the only normal you know is twisted, you end up twisted."

"That's nice and philosophical. But how twisted are we talking about? Enough to kill?" Zeke looked alarmed, but I pressed on. "If we can't escape our upbringing, and you said his father was violent, maybe Felix is, too. I know he set me up at the hospital."

"My friend who knows him well said Felix has seemed off this week. Less friendly, more abrupt. Secretive."

A hand fell on my shoulder, making me jump. Mike motioned with his other hand toward our racecar. "Saddle up, cowboy."

"With you." I made a zipping motion across my lips to Zeke. Zeke nodded. "Make me proud."

I'd do my best. For myself, my team, Zeke, and other supporters—and for women everywhere who didn't get enough respect. Time to channel my mad into some driving.

Chapter Thirty-four

"Clear of traffic from Turn 1," Bruce said, as I exited pit lane, only moments after the qualifying session began.

I accelerated through the gentle curve of Turn 2 and into the right-hand Turn 3. Pushing where I could, careful with my cold tires. Desperate to know if the car was as good as it had been before my excursion over the curbs and grass that morning.

I touched the brakes slightly on my mark at the top of the hill, to balance the Corvette for Turn 3. Wheel to the right for 3, carry speed through the corner. Right wheels onto the curbing, accelerating. Sweep through Turn 4, feeding throttle on through the turn. The track falling away, turning to the right. Lift slightly. No brake. Accelerate down the hill into the Esses. Right-left-right. Try to make it a straight line. Accelerating.

Hard on the brakes, pressing myself forward against my belts. Downshift to fourth, still braking. Release and turn left. On the throttle from the apex of 5. Run out over the curbing to settle the car. Wheel straight, upshift to fourth. Fifth. Full throttle. Sixth. Foot to the wood.

Rushing down the incline to Turn 6, still accelerating. Watching for my braking point out of the corner of my eye. There, braking hard. Downshift. Still braking. Downshift. Release brakes. Turn the wheel to clip the apex of 6, the banking helping me carry speed. Accelerate hard. Stand on the brakes again—maximum braking for the slowest corner. Downshift. Release brakes. Turn in for 7, another late apex. Feed the throttle on while unwinding the steering wheel coming out of the turn.

By the time my hands are straight again, I've got my foot to the floor. Yellow car entering Turn 7 behind me. Upshift to fourth. Fifth. Foot planted. Sixth. Check mirrors. Clear. Drift to the right side of the track. Flying. On a long straight with nothing but throttle, the growling V-8 is my whole world. I take a deep breath, focus on relaxing. Focus on speed. Remember I love my job. Remind myself to be precise.

Over the crest of the back straight, barreling down the hill to the Turn 10 left-right complex. A Porsche ahead of me in 10b, must have been the first one out for quali.

Throttle planted, still at top speed. Accelerating. Picking up speed down the hill, looking at the ninety-degree 10a in front of me. Slamming on the brakes at the last possible moment, nose of the car dipping down. Downshift to fifth. Fourth. Third. Release brakes most of the way to roll through the turn. Off brakes at the apex. Square off the corner. Foot hovering over the throttle, wait until halfway between 10a and 10b. Now, foot to the floor.

Throttle on. Hands turning right. Slow in, fast out. Make this good, Kate. Pointed up the hill to the bridge. Yellow car closer behind me. Seeing nothing but bridge and sky. Standing on the throttle. Flying over the crest of the hill. World falling away. Upshift when the car settles again after going over the top. Diving down the hill. Upshift again. Stay straight as the track moves to the right. Still dropping in altitude into the right-hander. Grab sixth gear.

Touch the left side of the track partway down the hill. The car bobbles, unsettled over the bump. Glance at the dash: 129 mph. Turning right. Holding my breath. Clenching my jaw. Clenching my stomach and bladder muscles. Hold the line.

Trusting the grip of the tires, my mind questioning that wisdom. Hold it. Start/finish line coming. No flags showing. Making the turn. Barely breathing. Flat out now. Sure the car's about to slip. Through. Left wheels touch the paint at the outside of the track under the starter's stand. Pointing down the front straight. Foot still planted on the floor. Breathe again. Check mirrors. Move left on the track. Pits on the right flashing by. Yellow car still behind me.

About a second to collect myself, then watching for my Turn 1 braking marker. Attack the brake pedal, downshift. Release brakes, turn. Accelerate up the hill. Aim for the power pole to position myself on another blind hill. Turn 2. Then 3. Settle into a routine, talking myself around the track. Finding my rhythm.

After two laps, I radioed the team. "Car's good. Going for it after three, then doing two," I confirmed. Jack's plan, if the car didn't need adjusting, was for me to warm the car up with three laps, then do two as my qualifying effort. If those times were good, I'd pull in and let them stand, to save wear on the tires we'd start the race with. If times weren't what we hoped for, I'd try more laps.

I took deep breaths going down the back straight on my third lap. Focused on hitting 10a and 10b perfectly, and pouring as much speed on as possible up the hill under the bridge. Willed the car to hold down the hill through 12. Poured every bit of anger, frustration, and grief into concentration, precision, and speed.

The Corvette flew. I was lucky with traffic also, only having one close moment with the Saleen going through the Esses—but he went offline to let me by, obviously on his out lap and still getting up to speed.

I was in Turn 3 after my two flying laps, my speed notched down, when Bruce broke radio silence. "Second lap was 1:18:900." I nodded to myself, recognizing it as good enough for third on the grid the previous year.

Bruce spoke again. "First lap was 1:18:650. Currently P1. Bring it in this lap. And good job."

Currently pole position?

My voice contained none of the elation I felt, as I radioed back. "Copy."

I concentrated on hitting my marks the rest of the lap and came out of Turn 10b with about eighty percent of normal speed, pulling to the right and steering into pit lane.

Past the pit lane entry line, the car in first gear and the speed limiter on, I keyed the radio button again. "Am I staying in?" One strategy was to go out early and lay down a time, but be ready to go out again near the end of the session to try to improve it, if other cars surpassed us.

"Negative, shut it down and get out."

Mike didn't let me finish climbing over the wall into our pit box before grabbing me for a bear hug. He whooped and swung me around. "That's better than last year's pole time! A GT record!"

I pulled my helmet, HANS, and balaclava off. "It's not over yet, Mike." But I couldn't stop the smile.

The next fourteen minutes were some of the most fraught of my life. I squeezed onto the pit box with Jack, Mike, and Bruce, all of us watching video of different corners on the track with one eye and monitoring the timing and scoring screen with the other. Every car that flashed past us on the front straight was trying to beat my time. I'm not sure I breathed.

"Checkered flag," Jack reported. I lifted my head from my hands. I hadn't been able to watch Andy Padden inch closer to my mark in the waning minutes of the session.

Only those who'd started a lap before the checkers flew could beat me now. I gripped Mike's hand, and he chuckled. A minute later, the entire Sandham Swift crew cheered and pumped their fists. Andy pulled into the pits without any improvement. I'd done it: my first pole. I slumped back on the bench seat, elated and exhausted.

Jack turned to me and held out his hand. "Hell of a way to shut the doubters up. That's what I like to see. Now you've got a press conference to go to."

I jumped down and accepted hugs and high-fives from the Sandham Swift team, as well as congratulations from passing drivers. I made a quick call to Gramps to tell him of my very first ALMS pole and had just hung up when someone tapped me on the shoulder. I turned to find a woman in a pantsuit standing next to Jack. Plus a uniformed police officer at the back of the walkway.

"Kate Reilly?"

I nodded, fear overriding my euphoria.

"I'm Detective Barbara Hauk. Can you tell me where you were between the hours of ten last night and ten this morning?"

I didn't like the sound of this at all. "In my hotel room and here at the track."

"Can anyone confirm your whereabouts?"

I pointed at Mike. "He rode in with me from the hotel this morning at seven-fifteen. Since then, I haven't been alone. Last night, I was in my hotel room."

She made a note in her notebook.

Jack crossed his arms. "What's going on?"

The detective nodded at him, then looked me in the eye. "I understand you know Felix Simon?"

"Sort of."

"Felix Simon was found dead in his hotel room at 10:30 this morning. I'd like to know what you meant when you told him not to bother you or he'd live to regret it?"

Chapter Thirty-five

I froze. *Felix dead?* Murdered, if the detective was any indication. *But he was Ellie's killer, wasn't he?*

Jack put a hand on my shoulder. "In thirty minutes, she has a press conference."

I took pole, I remembered. *Press conference for pole sitters.*

The detective nodded. "Is there somewhere she and I can talk before that?"

"We'll all go back to our paddock," Jack said. I was glad he meant to be there.

"I'll need to speak with her alone, but you can be nearby."

I found my voice. "I didn't do anything to Felix. I yelled at him because he was being a jerk. I thought he'd tried to kill me." I faltered. "I thought he killed Ellie."

She closed her notebook. "Let's go."

I kept my eyes on the ground, mortified at being trailed through the paddock by a policeman. *Again.* I'd had enough of that after Wade Becker's death last year. I couldn't think straight, caught between elation over my pole position and fear of the cops and another death.

I was also pissed off at Felix for putting me in this situation—even in death he made my life miserable. *Classy, Kate. He's **dead** and you think about yourself.* But I couldn't pretend we'd been friends.

I drank another bottle of water while I stood in our hospitality area and talked to Detective Hauk, Jack watching us from the garage. The uniformed officer stood at the entrance to our space, like a big neon sign proclaiming, "Check it out: Kate's in trouble again."

I related my whereabouts, as well as names and contact information of people I was with throughout the morning. I explained again my "relationship" with Felix, consisting of a single on-camera interview and plenty of taunting from him.

"What about the voicemail you left him this morning? How did he set you up? What did you mean he'd regret it?"

I hurried to explain the proof of his role in reporters crashing my hospital visit, as well as my suspicion of his involvement in Ellie's death and two attempted hit-and-runs. "I wanted him to stop tormenting me—" *Too strong a word, Kate.* "—maybe not tormenting, but stirring up garbage about me. I knew he was responsible for some of it. I was letting him know I knew. Hoping he'd knock it off. But I wouldn't kill him to stop it—I told him he'd *live* to regret it, not die. That's…"

"That's what, Ms. Reilly?"

"That's crazy."

"And final." She looked at Jack, now hovering a few paces away. "I'll let you go for now, but don't say anything in this press conference. Word will get around, but don't you be the one to spread it." Detective Hauk fixed me with a stern look, and I nodded.

"I'll be in touch again." She left the paddock, talking quietly to the uniform.

Jack walked over and put his hands on my shoulders. "You OK?"

"I'll live. Unlike Felix, I guess. It's weird." I tried to feel sorry Felix was gone—I didn't wish death on anyone. But I had to be honest, a Felix-sized hole in my life was not a bad thing.

I fumbled for my cell phone. *Was the Ringer dead too?* My hopes were dashed by a five-minute-old post about cops in the ALMS paddock—wondering what "Kate Violent" had done now.

"Ten minutes to the press conference. I'll go with you."

I dashed into the motorhome and changed into street clothes, leaving my sodden racewear spread across the bed for Aunt Tee. I used the walk down the paddock and over the bridge to the media center to stuff shock, worry, and fear into a corner of my mind. To focus on happiness over my first pole and anticipation for tomorrow's race.

Only two reporters departed from the standard press conference script of "How was your pole run and how do you feel about your chances in the race tomorrow?" by asking about the recent public backlash I'd faced and if I thought this achievement would answer some of the critics.

It was easy to smile for that one. "Absolutely. All of the attention has been really upsetting. I understand not everyone will like me, but the questions about my ability to drive are especially disappointing. Call this my rebuttal." Some reporters and the other drivers on the panel laughed with me.

The Series media officer had to step in once, when a journalist asked why I'd spoken with police right after qualifying, to explain there would be a briefing as soon as possible. The media reps exchanged glances with each other, a few of them regarding me with suspicion. *There goes my reputation again.*

Jack and I were back on the other side of the track, halfway down the paddock to our garage, when I saw Juliana, walking alone, crying. I sent Jack ahead and went to her.

"Jules." I put my arm around her waist.

"Kate, did you hear? Isn't it awful?"

"Are you all right?"

She sniffled and dabbed at the corners of her red-rimmed eyes with a tissue. I was impressed with the staying power of her makeup, which hadn't run. "I was so mad at him this morning. Wondered if he was in that car yesterday. But knowing he was lying there dead—" her breath hiccoughed.

We'd reached Sandham Swift. "Come in and sit down?"

She shook her head and took a deep breath. Pulled her shoulders back and lifted her head. "Thank you, but I need to keep on with work. There's even more to do now."

."They'll give you someone to help cover the pits, right?" Typically two pit reporters split coverage of teams on pit lane between them, for the sake of logistics, if nothing else, so the physical area they had to cover was smaller.

"I assume so, but I have no idea yet." She gave me a hug. "Thank you, Kate. And congratulations on pole. You guys were hiding a little something in all those practice sessions, weren't you?"

"No comment." I smiled.

Another squeeze, and she was gone.

I had half an hour back at the paddock, during which I thanked every last member of the crew for making the Corvette so fast and balanced. Tom took photos of everyone standing together, and we posed for passing fans and media, as well. Every car was a potential winner before the race, but having demonstrated our speed, we could be rightly judged one of the favorites.

I'd said all the correct words in the press conference, including, "Qualifying position doesn't matter as much for a long race as it does for the sprint races." The sentiment was true. But deep down, I burned with hope. We had a damn fast car, and I was ready to race. I wasn't sure how I'd sleep for the anticipation.

Of course, there was work to do yet. First was the American Le Mans Series drivers meeting conducted by the race director who called the shots from race control. Everyone trooped over to the Administrative building across the track, up the hill from the media center, some walking the shortcut over the bridge, some taking golf carts the long way around. We crowded into a room that was too small for the number of drivers present, leaving half of us standing at the back and around the edges, eyeing those seated with joking threats.

After the opening prayer from the Motorsports Ministries pastor, the longtime Series race director, Guy Dinman, started with thank yous and compliments from the last race. He specifically mentioned thanks from the safety crew for drivers giving them room to work on the big accident in the Kink.

I flushed, realizing that was mine.

An amused voice rose out of the murmur of the room. "There are easier ways to meet Miles Hanson, Kate. I could've hooked you up." Andy, the jokester from the LinkTime Corvette team.

Everyone else in the room laughed while I cringed. *Too soon, Andy. Not funny yet.*

"Stay classy, people." Guy surveyed us. There were traces of humor in his voice, but we all felt the steel underneath. "Just a reminder. In this room and on that track, you treat each other with respect. It's your job to race and my job to deal with anyone who does something wrong. Keep it clean and polite, and you won't hear from me."

I ordered myself to relax as Guy continued with reminders about full-course-caution processes: where the pace car would pick up the race leader, where cars should slow (where the yellow flags are being waved, not only displayed), and where they should speed up (other areas, to collect in one pack). Guy went on with procedures for the race start and subsequent restarts, as well as reminders about pit lane speed and where the pit lane began on the downhill entry at this track.

I was still smarting with shame when Guy delivered a warning that applied to a different incident of mine. "I want to talk specifically about Turn 4 and the Esses. Prototypes get through there easy, don't need all the track. But the GTs, they're using every inch of the road—especially on the exit of the right-hander. Prototype drivers, you've got to be aware of that. Don't think you can slip past them there with no problem—we've seen more than one incident of that in practice already. Be aware, if I see a GT and a prototype tangle there and someone goes off? I won't even review the tape, I'll hand the prototype driver a penalty. So watch yourselves in that area, and everywhere else."

He wrapped up with a warning about trips into the gravel—telling us he'd be in no hurry to retrieve multiple offenders. Then he closed his notebook and leaned forward on the podium, his eyes sweeping the room again. "Bottom line, with all due respect, try to keep your car on the track, and we'll be fine. Have a great race."

The meeting broke up with a few people clapping and others chuckling. The buzz of conversation was high, and as I turned to follow Leon out the door, I finally made out the words being whispered around the room: *Felix Simon dead.*

Outside, I was surprised to see Dominic Lascuola standing near two other Benchmark Racing drivers in a golf cart.

"Kate." He stepped forward, hand outstretched. "Sorry about this morning. I'm not used to the track."

I shook, wary. "Sure. No harm done, in the end."

"I'm glad your car's all right. Good job on pole." He smiled, looking very like his sister, only with short blond hair instead of her ponytail. But while I thought of Colby as open, straightforward, and honest, her brother seemed closed in. Calculating.

"Thanks," I said. "Good luck in the race."

"You, too. I'll be sure to leave you the track space you need."

Was that a threat, a taunt, or a simple statement? I didn't know, but I'd keep my distance, on track or off.

Chapter Thirty-six

Zeke knew more about Felix when I saw him in the paddock after the meeting.

"It's so odd." He ran a hand over his face and shook his head as if to clear his mind. "We weren't close mates, but I knew him, and he's…gone. I understand now how you feel about Ellie."

"Shocked, upset, angry, afraid for yourself. Guilty for not being nicer, friendlier, more something?"

"Exactly."

"What happened?"

"He didn't show up here, didn't answer his phone, and didn't answer the door at the hotel, so they got management to open it and there he was on the couch."

"Do they know how? Did he have a bad heart or a blood pressure problem?" *Who are you trying to fool, Kate? Detectives don't come out if the man had a heart attack.*

"Don't think he had a heart problem, since he told me how his life improved with his magic pills for—" he looked around, then leaned closer and whispered, framing the words with finger quotes "—erectile dysfunction."

I waved my hands in front of my face, trying to dispel the idea of Felix and sex. "Don't put images like that in my head."

"Sorry." He looked the opposite. "All I know is he was on the couch, not a mark on him. Looked peaceful."

"Sounds like Ellie." I spoke without thinking.

"You think they're connected?"

Did I? "If whoever killed Ellie was aiming at me, there would have to be a connection between me and Felix."

"Can't imagine what that would be."

We were interrupted by Tom walking toward us, from the direction of the Sandham Swift paddock. "It's six-thirty. Time for the auction."

Zeke greeted Tom, then spoke to me. "You donated something?"

"A ticket to the banquet as my guest—the team's guest. It was a better idea a month ago when they asked." I looked at Tom. "Maybe not a great idea now that I'm the most suspicious character around."

Zeke shook his head. "You may be the flavor of the month, but the shadiest guy is the olive oil king down the paddock."

"What's wrong with him?" He was a gentleman racer who supplied the team he ran with the best equipment and most opulent paddock setup.

"Money laundering is what I hear," Tom answered. "I don't ask."

Good plan. Zeke gave me a hug goodbye, and Tom and I headed to the Winner's Circle.

"@katereilly28: Hoping to raise money for a good cause in Andy Padden's charity auction. Come out and bid on a ticket to the #ALMS championship banquet."

The event benefitted a Georgia-based foundation for juvenile diabetes that Andy started sponsoring after his nephew nearly died from the disease. Savvy fans knew this was where to score unique collectors' items, as Andy stipulated everything up for bid was used by drivers in races or would provide a one-of-a-kind experience. Though the audience was small—fifty or sixty bidders—their pockets were deep.

Tom and I were there because Sandham Swift donated something unusual: a ticket to the American Le Mans Series Night of Champions banquet on Sunday night. The plan was Tom would talk logistics with the winning bidder, and I would remind everyone they'd get a rare inside look at the racing world, plus rub elbows with drivers and media stars.

Andy, as auctioneer, had gotten the bid to $600 when he called me to the stage. He slung an arm around my shoulders and bellowed, "Who wants to sit with our Kate at the banquet? Who wants to be her date for the evening?"

I tried to keep the panic I felt off my face. I elbowed him.

"What's that?" He looked at me and spoke into the microphone.

"Sorry, no date. But a seat at our table, yes."

He turned to the crowd. "A seat at the table, couple photos, conversation—close enough to a date for me! What am I bid to see Kate prettied up—you going to wear a dress, Kate?" The last bit was to me, of course.

I nodded, looking to Tom for help. He looked as alarmed as I felt.

"Photos with Kate in a dress! What am I bid?"

Is this tailor-made for a stalker or what? How the hell do I stop it?

Easier to stop a freight train. Andy released me and moved to the front of the stage, looking back and forth between two bidders. He drove the total to $1,200, where it got harder and harder to get more out of either man. They both looked familiar, though neither looked scary. Tom stepped to the stage and called Andy over.

Andy conferred with Tom, then turned to the audience. "Unbelievable! A question for our two bidders. What if I could get one ticket for each of you? Would you each agree to pay twelve hundred dollars. Remember, it all goes to a worthy cause, and you get a once-in-a-lifetime experience of the ALMS championship banquet with Kate and the rest of the Sandham Swift team."

Both men nodded, and Andy crowed, "Thanks to the generosity of Sandham Swift, I have two tickets. Sold! To two lucky gentlemen. Please see my assistant and Tom for payment and ticket information. Thank you to Sandham Swift and Kate Reilly!"

I hustled off the stage and grabbed Tom's arm, hissing in his ear. "Get their e-mail addresses."

When I followed him over to congratulate the two men, I recognized them both from the mall event the weekend before: George Ryan and—I had to sneak a peek at Tom's notes—Jeff Morgan. *Nice, normal guys? Stalkers? At least George was familiar.*

"Congratulations." I shook hands with each of them as Tom related details of where to be on Sunday and how to dress. I glanced at Tom's notes again. Neither e-mail address was anything I recognized.

"I'm so excited, this will be so cool. And I'll get to sit with my favorite team," Jeff said.

George Ryan laughed, a nervous, awkward sound. "I guess you'll have two dates, Kate. I hope we don't have to fight each other for you."

Tom took charge as my skin crawled. "If it's a date at all, it's one with the whole Sandham Swift team, and there are plenty of us to go around. Thanks again for your donation to the cause, and we'll see you Sunday evening. Look for me, and I'll have seats saved for you."

As we walked away from the Winner's Circle, Tom finished his sentence, for my ears only, "… as far away from Kate as possible."

I shuddered. "That was creepy. What was Andy thinking? A bachelorette auction with me as the only prize? It's flattering, maybe? But no thanks."

"Can't argue with the outcome. Twenty-four hundred dollars is a nice donation for his charity."

"You have to stick by my side all night."

He cocked his head. "Won't that be Stuart's role?"

I sighed. Tom was one of the few people who knew about my relationship with Stuart. "First, I'm sure he'll be busy at the banquet. Second, not ready to go public."

"OK, I'll be next to you."

"I'm not getting in the way of you bringing a date, am I, Tom?"

"You're the only woman I will ever love, Kate." He clutched his hands over his heart and fluttered his eyelashes dramatically at me.

"Cut the crap, Romeo. I'll see you bright and early tomorrow morning."

He laughed, and we parted ways for the night.

Chapter Thirty-seven

Over dinner with Holly at a bar and grill along Old Winder Highway, I finally had a chance to talk about Felix. "Two questions. Why would someone kill him? And do we think his death is connected to Ellie's?"

"He was a jerk to you." She waved a french fry to stop my protests. "You didn't kill him, but maybe someone did—like your stalker."

"Can we not say 'my stalker?' We don't know I have one. Anyway, being mean to me isn't much of a reason. Do we think Felix and Ellie's deaths are connected? Maybe it's a coincidence?"

"On one hand, deaths at two successive race weekends can't be coincidence—thank goodness this is the end of the season, because I'd hate to see what happened at the next race. On the other hand, I can't think what you and Felix have in common to make someone that angry at you both."

"And Juliana. Someone's after her, too."

"I know, maybe Felix killed Ellie and tried to run you and Juliana down, and someone killed him for revenge."

"But who? Me? Juliana? Ellie's husband who's at home dealing with twins? None of it makes any sense." I took a bite of my blackened salmon and thought about Felix. "I remember Felix saying he wasn't the only one after me. Plus he was acting secretive this week—but that's third-hand news. Maybe he knew something about Ellie's death—or who's after females at the track—and he was killed to keep him quiet."

"That big watch was new this week."

"Was it? A race-winner's watch. Did he ever win one?" The biggest Series sponsor, Kreisel Timepieces, was a luxury watch maker that handed out special watches to all race winners—a design that couldn't be purchased, only won.

"The company's only been giving them out for seven years. Felix hasn't raced in that time, so he couldn't have won it. To be fair, I've seen those watches in fundraising auctions before, donated by a driver. Or he could have been given one by the company."

I set down my fork. "Or he could have blackmailed someone for it."

"Maybe he saw something at the Tavern that night." Holly paused, handing her empty plate over to the waiter. "I think the manager of the team next to ours was friends with Felix. I'll see if he knows anything."

"Thanks. Did you find out anything about Colby and her brother?"

She nodded. "They were in Elkhart Lake that weekend, and even at Siebkens, but outside on the lawn eating ice cream. No one remembers seeing them inside the Tavern, which doesn't prove anything. You have to consider them."

"She seemed so nice."

"Everyone says she is. But her brother's a real hothead—loses his temper in and out of the car. Very protective of his baby sister."

"By now, I shouldn't be surprised people who don't know me don't like me." I looked at the time. "Now to meet some more."

My final obligation that night was my father's bank party, and I'd roped Holly into joining me. I was going because I was curious about my father's life. His family. But I wished I could observe anonymously.

"Only the two cousins dislike you, right? Maybe they won't be there. Besides, you already decided to do this. Let's get it over with."

We drove down the highway to the Chateau Élan Winery, where a couple hundred people filled its main room. Most wore suits or dresses—or all black, like Holly. I stood out in my khakis and white team polo shirt, though I recognized three other drivers in the crowd dressed as I was.

"I'm getting wine," Holly announced, drifting to a table at the right of the room.

I clamped a hand on her arm. "Don't leave me."

She looked past me, speaking quietly. "I need to get out of your way right now. I'll be here when you're ready."

I turned to find my father, looking relieved and nervous. "Thank you for coming."

"I can't stay long." *Damn it, Kate, you didn't need to start off negative.*

"I know. Race day tomorrow. I'm glad you stopped in." He took a deep breath. "Let me introduce you to my family."

I wasn't sure what to say, but I followed him to the back left corner of the room where five people sat at a table littered with half-full glasses of wine and empty appetizer plates. My father walked directly to a petite, blonde woman and touched her shoulder.

"Amelia?" As he spoke—no, as we approached, the table fell silent, the relaxed, jovial atmosphere turned tense. Wondering.

Exactly how I felt.

Amelia stood, smiling and reaching out her hands for mine. She looked younger than the mid-forties she must be.

"Katherine." Her voice was low and calm, her gaze direct. "I'm so glad to finally meet you." She drew in breath, as if to say more, but pressed her lips together and smiled instead, squeezing my hands.

I was grateful for her welcome, but I still felt like turning and running. "It's nice to meet you, too." I tried for a smile.

She released my hands as two others approached. The female was enough like her mother to have passed for twins: blond, slender, fine-boned, and the same couple inches taller than me. She'd also inherited our father's eyes. They were blue and wary, probably like mine.

"Lara," she said, shaking my hand.

"Katherine." I shrugged. "Kate. Whatever."

"And I'm Edward, Eddie, whatever." I heard laughter in the voice of my half-brother, as he stood beside his sister and offered his hand in turn. He took after my father in coloring, though he looked more like his mother around the mouth. He was six inches taller than everyone else and comfortable with his gangly limbs.

"Nice to meet you both."

"Interesting, isn't it?" Eddie grinned.

I nodded. "It looks like a great party. Are you all here for the whole weekend or only tonight?"

Amelia spoke up first. "We'll all be at the race tomorrow, but these two head back to school on Sunday. I'll stay with James for the banquet Sunday night."

"Good job on the pole position, by the way," Eddie put in.

"Thanks. It's a nice boost after the last race."

A new voice joined the group and finished my thought. "And everything since, no doubt." One of the other men at the table had risen and joined us, standing to my left on the other side of my father. His words were neutral, but his face was cold.

My father shifted to include the newcomer in our small circle. "Katherine, this is my nephew, Holden Sherain." My father gestured to the remaining man at the table, and at his approach, introduced me to another nephew, William Reilly-Stinson.

Great, both of the disgruntled cousins in one place. They both looked familiar, but I figured a look in the mirror would explain why.

William Reilly-Stinson smiled and said, "Call me Billy," reaching around Holden to shake my hand. I didn't trust his apparent friendliness.

Holden didn't bother to shake, simply nodded at me, a gesture I returned.

My father cleared his throat. "Katherine, are you ready for the race tomorrow?"

"As ready as we can be for a race this long. We've talked through contingency plans. A lot of it comes down to who's lucky and who's most prepared to deal with the unexpected."

As my father, Billy, and Eddie peppered me with questions about my qualifying laps, the crash at Road America, and plans for the next day's race, I switched into "racecar driver entertaining sponsors" mode, trying not to think about the emotional complications of the group in front of me. But Holden, Lara, and Amelia didn't speak, only watched me intently. That was unnerving and exhausting. After a few minutes, I glanced desperately around the room for Holly. She was at my side moments later.

I introduced her and apologized for having to leave. I shook hands all around again—though not with Holden, whose expression never wavered from something close to contempt. And not with Amelia, who leaned over and pressed her cheek to mine instead, whispering, "I'm so glad to meet you, because you mean so much to him."

I masked my surprise. "Thanks."

My father walked us to the door and kissed my cheek once more. "Thank you again for coming. Good luck tomorrow, we'll all be rooting for you."

I couldn't help myself. "All?"

"Most." He sighed.

"Were you able to find out if they—my—your nephews could have been in Elkhart Lake or Atlanta the last couple weekends?"

"I only confirmed Holden in Boston for the first weekend and Billy for the second—strange in itself, since they're usually regular with schedules and activities. I made some inquiries… this might not be the time."

Holly caught on faster than I did and excused herself with a wave, saying she'd meet me at the car.

"And?" I asked when she was out of earshot.

"I'm still digging into specifics, but it appears Holden and Billy have been quietly bankrolling a number of new businesses."

"Like angel investors?"

"Perhaps that's the idea. But these are high-end restaurants and fashion or art boutiques—which carry an enormous risk factor as potential investments. And results have been poor so far."

"Big points for style and power though."

He rubbed a hand over his face. "Yes, I'm beginning to suspect the role of provider is more important to them than a shrewd return on investment. I'm also concerned they may be spending beyond their current means—"

"And looking for other sources of income? The money they think I shouldn't inherit? Didn't you say there'd be no money for years?"

"Not until I'm gone, correct, though they may be borrowing against future expectations, in addition to spending their own money. Listen, let me pursue the question of what they might be involved in. I guarantee you if they're at all involved in what's been going on around you, the authorities will know immediately."

I nodded. "I won't spread it around. But I'm not going to shield them if the police ask me something."

"That's all I ask. I'll let you know what else I uncover."

It took until Holly and I drove through the main gates of Chateau Élan for me to release the breath I felt I'd been holding for the past half an hour.

Holly nodded. "Kate with family, that's something different."

"I can't see them as family. They're a mixed up collection of people—some may be supportive, but some have motive." I related what my father had told me about the cousins. "I'm not sure I trust *any* of them."

Holly laughed. "Sugar, dysfunctional is the definition of family. Get used to it. You're the long-lost daughter."

"Not dealing with that. Not until after this weekend. Maybe not ever."

She studied me. "You're angry."

"I can't deal with these emotions on top of everything else." I hit the steering wheel with my hand. "Everyone wants more than I can give. My father, Stuart, fans, the Ringer. And maybe those cousins are trying to kill me to get something I don't want anyway? It's too much. I can't do it. What energy I have, I'm focusing on the race. No one gets anything until after that."

As if on cue, my cell phone rang. I nodded to Holly, who picked it up from the center console. "Stuart," she said.

I shook my head. The only way to hold myself together was to shut everyone out.

"Do what you gotta do." Holly set my ringing phone back in the console and turned up the radio.

Chapter Thirty-eight

My resolve to focus on racing was tested twice the next morning before I reached my team paddock. First, my father cruised past me in a golf cart, as I walked down the hill from the field I'd parked in. He thanked me again for attending the party, but stopped talking when I held up a hand.

"After the race. Tomorrow. But not now, OK? It's too much."

He nodded, though his expression signaled he struggled with some emotion. "All right. Have a good race."

Was that anger? Disappointment? I squelched my guilt. I heard an engine fire up in a garage below, and my blood hummed in response. Race day.

My second hurdle was Stuart, stopping in front of me in the paddock, looking concerned and frustrated. *Focus on the race, Kate! The race. Cope with this later.*

He raised an eyebrow at me. "Did you get my message?"

"I haven't listened to it yet." I raised my hands. "I feel like a jerk, but I'm on overload. It's all I can do to hold myself together. I'm sorry."

"The message tells you Miles Hanson will be here today on the pre-race grid. He specifically requested a photo with you, to quell dissent in his fan club. Be prepared for that." He paused, his face stony. "I suppose you'll let me know when you can *deal* with me. Have a good race." He turned and walked away.

I stood with my eyes closed for a moment, not liking myself much. I shook my head and continued on to the Sandham Swift paddock. Two men stood at our rope barrier, and I nodded to them as I reached out to unhook the line, my mind preoccupied with the schedule of events for the morning, which would unfold at breakneck pace.

Movement to my left. A snarl. "Bitch!" Someone shoved me.

I stumbled sideways from the impact. Caught myself on the rope, pulling the stanchion over so it hit the ground with a clang. People rushed from all directions. A crew member shouted. I heard a scuffle. A punch landing on flesh.

I staggered into the garage and leaned against the Corvette abandoned by the five crew members now in the paddock lane. Tried to make sense of what I saw. Four Sandham Swift mechanics had subdued the two men I'd passed—one of whom pushed me. Another, Alex Handy, led a third guy into our paddock. I recognized him as one of the winning bidders from the auction the night before, now sporting a split lip and a half-wet t-shirt.

I crossed to him. "Jeff Morgan, right?"

He nodded and tried to smile. "Ouch."

Aunt Tee handed him ice wrapped in a towel for his lip. Tom ran up with a security guard who asked what happened.

"Someone shoved me and then there were people everywhere," I said.

Jeff lowered the ice and spoke carefully. "I saw the whole thing. She walked past them and one guy called her a bitch and shoved her. I went to stop him, but the second guy punched me. Then the crew tackled them both." He turned to me. "I tried, but I couldn't stop them alone."

"Of course you couldn't," Aunt Tee soothed. "There were two of them."

I shook my head. "It's not your fight, but it was nice of you to help. Thank you."

"What kind of fan or friend would I be if I didn't stand up for my favorite driver? I'm glad I was here."

The security guard spoke again. "Any idea why that happened?"

"They were wearing Miles Hanson gear," I pointed out. "Miles Hanson plus beer is my guess."

Jeff lowered the ice pack again. "I can confirm the beer because most of it ended up on me. I'm going to smell like a brewery today."

Aunt Tee patted his shoulder. "No, you won't. The least we can do is give you a fresh shirt. And you can clean up in our motorhome."

She led him inside when the security guard left. As I thanked the crew who'd come rushing to my aid, Mike and Leon arrived, allowing the mechanics to recount the incident blow-by-blow. I saw the door of the motorhome start to open, and I scurried into the transport trailer's office, hissing at Mike and Leon to come with me.

"You hiding from someone then, Kate?" Leon pulled down two of the slats on the blinds to look out.

"Stop that, or they'll see."

Mike flopped onto a couch. "Sounds like this guy was a hero. Shouldn't you be thanking him?"

"I did, but he acts like he's got a crush on me, and it's better to keep my distance from those. Besides, he'll get more attention tomorrow night at the banquet."

Leon cocked his head. "What's that?"

"He's one of the two guys who won our banquet tickets in the auction last night."

I wasn't able to avoid Jeff Morgan entirely, because Leon and I passed him on our way to the pits less than an hour later. Jeff waved to catch my eye, and raised his camera for a photo. I poked Leon and we both smiled and waved. But we kept walking.

"He wanted you to stop," Leon murmured.

"Keep moving."

Mike followed us some minutes later, still in street clothes. The warm-up session was only twenty-five minutes, and only Leon and I would get behind the wheel—Leon, since he had less experience here, and me, because I'd be starting the race.

Jack instructed us to take only as many laps as we needed to get comfortable, repeating an oft-heard mantra in racing: "Nothing good ever happens in warm-up." We each took three or four laps and kept our noses clean. Overnight showers had washed away a lot of the rubber laid down the past two days of practice, which meant less grip for our tires. I was glad to know the current condition of the course.

After warm-up, the car stayed in the pits with the crew while the drivers went back to the paddock with Jack and our crew chiefs for a five-minute check-in and some quiet moments before the race countdown began. Jack made last-minute points—primarily to me, along the lines of "Pole position is great, but don't throw the race away trying to stay in front."

"I gotcha, boss. 'To finish first, first you have to finish.'" Another racing maxim. "I'll hand the car to Mike in pristine condition, if it's the last thing I do."

I left the paddock for pit lane before Mike and Leon, because, as starting driver, I'd drive the car out of the pits, around the track, and into grid position on the front straight, where the others would meet me. I was thinking about the upcoming photo opp with Miles Hanson when a well-tailored suit got in my way.

Holden Sherain stood in front of me, his expression saying I was a bug he wanted to squash.

I sighed. "Hi, nice to see you. I have to be going now." I moved to step around him, but he grabbed my arm and leaned in close.

"Busy Ms. Racecar Driver, aren't we? Watch your step, because I'm on to you."

He'd have made more sense speaking Greek. "What?"

He narrowed his eyes. "I'm keeping an eye on you—everywhere you go, I'm watching. Don't think you can waltz in, pretend to be part of the family, and scoop up some money without any questions being asked. Without proof. You little nobody—"

I wrenched my arm from his grasp and stepped closer, invading his personal space and making him flinch. "Listen, asshole. I don't have time for this shit. I didn't ask for family, money—or *you*—and I don't want any of it. Stay the hell away from me."

I didn't look back as I entered the safety of pit lane.

Chapter Thirty-nine

I fastened my chinstrap, shaking my head over Sherain's animosity, and considered what he'd said. "Everywhere you go, I'm watching." Was he following me? Having me followed? Trying to kill me?

I banged my palm twice against the side of my helmet. *Enough, Kate. Save your energy for the race.* I climbed back into the Corvette.

At Bruce's signal, I pushed the ignition button.

"Pit exit open, Kate," he radioed.

When the crew member at the front of the car waved me on, I pulled out, slotting into an opening in the line of exiting cars. We had two minutes to get all cars out of pit lane and onto the track, per the minute-by-minute schedule race organizers followed pre- and post-race. I'd caught a glimpse of the three-page agenda once and was astonished to see tasks and activities in increments as small as thirty seconds. I was even more amazed everything happened on-schedule—or close enough to it for the race to start on time.

I followed a prototype around the track at a reduced pace—something a bit faster than the sixty miles per hour we'd do under caution—feeling excitement and anticipation well up inside. We had a great car. Anything could happen.

Five minutes later I was waved into the first position in class on the grid. I shut the car down, hauled myself out, and set my helmet, gloves, balaclava, and earplugs on the seat. Ahead of me were the prototype classes, all cars backed against the right side of the track, parked at a forty-five degree angle. Behind me were the rest of the GTs, the sportscars. Within a minute, our whole team was lined up next to the car across the grid, as a local minister gave the invocation. The national anthem followed as paratroopers descended, one trailing a large American flag.

"@katereilly28: Gorgeous weather for race day, with no rain in sight. Ready for good, hard racing here at Petit Le Mans."

The next activity, an hour and fifteen minutes before race start, was opening the grid to the public. Thousands of race attendees poured onto the track to get close to racecars, drivers, and teams. Hundreds of photos were taken from every direction. I stood against the track wall at the rear of the 28 car with Leon and the crew. Jack stood at the front, accepting congratulations and good wishes. Mike was off on a parade lap around the track.

I looked around at the mass of humanity, blue skies, and flags lifting in a light breeze. I smelled race day: fuel mixed with hot metal, rubber, and concrete, plus a dash of sweat, sunscreen, and cigarette smoke. There was nothing like it.

Steve and Vicki from Active-Fit appeared, Steve stopping to talk to Jack and Vicki making her way to me for a good-luck hug. We stood together, watching the crowd and commenting on the more outrageous outfits—baseball hats covered with pins, neon-patterned leggings, a bikini—and saw Juliana go by.

Vicki snapped her fingers. "I remember where I met her. I was judging a regional pageant, and she'd won the year before, then gone on to win Miss Alabama. She was quite the celebrity for that, if not—"

Tom interrupted us, waving at me from the front of the car to take a photo. I went forward to pose with George Ryan and the car, while George told me how excited he was for the race and the banquet. He wished me luck twice, shook my hand, then left.

I returned to Vicki. "If not what?"

She grimaced. "She had a cloud around her at the time—all rumor, but you know how that can stick to someone."

"Sounds familiar."

"I suppose so. At the time, she was suspected of doing damage to her pageant competition."

"What does that mean?"

"Lipstick smeared on a dress, shoes missing, laxative in orange juice, pepper spray in makeup. That kind of thing."

"People do that?"

"Weird things happen in pageants—they're competitions, and some people are obsessed with winning. Same as in racing."

"Wild. I don't believe it of Jules—but her mother could have been responsible. She was twisted, that's for sure." I started to wonder exactly how much Juliana's mother might have influenced her, but my mind went blank when I saw a disturbance in the paddock crowd. A swelling of energy and excitement heading my way. I felt jittery. I knew what was coming. Who.

Sure enough, the focal point was Miles Hanson walking down the grid, his left arm in a narrow sling. Like a boat, he left a wake of people tumbling over each other to keep up with him, take his photo, be near him. At least a dozen official photographers—and several score unofficial ones—clicked away on their cameras. Somewhere in the scrum was a guy Jack hired to get official shots of this meeting.

Miles Hanson was your typical tall, dark, and handsome. Tall enough, anyway, at five-ten, with a streamlined build that suggested many hours spent in the gym. Dark in coloring and hair—the kind of perfect, wavy hair that made most women jealous. And light blue eyes.

Even more compelling than Miles' looks, however, was his story. He'd grown up in a racing family, the star of which had been his father, Hank "Handy" Hanson. Handy spent most of his career as a crew chief in NASCAR, taking three different teams to championships before taking a pay cut to manage his son's team for Miles' first full year in the Cup series. Together, Handy and Miles steamrolled the competition with the combination of Handy's almost mystical understanding of the mechanics of racecars and Miles' stunning driving talent. Miles had sewn up the rookie of the year title and was looking for his second race win when tragedy struck. NASCAR was at Martinsville, in Virginia, five races left in the season. Miles led the race, and eventually won it, unaware Handy had suffered a massive heart attack and died atop the pit box with three laps to go. NASCAR fans mourned with him, as he endured public heartbreak and kept racing.

Miles had a story, looks, and oodles of charm. The undeniable "it" factor. Plus talent to spare, as his two NASCAR Cup championships attested. All by the age of 28. I didn't disagree when Holly called Miles Hanson potent.

I held my breath as he approached Jack, shook hands, and turned to the cameras with a smile on his face. Their hands still joined, Miles nodded at Jack and said something I couldn't hear, but that made the audience laugh.

Then Jack stepped aside and Miles headed for me—though the cameras and fans had to stay where they were at the front of the car. Vicki faded away to stand with our crew, and I reminded myself to breathe.

I wasn't star-struck. I respected him as a driver, but I wasn't awed by him the way I would be if Phil Hill or Janet Guthrie appeared in front of me. What did nearly strike me dumb was Miles Hanson's charisma. His presence was magnetic. And by God, he was good looking. I swallowed, and ignored the voice in my head wondering if he was here to spit in my face and make people hate me more.

I held out a hand, which he ignored, folding me in for a hug.

"Helluva way to meet, isn't it?" He whispered in my ear. I felt a laugh rumble in his chest.

"Yeah. It's really great of you to be here. How're you feeling?"

We pulled apart, and he kept smiling. "I feel fine. Wishing I could be in a car."

"About the race—"

"We both screwed up, didn't we?"

"Sorry."

"Well, hell, me too." He looked past me to the Corvette. "Though seems like you're doing better than I am with it. Nice job on pole."

I started to cross my arms over my chest, then thought better of it, as we were the focus of many eyes and cameras. "Thanks. It hasn't been a smooth ride for me either."

He ran his free hand through his hair. "I'm sorry about that. I've been trying to get the message out to not be mad at you, but it's hard to reach everyone. Or convince them. Picture's worth a thousand words, though, right?"

We were interrupted by two unexpected, unconnected arrivals: Holly and Nash Rawlings. Holly hung back while Miles waved Rawlings over and introduced us.

Rawlings looked calm and polite this time, and he reached for my hand. "I'm so sorry, Kate. My enthusiasm and emotion got the better of me. I was just so worried about Miles, I wasn't sure what I was saying." He sounded like he'd memorized the words.

I shook Rawlings' hand as Miles spoke. "We sat down and watched the video, and I explained how we were both at fault. Why no one should be upset with you."

Rawlings bobbed his head in agreement. I didn't buy the act. Wasn't sure the guy in front of me hadn't been responsible for death threats or worse. I made myself smile at both of them. I believed Miles, but not necessarily Rawlings.

I glanced to where Holly stood talking to Vicki and some of the team. I made a "come over" gesture with my chin, and Holly approached, tossing her head and making her red curls bounce. I introduced her to Miles and left them to charm each other.

I turned to Rawlings. "So I'm not a—what was it?—decoration in the way of real racers on the track?"

He flushed, turning red the way I'd seen him at the last race. "No. But I'm no redneck either."

Touché. "Sorry, what came out wasn't what I meant."

"Same here."

"You really rallied the troops to hate me though."

"Miles has millions of fans. They get angry if he's hurt." The traces of warmth and contrition I'd seen in his face were gone now, though he wasn't angry.

I understood Rawlings only apologized to me because Miles wanted him to. Maybe he really got that it was a racing incident with both of us at fault. But I also knew if he had it to do again, even knowing Miles didn't blame me, Rawlings would react the same way. Would draw the wrath of NASCAR legions down on my head with no hesitation.

Fine. I didn't like him either.

I nodded. "I'm leaving it to the police to track down who sent me death threats in e-mail. But I appreciate you being here to help stop those kind of attacks."

He swallowed at the mention of the cops, but showed no other sign of distress. "Sure, glad I can help." I pegged him for an instigator, but not a sender of threats himself.

"Maybe we can get a photo, the three of us?" I gestured to Miles.

When Rawlings agreed, I handed my phone to Holly and stood between the two men for shots from a dozen cameras and phones around us.

"Can we get just Kate and Miles again?" called an official media photographer, identifiable by his blue vest with "Press" on the back. Rawlings moved out of the shot, and Miles squeezed the arm around my shoulder, muttering, "This should shut everyone up." I glanced up at him, and he grinned at me.

He looked at his watch two minutes later, stopping the photo barrage. "I've got to get down to say hey to the LinkTime guys. Kate?" He turned to me and held out his hand. "I'd race against you any time," he said as we shook. "Maybe on my turf."

"I'm game."

"In fact, come out to a race sometime. Be my guest—guests," he amended, winking at Holly. "We'll see if we can get you a seat in a stock car."

"Any time. And Miles, thank you, sincerely."

He shrugged. "Racing's a family. We look out for each other." He laughed suddenly. "I call it the brotherhood. Guess I'll have to change that."

Holly smiled. "Sugar, call her Brother Kate."

Chapter Forty

"@katereilly28: Thanks to Miles Hanson for stopping by pre-race grid today. Will race each other again some day. [pic]"

As Miles left the Sandham Swift area, Scott Brooklyn approached and, to my surprise, gave him a back-slapping hug. Also strange, Scott wore an SGTV firesuit and was accompanied by a cameraman.

Mike returned from his parade lap around the track, followed closely by Zeke, who made his way to me and asked what I thought our chances were for the race. He told me to go kick butt, and hurried away to his next quote as Juliana appeared. She waved to Holly, who still stood nearby, and beckoned her cameraman forward, putting her right arm around my shoulders so both of us faced the camera.

"I'm here with Kate Reilly, who set an electrifying mark in qualifying for her first pole position in the American Le Mans Series." She stepped away, the camera remaining focused on me. "Where did that come from, Kate? Did you feel like you had something to prove after the last race?"

I smiled for the camera. "I sure did. I focused all that frustration on laying down a good lap. But the biggest credit goes to the Sandham Swift team, because the BW Goods Corvette they gave me was fantastic."

"Do you think you've got the car to win this race?"

"I'll leave predictions to you and the fans. I know we've got a fast car, and, especially with an endurance race like this one, it's all up for grabs. We need to stay out of trouble, run our own race—not get caught up in responding to what other teams are doing—and hope we get the lucky breaks, not the bad ones."

"I heard you had a visitor a few minutes ago."

"Yes, Miles Hanson was here, wishing us luck for this race, and making it clear we both messed up in the accident two weeks ago."

"One last question before I leave you to get ready. Tell our viewers what'll be going through your head as you come down the hill and see the green flag for the start of the race?"

The hair on my arms stood up with excitement. "Only one thing: Go like hell!"

She laughed with me, stepping close and putting her arm around me again. "This is Juliana Parker with Kate Reilly, pole-sitter in the GT class. Back to you in the booth."

Once the camera was off, she gave me a full hug and wished me good luck.

"Jules, what's Scott doing in SGTV gear?"

"Replacing Felix with me in pit lane. I'll take the bulk of it, and he'll fill in."

As Juliana headed down the grid, Holly stepped to my side again. "She'll be running her own race in the pits. He'll be there to help, but he won't have done the background research."

"Sounds like a lot of work."

"She'll pull it off. Do her own job and help the rookie—"

"Who she's dating."

Holly raised an eyebrow. "Interesting."

"Why was Scott with Miles?"

"They're cousins. Best friends since grade school, I heard."

"Ladies and gentlemen," boomed the track announcer, "please clear the grid. All non-essential personnel, please make your way off the grid."

"Gotta go," said Holly. "See you." She took off down the grid to her team.

"Wait!" The cry came from the crowd in front of our car. I looked over to see Jeff Morgan bouncing on his toes in front of Tom, darting anxious glances my way.

Tom turned, looking a question at me, and I nodded. I couldn't shut down the guy who'd taken a punch for me this morning. Tom captured the two of us standing in front of the Corvette with Morgan's camera.

Jeff was estatic. "Thanks, Kate. I'm so sorry I was late. I was talking with some other people who are fans of yours— we've got an unofficial fan club going. Next thing I knew, I was running down here to make it. I knew you'd make sure I got a photo. You're so good to your loyal supporters—not like some who don't realize drivers wouldn't be anything without fans behind you. I'm glad we'll be able to talk more at the banquet tomorrow."

I tuned him out. *Time to get ready. Time to get in the car. Racing!* I shook Jeff's hand, and Tom ushered him away, as we heard the second call to clear the grid. Up and down the line, drivers donned helmets, opened car doors. The crowd moved along, stragglers pausing to take last-minute photos. Series staff shooed everyone around or over the walls separating the pits from the track.

I taped my earplugs into my ears, and pulled on my balaclava. Tucked that into my firesuit, and patted down the Velcro tab holding the suit closed across my neck. Bubs, our driver-change helper, handed me my helmet and HANS, already attached. I slipped the HANS over my shoulders and pulled my helmet on. Fastened the chinstrap. Handed my phone to Bubs to take back to the pits for me.

Third call to clear the grid. The only stragglers I could see were at either end, waiting to file out through a small opening or to climb over the wall on a ladder. The announcer kept talking, introducing different officials and VIPs. Bubs handed me my gloves, then opened the car door.

I felt a hand on my shoulder, turned, and saw Jack, Mike, and Leon. Jack leaned close, patted the top of my helmet. "Be smart into Turn 1. Go get 'em." Mike and Leon gave me thumbs-up and smiles, then followed Jack and the rest of the Sandham Swift guys over the wall into pit lane.

I climbed into the car, settled myself, fed the belts into Bubs' hands. He strapped me in while I connected the drink tube. He plugged in my air hose and radio cable, gave me a thumbs-up, and withdrew his head and shoulders from the car, fastening the window net on the way out. I took the steering wheel off the ceiling hook, centered it, and snapped it into place on the column. Radio check with Bruce in the pits.

The final call to clear the grid. We waited, Bubs in the open doorway.

I heard more announcements, but couldn't distinguish words. Didn't want to. I focused on the small track map taped in the center of the wheel—there not because I didn't know the track, but in case any of us got turned around or disoriented and needed a reference. I thought through a lap. Thought through the first corner. My heart rate increased. Excitement, nerves, joy, anticipation coursed through my veins. I took measured breaths to stay calm.

It was time. Faint words from the track speakers. Bubs circled his finger in the open doorway at the same time as Bruce called over the radio, "Start your engines."

I pushed the button, and my C6.R roared to life. Bubs gave me a thumbs-up, then shut the door with a thump. I knew he and the crew up and down the grid would hop over the wall back into pit lane, leaving the front straight to the parade cars, pace car, and racecars. It felt like I sat there forever, car rumbling and shaking under me, before the last prototype in line pulled away on my right. Then it was my turn.

I accelerated away from the wall and followed the line of cars into Turn 1, all of us weaving back and forth, scrubbing our tires to keep them clean of debris. Scrubbing was more important during cautions, when tires were hot and more likely to pick up the dirt, rocks, and "marbles" of tire rubber that accumulated off the racing line and prevented maximum grip. Fresh, cold slicks were less likely to pick up debris, but we didn't leave anything to chance—and if swerving around put some heat into the tires sooner, so much the better. We'd take every speck of racing advantage.

Going out of Turn 10b, up the hill to the bridge, Bruce on the radio: "Parade cars off, one more lap behind the pace car, Kate. You'll bunch up going into 10, and pair up going up the hill. You stay to the right."

I pushed the radio button. "Copy." As I rolled down the hill to Turn 12, I could see the pace car leading the line of racecars in the middle of the front straight. I also caught a glimpse of the parade cars—track or Series cars sent out ahead of the field for the first lap to give VIP passengers a thrill—in pit lane.

One last lap around the track, scrubbing tires, focusing on the pavement—looking for debris to avoid, verifying the consistent surface—and warming up my brakes with quick bursts of speed then hard braking. Down the back straight, we got closer together, Andy Padden's blue LinkTime Corvette nosing up on my left, forming the other half of the GT class front row. I stayed ahead through the narrow Turns 10a and 10b, then lifted fractionally off the throttle as I turned up the hill, my nod to lining up together.

The fastest prototypes had already disappeared under the bridge, over the hill. I pulled up as close to the prototype in front of me as possible—still staying right, giving Andy the chance to get beside me.

"Leader coming down the hill," Bruce notified me.

I pressed on the throttle, accelerating behind the prototype.

"Number 64 outside." Bruce saying Andy was next to me.

I didn't look for him. Didn't think about him. Thought about getting over that damn hill and down the other side to take the green as fast as possible.

"Green, green, green," I heard from Bruce.

I swept down the hill, leading the class. Stayed right, as close to full speed as possible. Green flag waving. My heart pounded in my ears. Through the corner. Foot to the floor down the front straight. Willing my Corvette to out-drag Andy into Turn 1.

Racing.

Chapter Forty-one

In front of me, prototypes jockeyed for position, playing chicken for the racing line through Turn 1. The biggest danger to me—to any of us starting in the second half of the field—was a spin or wreck by the cars ahead of us. We had some room to maneuver or stop, but not much. We took it on faith they'd behave and keep the track clear for us. This time they did.

A blink of an eye and I'd reached my braking point for Turn 1. Blue in my side mirror meant Andy next to me. I stayed in the center of the track. Glanced left. He wasn't even with me or ahead of me, so I had the line into the turn. I braked as hard and late as possible, downshifting twice to fourth gear. Off brakes, turned to the apex, accelerated out.

Andy in my rear view, tucked up behind me as close as if we were parked at a curb. I smiled. *Still P1, Kate. Stay on top this lap*. Fighting hard to keep the lead from lap one wasn't our strategy for this long race. But dammit, I wanted to go on record as leading a lap. Andy would *really* have to earn his way past me.

Up the hill to 2, staying straight as the track starts to bend to the left. By the first white line across the track, turn left to the apex. Downshift to fourth. Set the wheels right next to the curbing at the apex. Barely any turning to the right for 3, right wheels on the curb. Down to 75 mph. No flags from the corner workers. Andy still on my tail. The prototypes ahead of me, with lighter weight and greater downforce, had put distance between us.

Accelerate out of 3. Turning left around the arc of 4, upshift to fifth right after the turn. Hands right, aim at the first right-hand curb of the Esses. Hesitate on the throttle. Accelerate. Touch the paint at the right-side curbing. Swing hands left. Touch paint at the left-side curbing. Upshift to sixth. Car at the bottom of the valley, pointing up now. Touch 120 mph. Waiting, waiting—then heavy on the brakes just before the right-hand curbing at the end of the Esses. Downshift twice. Turning left. Apex—and throttle.

I tracked out from the turn wide right and used all of the exit curb. Foot planted on the floor. Upshifted to fifth. Then sixth. Drove my line, trying not to look in my mirrors in this key passing area. I hit 135 before braking.

Andy swung right, filling my mirror as we braked for 6. I downshifted twice to fourth gear, braking hard and late. He wasn't close enough to take the apex away from me, and I swept right, touching the paint of the curb with my right-side tires.

Full throttle for a few heartbeats, then full braking, downshifting to third. Focused on hitting my early braking point, clipping the apex, getting smoothly on the throttle. Slowest corner on the track, 55 mph. No flags. Standing on the throttle for the drag race out of Turn 7 and down the long back straight. Using every bit of revs I can in every gear, upshifting, wringing out as much power as possible.

I knew Andy would attempt a pass at the end of the straight, and it was too early to play blocking games. I stuck to the line I'd drive if I were alone, drifting to the right side of the track halfway down the straight, upshifting to sixth, top gear. One eye on the track ahead, one eye on the blue car behind me. Andy pulled left, filling that mirror as we reached 160. Both of us braking and going down three gears for 10a. Not close enough to make the pass. Release the brakes, turn left for 10a, 72 mph. Get on the throttle slowly, turn right for 10b. Put the power down, pointing up the hill. Upshift to fourth. Flash under the yellow block on the bridge.

Shifting to fifth as soon as the car settles over the crest of the hill. Pointed at striped curbing on the left side of the downhill. Sixth. Absorb the bumps in the track. Turn right, just past the curbing where the track starts to flatten out. Foot still to the floor. Turning right. Start/finish line, no flags, 136 miles per hour.

I led a lap at Petit Le Mans!

I clamped down on those thoughts and focused again on the track. Andy was still behind me, ready to pounce. I hurtled down the front straight. Watched for my braking point for Turn 1. One lap down. Thirty or forty more to go in this stint.

Andy laid back after the first lap, sticking with me, but not hugging my bumper or hounding me, for a good twenty-five minutes. Then he got by me on the heels of the race leader as we went into Turn 10a. Nothing I could do to block him, short of moving over and hitting him, since he was tucked up in the draft behind the faster, lighter prototype I was letting by.

I hit the wheel in frustration, but settled in to follow him as closely as he'd followed me. I dogged him for the next twenty minutes, ready if he made a mistake, until a yellow flag for a Porsche in the gravel at 10 cut short our fun.

After the field collected behind the safety car and the prototypes had pitted, it was our turn in the GT classes. Jack confirmed we'd change to Leon, because this first pit stop was happening under yellow—if the first stop I had to make for fuel, usually around the hour mark, was under green, I'd have stayed in for another stint. I had my cables unhooked and my belts loosened as I stopped. I pulled myself out of the car seconds later, grabbing my seat insert, then got out of Leon's way.

I walked quickly around the back of the car, past tire changers poised with their air guns ready for the fuel to stop flowing. Hopped over the wall into our pit box to the sound of the air jacks deploying and tires being changed. Before I had my helmet off, Leon roared away with fresh tires and a full tank of fuel.

Aunt Tee waited, as always, with a wet towel and a cold bottle of water. I needed both of them. The day had heated up, though a breeze kept the humidity down—out of the car.

Ambient temperature was in the low eighties, and the cockpit of the car was probably thirty degrees higher and humid. I drank the water down and rubbed the towel over my face. Aunt Tee took my helmet and put it on the drying machine at the back edge of the pit space. I hung the towel around my neck, then unzipped and struggled out of the top half of my firesuit, knotting the sleeves around my waist. I was still covered by a sports bra and a regulation double-layer Nomex shirt, but I felt better.

I looked up at Jack, Bruce, and Mike, all sitting on top of the pit box command center, monitoring Leon in the car. Mike smiled and Jack waved me over. I climbed up two steps and hung off the side of the cart, as there was no room to sit on the bench seat with them, plus Walter and Paolo from the 29 car.

Jack pulled his headset off the ear nearest me. "How was it?"

"Fun. Car's still fantastic. Sorry about getting passed."

He shook his head. "Too early to worry. If the car's still good, we're good."

I gave him a thumbs-up and moved around behind the cart, joining the rest of the crew and Aunt Tee, who offered me another bottle of water. We watched the monitors, waiting to go green again.

Right before the field passed the pits under yellow for the last time, I heard my name from the other side of the cart. I leaned around and saw Juliana waving furiously.

I crossed to her, untying my firesuit sleeves and shrugging the top half of the suit back on.

She spoke as soon as the field passed. "Quick on-camera?" I nodded, and she spoke into the mic to the booth announcers. "Ready here."

Thirty seconds later she glanced at me, then started speaking. "I'm here with the pole sitter from the GT class, Kate Reilly. Kate, how was your first stint?"

"Lots of fun. It doesn't get better than starting on pole—except starting on pole and making it through Turn 1 with no incidents, as we did today. The Sandham Swift team gave us a fantastic Corvette this weekend, so we're out there trying to show our sponsors—BW Goods, Active-Fit, Leninger's Auto Shine, among others—a good time."

"Looked like you played tag with the LinkTime 64 Corvette."

"We had a good time. I have nothing but respect for those guys on the factory Corvette team—great drivers and nice guys. We got a little racy there, and it was good, clean fun. Neither of us is going to mess up a car this early in the race. There's still a long way to go."

Juliana nodded and turned to the camera. "That there is. Thanks, Kate, and good luck with the rest of the race. Back to you in the booth."

Chapter Forty-two

I watched Leon put a few green-flag laps in, his pace similar to mine and Mike's. All we could do was stay close to the leader, tick off miles, and hope little went wrong. In any race, but especially an endurance race, the question wasn't *if* something would break or go against us, but *when*. We hoped it would be minor and easily fixable.

After I finished another bottle of water, it was time to change out of my wet clothes and fuel back up with lunch at the motorhome—also the site of a real bathroom. Porta potties were fine for male drivers and crew, who didn't have to peel their entire firesuit off to do their business. Or for when time was tight. But I opted for a real bathroom whenever possible.

During one of the sprint races the American Le Mans Series ran, which lasted two hours and forty-five minutes, I'd never dream of leaving pit lane in case I needed to get back in the car. But here, if things ran to Jack's plan, Leon would do a double-stint of two hours, then Mike, who sat ready on the pit box, would do the same. I wouldn't be in the car for a while, and it was my job to be rested, nourished, and hydrated by then.

I stepped up onto the command center again and leaned close to Jack's ear. "I'm going to the paddock for lunch."

Jack shouted back. "We'll get you if we need you. See you in a bit."

I hopped back down and told Aunt Tee my plan. She decided to go with me, and we headed to the exit five teams down. The noise level wasn't much better a hundred yards away in the pad-dock, but being inside the motorhome dulled it to a bearable roar. I changed into a dry set of gear, then opened a laptop on the kitchen table to connect to streaming audio of the track announcer. Aunt Tee got out supplies to make me a sandwich, and I remembered I should tweet something.

"@katereilly28: Great first stint at #PetitLM in Sandham Swift Corvette. Car going strong, Leon Browning in now. Fingers crossed."

"That new young man seems to be doing a good job reporting in the pits today," Aunt Tee commented as I finished typing.

"Scott Brooklyn?"

"That's him. It's too bad he didn't have a job or a ride this year, but perhaps the silver lining of Felix Simon's passing will be an opportunity for another nice person."

I made a noncommittal noise as I scrolled through my Twitter feed.

Aunt Tee warmed to her topic as she put mayonnaise and mustard on rye bread. "I hope Scott can make the most of the opportunity. I've often thought he—and so many others trying to break into racing—must be quite frustrated. Even troubled. Though talk about troubled…Felix Simon was one for the books."

I paid closer attention to her. "You thought Felix was troubled? Everyone else thinks he was the nicest man they'd ever met."

"He hadn't an ounce of respect for women. I saw that, even if the men around here didn't. Though he was always polite and friendly to me."

We both stopped what we were doing and looked to the laptop as the excitable announcer's voice rose further:

"The number twelve car is shedding carbon fiber down the back straight, as the right rear tire has come apart at the seams and is tearing up the bodywork. Debris all over the racing line—double-yellow flags! Full course caution. Now fire at the back of the car! Undoubtedly from oil or fuel lines torn open by the tire carcass.

"The driver, Eddie McAlister in one of the Turner Racing Group Porsches, keeps going in the car—does he know he's on fire? He seems to, because he's pulled to a stop in front of a stand of corner workers, and we hope they're ready with an extinguisher. Now that he's stopped moving, fire sweeps forward in the car—get out quickly now, Eddie! There, he's opening the door and pulling himself out. He's on his feet and away from the car as the safety truck pulls up with larger extinguishers than those brave corner workers have. Sad for Eddie and the team, but I think their day is done."

"Glad he got out," I said. "Why do you say Scott Brooklyn is troubled?"

She rinsed two leaves of lettuce. "It must be difficult when the breaks don't go your way. So many of these boys are equal in talent, but some get attention and some don't. Often it's down to bad luck or good, I think."

"He seems to be good natured."

"I agree. I have no reason for saying so—and I trust you won't spread the idle gossip of an old lady—but I've always wondered if there was more boiling away under the surface because his ambitions have been thwarted so often."

"Now you've got me spooked. And you're hardly an old lady."

"He's no different than dozens of other boys out there pounding the pavement each race weekend." She set a plate down in front of me with my favorite sandwich: turkey and Swiss on rye. She turned to wash a bunch of grapes as I took the first bite and made happy noises.

"Personally," she went on, "I think Scott can make it bigger behind the microphone than the wheel. His sparkle shows on camera."

I swallowed a bite. "He's dating Juliana."

She raised both eyebrows in surprise. "I hope that works out for him this time. He dated Ellie also, you know."

"He told me he only met her once."

"Maybe he's still upset about it. That Ellie—rest her soul—she was a heartbreaker." She saw my confusion. "She wasn't malicious. She was sweet and gracious, but also so private and closed-in. I knew quite a few young men who fell for her and were quite hurt by her lack of real interest."

"Like who?"

"Scott, for one. Zeke. Duncan Forsythe. Stuart." She eyed me, and I nodded to indicate I knew. She named half a dozen other men, including Holly's boss, the team manager at Western Racing, and some reps from engine or car manufacturers.

The announcer called the green flag, and we refocused on racing. A short time later, Aunt Tee and I left the motorhome to return to the pits. She carried a plate of cookies she'd baked that morning to add to the pile of snacks for the crew.

A fan with a tight black shirt over a pot belly aimed a long camera lens through the chain link into the LinkTime Corvette pit space, and he swung the camera toward me, tracking me as we passed him. He lowered the camera to reveal a blond goatee and a wide grin. Then he waved.

He was gone before I realized he was the nameless guy on my possible stalker list. As Aunt Tee and I reached our pit space, I saw movement out of the corner of my eye. George Ryan stood on the paddock side of the fence, trying to get my attention. He held a weekend program and a pen above the fence for me, mouthing what looked like a request to sign it. He took my photo with a pocket camera, and when I finished signing, I posed so he could take another.

He couldn't look happier about getting a puppy on Christmas, and he mouthed "See you later," as I returned to the pits.

How many items have I signed for him? I could hear Gramps in my head, "Stop looking a gift horse in the mouth, Katie!" He was right. I shouldn't question anything my supporters and fans wanted. They cheered for me, and I appreciated them. Even if they were a little weird sometimes.

Chapter Forty-three

I saw Zeke approaching, his head bent close to that of a driver from another team. Zeke wrapped up his spiel as he reached me, stopping to shake the driver's hand. "Just remember, Zeke Andrews, Z-A—like A to Z, but in reverse."

In a flash, I remembered the Ringer's post about a possible source of trouble close to home, simple as A to Z. I waved at Zeke to stop, pulling up the Ringer site on my phone. I found the post and showed it to him.

He read it, then looked at me, stricken, which tied my stomach in knots. He led me away from my pit space to the fence and spoke close to my ear.

"It's not what it looks like. Give me a second to explain."

I made a "hurry up" gesture with a hand.

He sighed. "It's about Rosalie. I haven't told you about the part-time job she picked up this year. She's running Miles Hanson's fan club."

I pulled away, my mouth open in shock. "Miles Hanson?"

"She's done what she could to defend you."

Something in his voice made me look him in the eye. "Has she?" Though Rosalie was outspoken, I'd always thought her easily swayed by the loudest voice in the crowd.

"She tried to stop the witch-hunt." He rubbed a hand over his face and looked guilty. "This has been a mess. She's a mess. There are other issues, and she didn't do as much as I wanted her to with the fan club."

"Other issues?"

He cupped his hand around his mouth next to my ear, so no one could see what he said. "Emotional issues. All of a sudden she's insecure, doesn't want to leave the house. Worse, she's crazy jealous of anyone I talk to. Especially women. Even you. She keeps saying she's afraid I'm going to leave her."

I was shocked. "You'd never do that."

"Not until she drives me to it." He laughed, a humorless sound. "Never mind. That's what the damned Ringer post is about. What a shit-disturber."

I couldn't argue with that. I assured Zeke I would keep his secret, and he apologized. We parted because we both had jobs to do, not because anything was resolved.

I crossed back into our pit space and grabbed a radio headset to listen to transmissions with Leon, then found a seat facing the monitors. The ten screens on the back of the pit cart carried the same feeds as the ones suspended above the bench seat and desk where Jack and the others sat. One showed live timing and scoring, currently displaying Leon fourth in class; one showed the live SGTV feed; and the others carried camera feeds for different corners. They were arranged in order left to right across the top row of monitors, then left to right across the bottom. We had nearly constant video coverage of our Corvettes.

A few minutes later, just before the hour mark since the last pit stops, the crew of both cars stirred, pulling on balaclavas, helmets, and gloves. Uncoiling air gun hoses and inspecting tires. Similar activity happened up and down pit lane as teams readied for green-flag stops. Soon cars rolled by, engines sounding wounded with fewer cylinders firing under speed limiters.

Bruce kept talking to Leon, counting down the laps until he'd come in and telling him to stay in the car for a double stint, as planned. Two laps to go. Race still green. Crew in position, crouching on the pit lane wall with tires, air guns, fuel hose, fire bottle, and windscreen cleaner ready. Waiting. One lap to go.

"Pitting this lap, Leon," said Bruce.

"Copy," came Leon's response.

As Leon barreled down the back straight—race still green—
Bruce called again. "Pitting this lap. Stay to the right coming
out of 10b."

Leon didn't respond, but did as told, pulling smoothly to
the right out of the flow of traffic and into pit lane. I imagined
him downshifting three times. Pressing the speed limiter as he
crossed the line marking the start of pit lane. Breathing. Less to
do this time through, since he wouldn't get out.

Bruce counted down, guiding Leon into our stall, where Leon
stopped and shut down the engine. The crew leapt over the wall,
and the fueler plugged the hose in. For safety reasons, while the
fuel flowed, only a driver or someone to help the driver—such
as cleaning the windscreen or buckling a driver in—was allowed
to touch the car. For those twenty-plus seconds, tire changers
crouched waiting and ready, air guns only inches from their
targets. The fueler disengaged and the other four crew leapt into
action, two men working each side of the car.

One pushed an air hose into the outlet to deploy air jacks.
Two others, one on each side, used air guns to remove wheel nuts
from the front wheels. In a single motion, each man pulled the
gun away with his right hand and pulled the tire off with his left.
The second man settled the new tire on the hub. Brrrrrrttttttt,
went the air guns, tightening the new wheel nuts. Two choreo-
graphed steps to the rear wheel, repeat. Four tires changed in
ten seconds. A hand up from the crew on each side when tires
were done, and the air gun man on the near side yanked the air
jack hose free. Leon fired the engine as the Corvette plopped
down on its tires, and he pulled away. All in thirty-eight seconds.

If my job was a marathon, the pit crew ran the hundred-yard
dash over and over.

Half an hour into Leon's second stint, Mike climbed down
from the top of the pit cart and high-fived me as he walked to
his pit locker for his gear. If we stayed green, he'd get in for his
own double-stint in thirty more minutes. Jack waved me over,
offering me the space on the pit cart Mike vacated. I'd just
climbed up the three steps when all hell broke loose on the track.

A gaggle of Porsches—some from our own GT class and some from the slower GTC or Challenge class—wreaked havoc through Turn 3, when two cars tried to fit into space for one. They touched. The car on the outside of the pair spun rear-out to the left, ending up stalled across the curbing on the exit of the turn. The car on the inside checked up from the impact, causing a Porsche behind him to punt him to the right, beaching him nose-in on the apex curbing. The third car, slowing up, was hit from behind, though he displayed admirable off-road skills going through the grass wide around the first car. A fourth car banged into the third and chose badly, opting to dive to the inside of the turn, where he was blocked by the second car and had to come to a stop and reverse to try again.

Bruce was already talking to Leon, who was in Turn 7. "Wreck in Turn 3. No flags yet."

More cars arrived on the accident scene. Two prototypes threaded the needle neatly in the slice of open track and continued on their way. The third prototype—the current race leader—wasn't so lucky, because the Porsche stopped on the outside of the track decided to move and tagged the leader, sending them both spinning.

Another prototype crested the hill and reacted poorly. He saw the action on the outside of the turn, and hit the throttle while steering to the inside—right into the stopped Porsches. He sideswiped the Porsche trying to reverse out of trouble and slammed into the one stuck at a right angle to the track. The momentum of the prototype carried it down the hill past the Porsche, taking the Porsche's right rear tire and suspension assembly with it, carbon fiber bodywork from both cars flying like confetti.

Before the car bits touched back to earth, our crew was scrambling for their equipment and helmets. The track would go full course caution. Since we were past halfway in the stint, the 28 would come in for fuel, tires, and a driver change. Mike was already helmeted and pulling on his gloves as the double-yellow flew.

"Full-course caution, Leon." I heard Bruce on the radio. "When pits open, come in for driver change." Leon was in Turn 12, and Bruce added, "Careful through the debris." Shards of carbon fiber were dangerous to tires. No matter how well course workers cleared the track—and they were good at their jobs— more than one car over the duration of the race would end up with a flat from debris there.

Our crew hustled and was ready two laps before the pits opened for the Le Mans Prototype classes. A lap later, our GT classes entered. I sat forward, tense, cracking my knuckles as Leon pulled the car in. Bubs and Mike went to work making the change. Leon out. Mike in. Fuel done, car up. Front tires done. Bubs slamming the door. Back tires done. Car down, engine fired, Mike away.

I sat back and breathed again.

Next to me, Jack pointed to the monitor showing a Ferrari following Mike out of pit lane. He pushed the transmit button on his radio headset. "Pit crew gained us a spot in the pits. We're out P3, ahead of the Ferrari. Good work."

The crew carried on for two minutes, shaking fists in the air, beating their chests, slapping each other's hands. *Sprinters winning the dash*. I was proud of them.

I looked at the circulating pack on the monitor again. Mike was only four cars behind the second GT in class, with the leader only five cars ahead of that. I nodded. Still in it with a fighting chance. Only five or six more hours of racing to go.

Chapter Forty-four

Pit lane was calm again in minutes, and I saw Juliana walk past our setup. Scott Brooklyn ran after her, stopping her in the 29 car's space by grabbing her upper arm. She jerked out of his grasp, and I could feel the anger she blasted at him from where I sat. I looked at them going toe-to-toe and worried for her. Then Scott pointed a finger in Juliana's face and said "No!" adding a downward slashing motion with his right hand.

He'd turned his back on her and continued on his way when he turned and saw me watching. His face hardened. I ducked my head to the timing and scoring screen, the tips of my ears warm. When I glanced back a second later, he was still staring at me.

My phone buzzed in my pocket, and I fished it out, grateful for the distraction. A text message, from Holly. "Good news: nice stint. Bad: check out new Ringer post."

I pulled up the Racing's Ringer blog on my phone. "Show Down on the Grid!" read the header, complete with the eyeball graphic. "NASCAR fav Miles Hanson took his life in his hands today, willingly getting close to Calamity Kate on the grid for Petit Le Mans. Calamity (who, I have to admit, deserves a Ringer shout-out for her pole position) must have benefitted from Miles' appearance. Everyone on the grid shined brighter in his presence, and those he granted the honor of a photo were extra lucky."

I looked up at the sound of a wounded prototype limping down pit lane to stop a few doors away from us. I wondered if the Ringer was serious or poking fun at the cult of Miles Hanson.

"Of course, Calamity was extra, extra lucky," the Ringer continued. "She got Miles' attention for EIGHT WHOLE MINUTES, and an apology from Miles' fan club president. But we and our Ringer Readers want to know: did Calamity apologize to the FC Prez for calling him a redneck???"

I guess the Ringer doesn't know everything. I accidentally hit a link and when I pressed the back button, the page refreshed, displaying a brand new post: "P.S. To Calamity."

I had to close my eyes and take a breath before reading.

"I hear you behaved well, so I guess you've got some class after all. I'd still watch out for that guy in the background." I studied the photo of Miles and me smiling full-wattage at the camera. Also there: Nash Rawlings, regarding me with hate-filled eyes.

I knew I didn't believe him. I switched to the photos on my phone for the shots Holly had taken. There were five, including one of Miles and me smiling at each other. I posted it to Twitter.

"@katereilly28: Nice to shake hands with Miles Hanson (and his fan club prez) today over racing incident. [pic]"

With the image of Nash Rawlings in mind, I surveyed the background of the photos for other revealing emotions, but didn't see anything out of the ordinary. Leon looked happy. The Sandham Swift crew looked relaxed.

My next swipe took me to the photos Tom had taken of me, Juliana, and Ellie at Siebkens Tavern, which I'd saved to my phone. This time, I looked at the background of both shots, and what I saw made my breath catch. Scott Brooklyn was in the wide-angle photo, somewhere on the other side of our table. So was the preppy, East-Coast guy I remembered—who I now recognized as Billy Reilly-Stinson. In addition, I saw not only Nash Rawlings in the crowd off to one side, but also Jeff Morgan, the super fan, hero-guy. I kept looking but couldn't find George Ryan in the shot, though I knew he'd been at Siebkens that night. All of them had been in close proximity to us—and our drinks.

Everyone who was out to get me in the same room that night? I'd said it myself: everyone at a Road America race weekend ends up in Siebkens. I shouldn't be surprised to have photographic proof.

Holly texted again. "Re. Felix. No new interests/topics other than you. But seemed more 'amused or smug' since Tavern night. Supports idea he saw/knew something."

That doesn't help much.

Jack flinched next to me, and seconds later, crew members scrambled to their feet, reaching for helmets and hoses. Jack pointed to one of the monitors, where SGTV helpfully showed the right front tire on our car sagging, then folding over from a puncture. Mike stayed offline and out of the way as much as possible, driving slower than race pace, but as quickly as he dared, back to the pits. My eyes were glued to the monitors, willing the tire to hold up, stay intact—above all, not shred into pieces, whip around with every revolution, and destroy body parts, as happened to Eddie.

"Ready for you, Mike. Take her easy," Bruce reminded him.

Mike didn't respond. I knew he was fully occupied with the fight to go slowly enough the tire wouldn't come apart, but fast enough to not lose many positions. For a racecar driver, there was no lap as slow as the one with a flat tire or a damaged car. I'd been where Mike was, and it was agonizing. I cracked my knuckles and reminded myself to breathe.

Three minutes later, he was back under way, and the race stayed green. We'd been lucky, with no damage to the car and the loss of only one lap to the leader. Only five cars remained on the lead lap, and we were the first car a lap down, along with three others in our class. We knew we'd have opportunities to make it up, through our efforts or through the leaders having issues of their own. An endurance race was a fight against attrition. Four GTs were already retired, and we weren't even halfway.

I stayed on the pit box for the next hour, willing Mike on as he clawed his way back to the leader and got our lap back when the leader pitted under green—because of our stop for the puncture, we were on a different schedule of stops than the leader and others in class. Then we got lucky with a full course caution caused by a prototype whose steering broke as he came over the hill and under the bridge. He arrowed straight down the hill, over the curb, over grass, and into the tire wall at the outside of Turn 12. The safety workers hustled and everyone watching held their breath—because it wasn't clear from the camera angles if the driver's head in its open cockpit was under tires or not.

It turned out he was stuffed against them and unable to get out of the car, but unhurt. Jack, who'd been around racing for decades, could tell that from the safety workers' manner. When the tractor tugged the car free, I did a double-take. It was Dominic Lascuola in the Benchmark prototype.

Payback's a bitch, I thought, then scolded myself for being ungracious.

Forty-five minutes later, I wondered if Dominic—or the universe—was getting me back. Leon had taken over behind the wheel under the long caution to extract the prototype and fix the tire wall it disarranged. He was twenty minutes into a green-flag run when we lost another tire.

Chapter Forty-five

"Shit!" Jack banged the edge of the desk with his fist. The only voice on the radio was Bruce's, telling Leon to stay offline, go slow, and come back to the pits. Leon had been brushed by a GTC class Porsche he was passing, and something on the other car must have cut our tire's sidewall.

The GT leader, a BMW, passed Leon on the back straight, putting us one lap down again.

"Careful, slow it down a little," Bruce cautioned, and I saw why.

The left rear—visible on the live SGTV feed—started to fray at the edges. Leon slowed further, to what looked like the pace of someone pushing a shopping cart. It was excruciating to watch, and it must have been hell in the car, with every nerve screaming to go faster. But Leon was smart. He didn't want to be the next car-be-que on the highlight reels, and he knew we could recover from laps lost with an undamaged car.

Our crew was in their places, fresh slicks with the tire changers on the wall, hoses in hand. I saw they'd readied tools to cover a variety of contingencies, because at this point, they didn't know what they'd face when the car crawled into the pits. They had to be prepared for anything from cutting away body panels or torn rubber to replacing suspension components or a brake assembly.

Race still green. The GT leader swept by on the front straight as Leon pulled the car to a stop in front of us. Two laps down. We stuck to the routine of fuel first, then tires, hoping for the best. Twenty seconds for fuel, during which as many crew as could get close peered at the damaged tire, inspecting without touching. All of us in the pits watched the SGTV feed, because the action was on the far side of the car from us. Fuel out, jacks down, car up, front tire changed. To the back tire. Damaged rubber off. A crew member shoved his head in the wheel well for an inspection, then pulled back and settled the new tire on. He raised his hand. Car down and away.

"No damage, Leon, good work. Go make it back up," Bruce said. I slumped with relief, then felt a surge of adrenaline. *We're back in it.*

Twenty minutes later I climbed down from the pit cart to start the process of getting ready to be in the car next. First, a trip to the porta potty, since I didn't want to be as far away as the motorhome. Some stretches and deep-knee bends to loosen my muscles. Then I deposited my phone in my pit locker and collected my gear.

Nash Rawlings walked by, suited up in LinkTime colors. He saw me watching him and managed a smile that was more grimace, as well as a jerk of his chin that passed for a nod. I stepped over to him, helmet, gloves, and other stuff still in my hands.

He looked unwilling, but stopped.

"I saw a photo of you in Siebkens Tavern that night after the race," I shouted in his ear, then stopped, not sure where I was going from there. *Think, Kate!*

He pulled back. "So?"

I didn't like getting as close to him as a conversation in the pits required, but I'd started this and I'd finish. "Did you talk to the cops? To help them figure out who was in the room and who was close to our table. My friend died from something in a drink—they don't know who put it there, so all information helps. Maybe you saw something useful." I was out of breath by the time I finished, from the effort of shouting above ambient noise.

"I'm not sure why it's your business. I hope you don't think I had anything to do with it—what would I have against your friend, anyway?" He pulled back to give me a sly look. His face was too close to mine for comfort. My skin crawled.

"Yes, I talked to them," he said. "Is that all?"

"Do you live full time in Atlanta?" I was guessing.

"Yes, why?"

"Just curious."

He looked at me strangely and left without another word. He didn't like me, he'd been near our drinks at the Tavern, and he lived in the Atlanta area. He was my new prime suspect. *Later, Kate. Racing now.*

I turned back to the monitors behind the pit cart. I handed the radio headset to Aunt Tee and secured my earplugs with tape. I had my helmet, HANS, gloves, and balaclava handy—but I delayed putting them on.

Leon's fuel level got lower and lower, and still no yellow flag. The crew stirred to ready themselves for a green-flag stop. We didn't like doing a driver-change under green, because if anything went wrong and took more time, the impact was greater while the other cars were at full speed. However, our plan was for me to get in the car now, so we were going for it. We'd simply have to be careful.

Ten laps from Leon pitting. I helmeted up and climbed on the wall with the crew, at the left end of the lineup, ready to run around the back of the car.

Five laps. I focused on the driver change process, repeating it to myself, visualizing everything happening smoothly. *Run around the back of the car, Leon out, put my seat insert in. Right leg, left leg, slide through into seat. Lap belts, shoulder belts—over HANS. Plug drink tube in. Bubs clicks the belts. Steering wheel. Radio check. Car in gear. Bubs done with belts, window net, door. Watch for the air-gun guy to move forward to the air jack. Push starter button.*

Leon entered pit lane. The rest of the world disappeared and then I was moving. Forty-some seconds later I drove down pit lane in the car, cinching my belts down. My finger hovered over the speed limiter, ready to release it.

There's the line. Limiter off, car into second gear, foot to the floor. Bruce in my ear telling me the track is clear. Third gear. *Go like hell, Kate.*

My stint was eventful in a good way. Immediately after I got in, race control threw a double-yellow to retrieve a driver who'd gotten into Turn 10a too hot and stranded his car in the gravel. We stayed out, and I got a lap back on the leaders. That put us in sixth, on the same lap as positions four and five.

On the last lap before going back to green, Bruce spoke, "P5 four cars ahead of you, P4 six cars ahead of him. Go show everyone pole position wasn't a fluke."

"Copy." My heart rate was high. *Bring it on.*

Eight laps later I slipped past a Ferrari into Turn 6 for fifth.

Fifteen laps more and I dogged the back bumper of the Porsche in fourth. I nipped at his heels for three or four laps, unable to force him into a mistake. Then I held back, watching for his strengths and weaknesses. I could go deeper into a corner before braking than him, and the discrepancy was greatest in the corner with the hardest braking: the 10a/10b left-right complex. That's where I pounced.

I shot under the bridge, an angry Porsche now in my rearview, and I imagined the high-fives in our pit box.

"Good work, Kate. P4 now. Settle in, keep pushing," said Bruce.

I kept up the pace for the rest of my fuel load, through a green flag stop for fuel and tires, and for forty-three minutes of my second stint. That's when the racing gods smiled on us.

Two prototypes leading the LMP2 class tangled at the top of the hill in Turn 2, collecting one of the LinkTime Corvettes in the process. The Corvette got off easy, able to limp back to the pits with a broken right-front suspension to be repaired. They could finish the race and earn points. The two LMP2s were in worse shape. One smacked into the tire wall on the left side of the track, breaking too many parts to continue. The other tipped up and barrel-rolled three times. The driver walked away, but track workers needed shovels to collect car parts. We were in for a long caution for cleanup.

Bruce radioed me news of the accident and the full-course caution. He also shared the best news of all: the race-leading LMP1 was two cars behind me, about to be picked up by the safety car. My job was to hurry around the track to join the back of the long line of cars—which put us back on the same lap as the GT leaders.

Racing also meant blind luck sometimes.

I picked my way through debris and safety vehicles in Turns 2 and 3, then floored it around the rest of the track trying to catch up. That's when Bruce relayed another piece of news. The LinkTime Corvette involved in the accident—which I'd passed between Turns 6 and 7, making its slow way back to the pits—was third in class. One lap later, I inherited that position.

"You are P3 now," Bruce said. "Pit with GT class for driver change."

I had three laps at slow speed to enjoy the track. We were officially in twilight, and the waning light made the racing more challenging, but made the cars look extra cool with headlights, reflective tape, and decals glowing. I'd been blinded by the setting sun between Turns 6 and 7 for the past half hour, but the trees finally blocked it, and I caught glimpses of a medium-blue sky with puffy clouds tinged pink.

The pits opened for the prototypes, and I spent my last lap behind the safety car focusing on pit stop procedure. Then I followed a Ferrari down pit lane.

A minute later, Mike pulled out for the run to the checkers.

Chapter Forty-six

I put my helmet, gloves, and other gear in my pit locker for the time being, gratefully accepting water and a wet towel from Aunt Tee. I wiped my face and neck, and felt a lot more fresh.

Juliana waved from the wall, and I went forward, finger-combing my hair, to give her my comments on the race, the pace of our car, and what we might see in the final laps. We'd raced for eight hours at that point, tallying approximately 825 miles on 325 laps of the circuit. That meant about another hour and a half to reach 1,000 miles.

She asked me to make a prediction, and I shook my head. "We might still see anything and everything. I hope you'll see us hang on for a podium!"

Juliana tossed me a smile and a "good luck" before hustling off to her next story. I briefed Jack and Bruce quickly on the car and my stint, then ran back to the motorhome to change into another set of dry racing gear. Once back in the pits, I grabbed radio headphones and stood behind the pit cart watching the monitors with Leon.

A crew member stood to get a snack and offered me his chair, but I declined. I'd stand, pacing and nervous, for the remaining laps.

Sometime later, I was distracted by a group on a VIP pit tour, garbed in matching red firesuits with big ALMS logos, led by a Series rep. They got closer, and I blinked in surprise, seeing my father, his wife and kids, and his angry nephews.

I kept my focus on the monitors as they approached, but turned and waved when they stopped behind us, their guide pointing to our display and shouting something in Amelia, Eddie, and Lara's ears. My father had no need for the tour or the explanation, and Holden and Billy stood to the side, giving me dark looks.

My father noticed their behavior and spoke sharply to them. They stepped apart and smiled at both of us. Like sharks. My father mouthed "good luck" to me, and I nodded before turning back to the monitors. Mike kept reeling off laps.

At a tap on the shoulder, I turned to find Billy looming over me, Holden next to him, the others walking away. I steeled myself not to retreat as Billy leaned close. "Just stay away from our family, little imposter, for your own good."

I had a hard time taking these pampered, rich kids seriously. "I don't need your advice," I spit back. "Get the hell out of my pit space. Or maybe I'll start asking if anyone else knows you were in Siebkens Tavern two weeks ago."

Billy reared back in surprise. Holden gave me a small, nasty smile, and pointed his index finger at me, thumb cocked to look like a gun. He bobbed his hand as if firing, while making a kissing motion at the same time. They walked away, chuckling.

Leon put a hand on my shoulder. "What the bloody hell was that about?"

"Spoiled brats who don't like me. Don't worry about it." I might suspect the cousins of wanting me out of the way, but I wondered if they could be responsible for the ill will raining down on me lately. I also didn't know why they'd have killed Felix. I shook my head to clear it. Focus on the car and the race. Deal with unwanted family later. Or never.

The whole team heard Jack's voice on the radio. "Forty-five minutes remaining." He meant we were in the fuel window to make it to the end of the race. Mike would stop under green in twenty minutes, just as fuel ran out, or under yellow between now and then for the last stop of the race. The crew started preparing.

"@katereilly28: One more stop for fuel/tires then good to go to the end of #PetitLM. Keep hunting them down, Mike! #hopingforapodium #afraidtosayitoutloud"

Ten minutes later the caution waved, for a Porsche GTC entrant with a blown engine. The pits were chaotic, every car in for service. All took fuel, some changed drivers, and most changed tires. Everyone in Sandham Swift congratulated each other on a perfect stop—and then we realized we were P4. A Porsche had leapfrogged us by taking fuel only.

Just like that, our podium finish slipped away. We were devastated. Every team member watched Mike with grim, laser-intensity focus, willing him to get the spot back.

He tried everything. For the next half-hour, he drove like his life depended on it, putting in lap times through traffic that rivaled my pole lap, even setting fastest lap of the race for the GT class. Six laps to go, he was nine seconds behind the Porsche, and try as he might, he couldn't make up more than a second and a half each lap. He pushed. We bit nails. Paced the pit walkway. Cracked knuckles.

Four laps, six seconds behind.

Three laps, five seconds.

Coming down the back straight, headed to the line for two laps to go, he flashed past a Porsche. Leon and I looked at each other.

"Wasn't that…?" I began.

Bruce, calm as ever on the radio. "P3 Porsche slow on the back straight, possibly out of gas. You're now P3, Mike."

We started to cheer, then realized we still had two laps to go. We didn't breathe until Mike was half a lap from the end. That's when I grabbed Leon's hand and followed the crew as they hopped the wall, ran across pit lane, and stood at the track wall along the front straight.

The overall winner tore past us, taking the checkers. Fireworks went off at the start/finish line. We saw the LinkTime Corvette in P1, GT winners. The BMW in P2.

And then there was Mike, blinking the lights for us as he roared past. I hugged everyone and didn't mind crying at the racetrack, because we were third at Petit Le Mans.

Back at our paddock an hour later, Mike's only disappointment was our trophies weren't cups for drinking champagne out of. Instead, they were glass replicas of a waving checkered flag on a globe, all on a pedestal with "Petit Le Mans," the date, our class, and our finishing position. Our third-place trophies were smaller than those for second or first, but we didn't care. We'd fought hard and pulled through for third against a tough, international field. Not only that, but our finish—and an early mechanical failure for another team—meant we'd taken second place in the season driver and team championships. The champagne flowed.

Anyone with a camera was invited in for photos of the car, trophies, drivers, and crew. That included my two journalist-buddies Colton Butler and Jimmy O'Brien. I even poured them plastic cups of champagne.

"Thanks again for that phone number," I said to O'Brien. "I still can't believe it was Felix, though I suppose I can't be mad now the guy is dead."

He looked confused. "Felix Simon? Can't be. It was a woman's voice. Why else would I think it was you who called?"

I was numb with shock, hardly noticing as they waved good bye. *It was Felix's phone, how could it not be Felix?* I smiled for more photos.

"You OK, Kate?" Tom handed me another glass of bubbly.

I snapped out of it as Juliana rushed in to hug me, Scott trailing her.

"Congratulations, Kate!" Jules danced me back and forth in her embrace.

I laughed with her. "Pretty awesome, huh? But how are you after that marathon?"

She waved Scott forward to stand with us. "Not bad, Scott was a big help."

He smiled. "Glad I could step in."

"Well, good for all of us." I snagged cups of bubbly and handed them over. "Time to celebrate!"

"@katereilly28: Kudos to Sandham Swift team and Mike/ Leon, great co-drivers. Third in GT at #PetitLM rocks! Sooooooo thrilling!"

Chapter Forty-seven

I made it to Centennial Park in downtown Atlanta the next morning by 7:30. Tired, but on my feet. Not even hungover. Even more amazing, Tom and Holly agreed to leave our hotel at 6:45 to go with me. Stuart also made a surprise appearance, showing up right before eight o'clock. I felt guilty, seeing him there. I needed to get my head straight and apologize to him. But not in the middle of hundreds of people.

I waited with my friends and the rest of the Beauté spokes-women and corporate reps—Lindsay Eastwood and others—near the Centennial Park Concert Stage, where the races would begin and end. The half-marathon had taken off at 7:30, with the marathon runner spokeswoman—Leslie something—and Tina the jockey joining that pack. The other four of us would go out with the 5K groups at 8:30: the soccer player and basketball player running it, the rower and me walking—with a thousand of our closest friends.

Early or not, the atmosphere was festive. The temperature was still cool, and the roads had been deserted, right up until we reached the streets around Centennial Park. The stage and multiple pop-up tents were festooned with balloons and ban-ners—predominately pink and white—and pop music with a quick tempo blared from the speakers. Under the tents, each event sponsor distributed samples and information: makeup and product brochures from Beauté, nutrition bars from a sports food company, sweatbands from an athletic gear company, and so forth.

After ten minutes of on-stage activities, during which an energetic female emcee introduced executives and spokeswomen, invited each of us to say a few words, and pumped up the crowd, we were instructed to line up for the race start.

"Someone gonna yell 'green, green, green' in my ear?" Holly wondered, as we followed an event volunteer to the head of the walking group.

Tom and Stuart chuckled.

As we reached the crowd, another walker attached himself to our group: my super-fan, George Ryan. He wore the same event t-shirt everyone else did and toted a camera, which he used to take a photo of me as I walked past him.

"Hi Kate," he said, his prominent Adam's apple bobbing as he swallowed.

"Thanks for coming out today, George." I shook his hand.

I heard Tom talking to George behind me as we approached the main pack of people—mostly women—waiting to walk the course. I felt the first flash of nerves at being a representative of an issue and an organization with so much impact. Then I felt proud to be able to contribute. I stepped forward and introduced myself to everyone in sight. I hardly noticed when the gun sounded for the 5K runners, when our group started walking, or details about the course, because I was listening to stories about why people were there and how breast cancer touched their lives.

The race route ended where we began, and we returned to the field in front of the stage for the presentation of medals to top finishers. I had no further duties, so I stayed in the crowd and applauded.

George touched my arm to get my attention. "I wanted to say good bye."

"There was something I wanted to ask you about, George. The other day you said something about drivers' personalities, how they can be different behind the wheel. That some will always be jerks. Who were you thinking of when you said that?"

"No one I'd consider a jerk. But you know, some drivers are really aggressive in the car, but not on foot. I figure, no matter how nice they are out of the car, they're going to be strong-willed. Maybe have a temper. There's a personality trait that will be the same, even when people act differently in the two situations. It's not a well-formed theory, sorry."

"Why didn't you think Ellie would keep driving? And how did you know Felix Simon and Zeke Andrews would end up in broadcasting?"

"I didn't think Ellie had the fire inside. Felix and Zeke?" He grinned. "They're hams. Always loved the spotlight."

"But not Scott Brooklyn?"

"There's something more private about him. I didn't peg him to be able to stand being around racing if he wasn't behind the wheel. I always thought he wanted it more than a lot of drivers, but he didn't know how to connect for it. But he's good on-camera."

"That's an interesting perspective." I paused. "What about me?"

"Too soon to tell."

I laughed and shook his hand. "Good answer. I can't think about the end of my racing career yet. Thanks again for coming this morning. It's really great of you to support the organization."

"Anything you support, I'll support. I'll see you at the dinner tonight."

He left as the crowd applauded the final winner. Two minutes later, the perky emcee closed by exhorting us to support our sponsors at their booths.

I snapped a phone photo of the stage and tweeted it:

"@katereilly28: Great turnout for Beauté and BCRF 5K downtown ATL. Thanks to all participants and supporters. Keep working on a cure! [pic]"

Stuart checked his watch. "I have to head back to cover some of tonight's details."

"Thanks for coming, Stuart." I paused, looked him in the eye. "I'm looking forward to more time to talk."

He nodded, but I couldn't read anything in his expression. He said goodbye to the others and set out across the park.

Holly, Tom, and I agreed to do a quick walk around the tents before we left. Near the BCRF tent, we ran into Juliana and a cameraman. Tom wandered off to a nutritional supplements table while Holly, Jules, and I compared notes on what we planned to wear to the banquet—I'd be in blue, Holly in black, and Jules in red for her role up on stage.

"I hope you insisted on a speaking role," Holly said. "Not the silent trophy girl."

Juliana laughed. "You better believe it."

"Jules," I lowered my voice. "Is everything good with you and Scott? Is he OK?"

She nodded. "Why do you ask?"

"I saw the argument you had in the pits yesterday, plus he's seemed frustrated recently. He could benefit from Felix's death if a spot on the broadcast team opens up next year."

Juliana looked annoyed, and I spoke again quickly. "I'm worried for both of us. I just found you again. I don't want to lose you also. I'm messing this up."

"How can I get mad at you for being concerned for me? Trust me, I'm watching out for myself." She put a hand on my shoulder and looked to Holly. "I'll see you later this evening? Looking fabulous?"

"Sugar," Holly drawled, "you can count on it."

Jules wiggled her fingers at us and took off.

I looked at Holly. "She didn't say anything about Scott."

"She sure didn't."

I looked around at the tents and the crowds. The pink and the purpose. "This has been great, but it's time to get back to the racing world and wrap up this season."

Tom walked up in time to hear my last statement. "Shall we go? The Night of Champions banquet awaits."

Chapter Forty-eight

We got back to our hotels a little before noon. Holly and I had an afternoon date at the Chateau Élan spa before the banquet that night, and she opted for a nap first. I was tired, but I knew the questions rattling around in my mind would prevent me from sleeping. One concerned something Ellie's husband Ethan had said, and I reached him at the cell number he'd given me.

When he answered, I heard a horde of children in the background, shrieking and laughing. "Is this a bad time?"

"I'm with my kids at a birthday party. Plenty of parents supervising, so I can talk."

"I wondered about something you mentioned. What was the new job you said Ellie looked forward to?"

"SGTV cooked up a gimmick. Ellie and Juliana were going to pair up to cover the pits next year. They were going to promote the heck out of them—"

"As the 'pit princesses.'"

"Right, you heard about it."

"Felix mentioned the term, but didn't explain. Any idea where he'd have been?"

"The booth, Ellie was told. Guess they'll have to figure something else out now."

"Was that the goal you said Ellie had found?"

"No." He paused. "The goal was a year of sobriety. Ellie was a recovering alcoholic."

I was stunned into silence.

"Surprising, right?" He gave a tired laugh. "I learned alcoholics are never who you expect."

"But, her job? Your twins?"

"She was high-functioning. She'd cut back during her pregnancy, and the babies were on formula from day one for other reasons. She went back to her habits after they were born. That's when I found out. She'd hidden it from me for years. From everyone."

"Was she drinking back when we were racing? I didn't see it."

"She was good at hiding it. They usually are. Racing's what started it—she said winner's circle champagne was a trigger."

I remembered my surprise the first time we had champagne in the winner's circle—I'd been fifteen. I'd taken a few sips, in between spraying the others on the podium, but Gramps quickly stepped in and took the bottle away. His later warnings to stay away from it until I was of legal age hadn't been necessary, as I didn't like the out-of-control feeling alcohol gave me. Later, I'd learned to enjoy a couple glasses of wine, but I'd never developed into much of a drinker.

"I can understand that. So she got sober. She was in the Tavern with us—but she ordered juice."

"She was really proud of coming close to her year mark. We planned a special celebration, just the two of us with Sammy and Chloe. She was following all the steps, including reaching out and making amends. I don't know all the details, but I know she'd reached out to a former fiancé who she said she'd treated badly."

I had to clear my throat to get the name out. "Stuart Telarday?"

"I think that was it. And I know it was important to talk to you and Juliana."

"Do you know who else she talked to?"

"I'm not supposed to know—or tell, since that's her private business. But I found her notes, and it can't hurt her now." He gave me a dozen names, among which I recognized Stuart, Zeke, Rosalie, Juliana, myself, and Scott Brooklyn.

"I don't know what she wanted to talk to me about," I said. "I don't think there was anything she'd need to make amends to me for."

"I don't know the details, but she'd had her heart-to-heart with Juliana, who forgave her. Ellie was glad to be free of that weight."

"You spoke with her when she was at the Tavern, didn't you?"

"Just before she died, yes. She was happy—thrilled at seeing the two of you. At being sober and part of the racing world again. At least she had those moments, and I have the memory." He sighed. "You know, there were times I wondered if my life would come to this. If I'd have to raise the kids without her. But then she got better…I wasn't prepared after all."

I offered him my condolences again, and we hung up. His information left me reeling. I wanted to talk to Juliana about her conversation with Ellie. I wanted to know Scott's connection to Ellie—since he'd told me he didn't know her. Most of all, I wanted to know why Stuart, once again, hadn't told me a key part of the story.

I put those questions aside and thought instead about the Lascuolas and the cranky cousins having been in Elkhart Lake and Atlanta. Dominic Lascuola particularly interested me, because he was one of only three people in both places who also had access to the race-winner's special watches. Scott Brooklyn and Zeke were the others. Unless there were other race-winning drivers out there who'd been in Siebkens and Atlanta and hated me. I wasn't sure I was getting anywhere.

I got up to make some coffee in the two-cup pot, hoping the caffeine would stimulate some brain activity. My cell phone rang as the coffee started dripping.

"Gramps."

"Katie, my love. How are you today?"

"Tired, but doing better now I've put coffee on. I'm more awake from the smell."

"Best drink in the world!"

I'd learned to love coffee from Gramps, who adored the taste and brewed it fresh all day long—caffeinated until noon, decaf after. Always black and hot, even in the dead of summer.

"But not that iced garbage," I parroted his favorite line.

"You know me well. Congratulations on the podium, Katie! All of you put in a hell of a drive. How'd you feel about leading the first half hour of the race?"

With Gramps I could crow. "Damn good—every second. Just wish I could have held on longer. That we could have won."

"Here now, don't be greedy. Twenty cars in that class, and you ended up third. In a major, worldwide race. Nothing to be ashamed of. Besides, you finished second in the championship this year. That's nothing to sneeze at either."

"You're right. It's something to keep pushing for."

"Good to have goals. Hang on, Katie, here's Vivien."

A rustling, then, "Congratulations, Katherine. I was so proud watching you take the green flag and lead those laps."

"Thanks—and thank you for watching."

She tsked. "Racing's not my choice, but it's yours, and I support you. I certainly won't miss when you're on television and you put on such a good show."

"Me being out front was pretty cool, wasn't it?"

"Pretty cool, indeed." The words sounded strange from her, and I laughed.

She went on. "We'll take you out to dinner to celebrate when you're back home. Do you know your plans yet?"

"I'll probably be a couple weeks yet. Beauté wants to do the photo shoot at the Sandham Swift shop in the next week or two, and…" *What to do about Stuart?*

"Will you spend time with that young man you've been seeing?"

Grandmother was no fool. "I think I will, for a couple days. We have to talk some things out, see if this is going anywhere."

"Parents always want their children to know the joy of head-over-heels love. But we also want you to think things through and choose wisely. The hardest thing is finding someone you can

trust as well as love. Someone who won't bow to other pressures."
She paused. "Be careful with your heart."

"I'm being very careful I'm not hurt. I promise you."

"Good, that's good."

"Grandmother? I mean that about Stuart and about my
father."

Silence. I closed my eyes, afraid I'd pushed too far.

Very quietly: "I know. Be careful."

More silence and then Gramps was back. "She's out of the
room now, Katie. I didn't hear it all, but it sounded like progress."

"It was. I love you both, Gramps. Make sure you tell her I said
that. I'll see you in a couple weeks for that celebration dinner."

"Bet your boots, we will. Now knock 'em dead at the party
tonight."

As soon as I set the phone down to pour myself some coffee,
a chime heralded a message from my PR team. Matt and Lily
announced media coverage of me had turned positive and
would keep on improving. Even on racing blogs. As proof, they
included a link to a Racing's Ringer post, which I clicked on
with trepidation.

"Food for Thought About Kate Reilly," the headline read.
"Ringer Readers, tell me, have I been too hasty in dismissing Kate
Reilly's abilities and potential? I watched her this race weekend,
and was grudgingly impressed with her driving ability and how
she handles herself. Hmmmm, do I need to rethink Calamity
Kate Violent? The Ringer does hate being wrong, but I hate being
a hypocrite even more. Tell me, Readers, what's your opinion?"

I almost fell over with shock. *What on Earth did I do to change
his mind?* The answer: nothing. I did my job, the same as every
other race weekend.

I raised my coffee in a toast. "Here's to you, Ringer, for finally
paying attention."

Chapter Forty-nine

By mid-afternoon, I was in heaven. Holly had booked the works for both of us at the Chateau Élan spa: massages first, then facials, then manicures and pedicures. All set up for maximum relaxation and prettification. We'd get ready for the championship banquet at the spa, then drive around the corner to the Chateau Élan hotel for the event. She was the mastermind. I went where pointed.

After our facials, we lounged in the wet eucalyptus steam room, which did a good job of clearing my sinuses, even if the rest of my body felt torpid.

"I can't remember feeling so relaxed, Holly."

"It's about time. How are you feeling about Stuart?"

I'd filled Holly in on my conversation with Ethan during our drive to the spa, and she'd obviously spent time thinking about it. As had I.

I looked at the clock. "We've been in here five minutes."

"Let's paddle in the whirlpool. You still have to answer."

"I know." I covered my bathing suit with a towel and followed her to the co-ed whirlpool, which was steamy and deserted.

I sank to my chin in the warm water and sighed. "Stuart and I need to talk, to spend time together when we're not in the middle of a race weekend. I'm going to stick around for a couple days in his guest room. Now that the drama has died down—"

"We still don't know who killed Ellie and Felix. Who tried to kill you and Juliana."

"I know, but at least the world doesn't hate me anymore—even the Ringer thinks he might like me. With the racing season done, I'll have space to think."

Holly moved to the other side of the pool. "You really need to figure out what you want from him."

"I'm just so twisted up about him and Ellie. Do I know him if I didn't know about their relationship? Why didn't he tell me, and why is it so important to me? Is this just my excuse to push him away? On the other hand, even marriages I thought were perfect have turned shaky—who says a decision I make will last anyway?"

"Who's got you rattled?"

"Zeke and Rosalie. He says she's changed a bunch in the last year. He's pretty freaked out. Get this, she's even jealous of me."

Holly shook her head. "She's not thinking straight."

"There's more: she's Ellie's husband's estranged sister, and she's running Miles Hanson's fan club."

"Maybe she tried to kill you."

"You can't be serious." I saw her shrug. "I don't believe it. She wouldn't do that. Besides, why would she want to kill Felix?"

"Blackmail. It's the only reason that makes sense for anyone killing him."

"I'll probably burn in hell for this, but I don't miss Felix at all."

Holly laughed. "Understandable. And a sad statement about him. He had his moments—he could be a nice guy and fun to be around. But I think there was pain underneath it all."

"Who do you figure they'll replace him with?"

"Scott Brooklyn would be the frontrunner now, wouldn't he?"

"I still think it's suspicious he's Johnny-on-the-spot, ready to capitalize on the elimination of two pit reporters. But Jules isn't worried about him at all."

Holly laughed harder this time, and I moved around, uncomfortable. I didn't think I'd said anything funny.

"Oh, sugar." She wiped tears from her eyes. "Don't you remember? Last year at Lime Rock, when you took Wade Becker's seat, you bristled when everyone pointed at you with similar suspicions."

I felt heat flood my face.

Holly chuckled at my expression. "I'm not saying you're wrong—I agree with you there's something not right with him. But the irony struck me as funny."

"Sure. Great. Now I'm mortified." I paused. "By the way, about possible suspects. Aside from the basics, the suspicious ones are Scott, Felix, George Ryan, Dominic and Colby Lascuola, and the cousins. Plus Nash Rawlings, the hateful fan club president. People who'd have access to a race-winner's watch are Zeke, Scott, and Dominic."

"And Rosalie," she added.

"Rosalie?"

"Sure, spouse or girlfriend would have access. Even sister, like Colby. And don't be so sure someone with money and connections in the Series couldn't get one—like your cousins."

"I still think it's Scott."

"Why would Scott be after you? Or after Juliana?"

I looked at her, my mind blank.

"I'm thinking about motives," she said. "Zeke: none. Rosalie: jealousy, Miles, whatever—but weak. Dominic or Colby: Colby would take your place. Cousins: money. But Scott? You're not in his way. Assuming he gets the job next year, Felix was in his way. Ellie was in his way. Juliana might be. But the drink that killed Ellie was meant for you, right? Why would he be after you?"

"Miles is his cousin."

"Revenge? Miles wasn't dead. A crazy fan I could see getting freaky and wanting revenge, but a family member? Another racer?"

"Jack said Scott might be someone he'd hire if I wasn't on the team. Or maybe Colby Lascuola. Or some others."

"Maybe Scott tried to kill you for your seat—except there was no guarantee he'd get it. Colby now, she might have gotten your seat and your sponsorship."

"*Someone* had a reason to try to kill me—twice—and kill Ellie by mistake."

"Scott trying to salvage the second career he sees slipping through his fingers is more logical than because you gave his best friend a concussion."

I worked it out. "If that's true, I wasn't the target. Ellie was."

"Could be."

"Does the whole thing make any more sense if she was the target? There's still the car in Atlanta and the damage to my suit and helmet. And the hospital press setup."

"None of those killed you, unlike the stuff in Ellie's drink."

Did I see a new pattern? "Like the guys shoving me yesterday, maybe the car and the rest of it was someone taking any opportunity for mischief? Then it's not about who benefits with me out of the way, but who benefits with Ellie gone."

"Scott for sure, at least if SGTV hires him next year. Probably not Dominic or Colby. Rosalie? Don't know. Zeke, probably not."

"Except he was someone Ellie was going to make amends to. I can ask him, and about Rosalie." I sighed. "This is still confusing. Does this mean I don't need to watch my food and drink tonight?"

"Get your own drinks, just in case. Now, enough. It's time to clean up before our manis and pedis. Then we'll get fabulous."

"You'll get fabulous. I'll get decent."

"In that dress? Sugar, you'll be phenomenal. Eyes will bug out of heads tonight."

I'd rather have that effect from inside a car than a too-tight dress. I didn't care what Holly said, I still wasn't good at the girly thing.

Chapter Fifty

"@katereilly28: Heading for #ALMS Night of Champions. Looking forward to celebrating with Sandham Swift and sponsors. Thanks to all for a great year."

I tugged my skirt down as Holly and I stepped away from the car.

"Stop that," she hissed.

I stopped, because tugging didn't help when the issue was cling. I wore a "bandage dress," which Holly had forced me to buy earlier in the year. Royal blue, knee-length, square neckline that wasn't too low cut, cap sleeves. Tight. Tighter than the fit of my seat and belts in the Corvette. I had the same issues breathing in this dress.

Holly told me that was nerves. Fear was another possibility, as I maneuvered on four-inch, glittery platform heels. Between the shoes and the dress, I had to slow my usual quick, heel-first stride. I had to mince. I felt like an idiot.

The expression on Tom's face changed my mind. He was the first person we saw, as we wove our way through class champion racecars on display to reach the grand entrance. His jaw actually dropped open in shock. "Holy shit, Kate, you look amazing."

Once again, Holly was right. Damn her.

I heard a whistle behind me and turned to see Mike wiggling his eyebrows. "You look like a dirty old man, Mike."

He laughed and pointed to my chest. "Where'd you get those?"

I looked down at my breasts, squeezed into view by the dress and the well-padded bra underneath. "Smoke and mirrors, my friend."

"Reilly, you look like a girl," Mike said. "This is strange for me."

I understood. Holly had done big things to my hair and used nine makeup products to give me huge, smoky eyes. "For me, too."

I looked at Holly, smug in her little black dress with a blousy top and a teeny, tiny, sequined skirt. "She looks great too, don't you think, guys? Fawn all over her a minute."

"She always looks like a girl. That's not a shock," Mike said, but they dutifully admired her before turning back to ogle me.

"You're enjoying this, aren't you?" I asked her.

"Absolutely."

I squared my shoulders. "Fine, let's do it." The four of us went in together.

We were looking at photo displays of great moments in ALMS history in the long entry hall when Stuart walked by with the president of Kreisel Timepieces. Stuart went from walking, talking, and collected to stock-still and dumbfounded in the space of a heartbeat. The sponsor looked over, checked out Holly and me from head to toe, and put his hand to his heart. He was French.

Stuart continued to look poleaxed. *Worth the price of the dress right there.* I waved at him as we made our way to the banquet hall.

"Banquet hall" wasn't quite correct, since the ALMS had taken over the Chateau Élan Inn for the night. On the ground floor of the three-story, glass-roofed atrium sat a stage, surrounded by more than fifty tables of ten. Each round table was dressed out in black linens, gold chargers under white plates, three sets of crystal glassware at every place, and glimmering candles.

We dropped Holly off at her table, nearer the entry-hall side of the room, then made our way to the other side of the stage. We saw evidence of three seats claimed at a table marked for Sandham Swift, and we pulled napkins out of glasses to reserve our own spaces. Mindful of the eager fans who'd be joining us, I put myself between Mike and Tom. We headed for the nearest bar, where we found Jack talking to Steve and Vicki Royal from Active-Fit.

Vicki and I stood back to admire the men in our group and around the room. "There's something about a man in a suit and tie, isn't there?" she mused.

I nudged her and nodded at Marco Orfanelli, the gorgeous, playboy Italian driver in the Series. "Or without a tie." Marco's dark suit matched his lush black hair, and his white shirt, unbuttoned to mid-tanned-chest, set off the blinding white of his perfect teeth. He saw us and smoldered, pressing a hand to his heart and blowing a kiss.

"Yum."

I laughed. "Stay away, trust me."

"Only looking. Two more handsome boys over there. Too young for me though."

I turned in the direction of her gaze and was startled to see the cousins, Holden Sherain and William Reilly-Stinson, holding drinks and watching us. They did look good, Holden dark and brooding, Billy fair and sunny. Both in the best-cut suits money could buy.

They headed our direction. I told Vicki I'd be back and took off toward the stage, hoping to avoid them. They changed course and intercepted me.

"We'd like to apologize for yesterday." Billy smiled at me.

Was he serious? Or worried I'd tell someone he was at Siebkens?

"Can we offer you a glass of champagne?" He held a flute in each hand and offered me one.

You've got to be kidding me. "No thanks, I'm good right now."

He looked disappointed, but regrouped. "What do you say to a cease-fire?"

"I say I wasn't shooting. But you're welcome to stop glowering at me." I looked at Holden, whose face had returned to that state. "Or making threats."

Billy elbowed Holden, then spoke again. "I'm sure you can understand, we're protective of our family."

"Because I'm such a menace." I looked at Billy, then Holden, then back to Billy. "Does he speak?" I jerked a thumb at Holden.

Billy's laugh sounded genuine. "Sometimes. Damn, if I don't like you."

"Then my work here is done. If you'll excuse me?"

They didn't move. In fact, Holden stepped closer. "What do you want?"

I met him glare for glare. "What do you think I want? More important, what are you willing to do to keep me from getting it?"

"I knew that was your style." He nodded. "I'll do whatever it takes to keep you from getting your hands on—"

I held up those hands. "You make nasty assumptions, and you're wrong. I'll tell you what I want: nothing. I want nothing of yours. Nothing from your precious family." I stepped closer to him and shoved my face toward his, my hands on my hips. "Get that? Now stay the hell out of my life."

I spun around and discovered my father.

"Katherine. Is everything all right here?"

"Fine. We're done."

Billy spoke behind me. "James, maybe you can help Kate understand—"

I turned and cut him off with a look. "We're done here. Would you *gentlemen* please excuse us?" I watched as they left, trapped by good manners. I saw Amelia watching us from the table they headed to, and I nodded to her in greeting.

"Is everything really all right, Kate?"

I turned back to my father. "I told them I don't want anything from the family, and they don't believe me. I don't like them. Or trust them."

"I can't argue or blame you." He frowned. "Holden is the oldest of his generation, and he's actively involved in the bank. Billy isn't, but they've been best friends forever."

"Thick as thieves."

"Yes. Holden…his mother is my younger sister, and I think she and my brother passed along their fears to Holden—meaning his life has been one big competition for his birthright. He's territorial."

"Is that why Billy called me an imposter yesterday?"

"That goes back to mistakes I made when you were born." He sighed. "Mistakes my father compounded, allowing himself to be influenced by various family members."

I remembered Grandmother's caution: "Someone you can trust who won't bow to other pressures."

My father started to speak again and I stopped him. "This isn't the place or the time." *Not to mention I'm not ready for this story yet.*

"You're right. Later. Short answer: Holden and Billy are parroting Billy's father's opinions—and they're wrong."

I thought of the stories I'd heard of Felix's father. Of Juliana's mother. "Parents can really warp their children's minds, can't they?"

"Much as we try not to, I'm afraid so." He smiled and caught my hands in his. "You look lovely tonight, by the way. Stuart can't tear his eyes away."

I turned and caught Stuart staring, as advertised. I looked back at my father. "We're good? I need to get back to my team."

"We're good. Congratulations on the season, Kate. Would you respond if I e-mailed you during the off-season to stay in touch?"

"Sure, we'll e-mail." I got out of there before he asked for anything more.

I rejoined Vicki in time to catch the fresh wave of gossip sweeping the room.

"It's about Felix," she whispered in my ear. "Died because of something or other combined with his little blue pills. I can't decide if the men are going to start cracking jokes about boners or take up a collection in sympathy."

"An erection killed him?"

"Something like that. Isn't that just—I mean, it's terribly sad." She held her composure for two seconds, before we both snickered.

"It's like men who die in the middle of having sex. Sad, but hilarious."

Vicki linked her arm through mine. "I think that's how they all want to go."

We looked at each other and started giggling again.

Chapter Fifty-one

I had to admit, it was fun watching our two guests, Jeff Morgan and George Ryan, having such a good time at the banquet. Andy Padden presented the duo with badges proclaiming them super-donors to his charity, which meant everyone treated them well. Many a team owner had raced and won championships in their day, and Jeff and George were in heaven getting insider access to a part of the racing world few fans penetrate. Their enthusiasm was infectious.

Sandham Swift had three tables right next to each other. Our crew chiefs, chief engineer, and their wives—including Aunt Tee—shared the other two with sponsors and the 29 car drivers, Seth and Lars, plus their spouses. Joining me, Mike, and Tom at our table were our two fan guests, Steve and Vicki, Leon, and the head of BW Goods and his wife.

I finished my dinner and slipped away to the bathroom in the hallway behind the stage. It was quiet back there, with only two other women in the bathroom touching up lipstick, and I was glad for the break from the buzz of so many people in one large room. I stepped out of the women's lounge to find Stuart loitering in the empty hallway.

He had his race face on: stern and businesslike. So I was surprised when he hauled me to him for a whopper of a kiss. He stopped abruptly and stepped back, leaning a hand on the wall next to us.

"I hardly remember who I am after that, Stuart." I wiped remnants of my pale pink lipstick from his mouth.

"Then we're even, because I lose my breath when I look at you tonight."

It wasn't lust—or not only—but raw emotion behind those words. I touched his cheek. "Am I still welcome to stay with you?"

He turned his face into my hand and kissed my palm, closing his eyes. It was almost unbearably sweet.

I heard voices coming down the hall from the banquet area, and I moved back. He straightened. "Yes. I'm glad we'll have some time. Tomorrow, then." He started to move away, then turned back with a wicked smile. "Bring those shoes."

I fanned myself on the way back to the ballroom.

As I walked around the edge of the stage, Juliana got the room's attention, announcing ten minutes to show time and directing everyone to make their trips to the restroom or call their bookies now.

To laughter from the room, she stepped down from the stage near where I'd paused. She smiled widely. "Holly was right, you did bring the fabulous."

"We can't hold a candle to you—wow!" She wore a floor-length, flame-red, strapless mermaid gown with a wide, black ribbon tied at the waist and trailing the ground. She looked old Hollywood glamour, with smooth, curled hair, red lips, and curves to die for. "I want to be you when I grow up."

She laughed, and what must have been diamonds shot fire from her wrist as she pulled her hair over her left shoulder. "We have to give the crowd their money's worth, you know."

"Better you than me. I'm already tired of the double-takes at my chest."

"Don't joke." She pressed a hand to her stomach. "I'm trussed up so tight in here, laughing might split something."

Scott appeared behind her, from the tables in the center of the room, sliding a hand around her waist. "Hello, gorgeous," he said to Jules. Then he turned to me and his eyes widened. "Well, hello, gorgeous to you, too."

I wanted to roll my eyes. "Thanks, Scott. Lookin' good yourself. And great job yesterday. Any chance they'll hire you full time next year?"

"Nothing's settled, but we're talking. Thanks for asking."

"You'd make a good-looking pair in the pits. Put the rest of us to shame."

"I can't compare to this goddess of the airwaves, that's for sure." Scott beamed. Why shouldn't he? Job prospects looking up, most beautiful woman in the room on his arm. What was there to be unhappy about? But something didn't sit right with me.

"Follow my lead and you'll do fine." Juliana looked fondly at Scott. "The first step is being a sweetheart and getting me another glass of champagne while I freshen up before the show starts."

He departed, and I took my cue. "Knock 'em dead, Jules."

"I intend to." A quick hug, and she slipped around behind the stage.

Half the members of the audience were standing, whether stretching their legs, getting another drink, or moving to another table to shake someone's hand. Making deals. Racers were the biggest bunch of wheelers and dealers I'd ever seen, and ninety percent of the business of racing happened at the races. The rest of the year happened in slow motion compared to what got settled at a race weekend. Tonight would be more about starting conversations than closing deals, but I imagined plenty of ventures would be conceived in the free-flowing alcohol here.

I saw Zeke and Rosalie a few tables away and went to say hello. They both got up to hug me, and I wondered if Rosalie would be mad at Zeke for doing so. I tried not to feel awkward with her.

"Are you having a good time?" I asked.

Zeke nodded. "Good so far." He looked to Rosalie, who shrugged.

"I spoke with Ethan today," I said. "He seems to be doing all right. I'm sorry for your family's loss, Rosalie."

"Right, thanks." She saw Zeke's expression. "What? I'm not going to pretend we were friends. We didn't like each other. I thought my brother could do better. And the drama she put him through…" She sat back down.

"I heard about that," I murmured.

"She was your friend, right?" Rosalie asked.

"Years ago. I didn't know her recently."

"Trust me, she had issues, I always knew he'd come to grief with her." She looked disgusted. "You'd think after I practically raised him, he'd listen to me, but no."

Zeke sat down and put a hand on her knee. "Rosalie was Ethan's caretaker for most of his childhood while their parents worked. Ellie was a sore point with them."

Rosalie snorted. "She's why he wouldn't talk to me all these years."

"That's too bad," I said.

Zeke looked at her with concern. "At least you're talking now."

Rosalie reached for her wine glass and took a big sip. She looked down at my shoes. "You even have glittery feet, Kate. You're so dolled up, I hardly recognize you."

What did that mean? "You guys look great also," I returned. True for Zeke, but not Rosalie, who looked sloppy, uncaring in her shapeless black dress.

She took offense at something she saw on my face—sympathy? pity? concern?—and turned sharp. "This has been great, Kate. Hope it won't be so long the next time."

Clearly dismissed, I made my excuses, shooting a confused look at Zeke. I saw an apology in his eyes and hurt for him, wondering where his vibrant, engaging partner had gone. I'd always admired her take-no-prisoners attitude, but she had a harsh edge tonight.

I detoured to the bar for champagne to improve my mood, and ran into Colby Lascuola on the same errand. She was at a table near ours with her brother and his team, and when she pointed him out, he returned my polite wave with a similar lack of enthusiasm. I looked forward to keeping in touch with Colby. Dominic, I still didn't trust.

Before I could sit back down, our fan guests insisted on full-length photos with me. With Tom acting as our photographer, they posed with me separately, then together, each with an arm around my waist. The single camera bred more cameras, and before I knew it, Andy Padden was there taking a shot for his charity site, and a multitude of others held up phones for photos.

"It's like they're paparazzi," said Jeff. "We're famous because of you, Kate." He hugged me a little, leaning in.

That was too familiar, at least while I felt unlike myself in this dress and heels. In a firesuit in the paddock, I might feel better about it. But my physical and psychological space was under attack.

I popped out of their grasp and grabbed Mike's arm. "Mike should be in this."

He got the message from my death grip and inserted himself beside me for the next round of photos.

Before he sat back down, Jeff pulled a pen and a business card from his pocket. "Could you sign and date on the blank side of it—and put 'ALMS Night of Champions' also? I'll frame this with our photo."

"Sure." I flipped the card over and read "GMR, Geoff Morgan, Owner." I blinked. "I thought your name was with a 'J.' What's GMR, anyway?" A warning bell went off in my head. My potential stalker's e-mail address included "gmr." I wondered if that was Geoff. Wondered about George's middle name. I struggled to keep a smile on my face.

"That's my company: Geoff Morgan Restoration. I restore antique furniture and household goods."

I signed and handed the card back to him. When Geoff returned to his seat, I thanked Mike for stepping in.

He chuckled, a rumble low in his throat. "You looked wild-eyed."

"It's different if these guys want to be 'best buds' with me than with you. There are different personal space issues because I'm female—men get more comfortable and touchy with a girl than with another guy."

"I never thought about that. Makes it tough, doesn't it."

"To have boundaries without being offensive? Yeah."

Just as the room hushed, because Juliana and Benny Stephens, the booth announcer who'd emcee with her, stepped forward to the mic on stage, Geoff blurted out, "Oh Em Gee!"

Everyone laughed, and Geoff turned beet red, waving a hand and apologizing.

Benny welcomed everyone and introduced himself and Juliana, outlining the program for the rest of the evening. I was distracted by Geoff excitedly pointing at something being passed to me. It was his phone, displaying a photo of the three of us.

I didn't understand until I saw the eyeballs-in-a-car graphic sitting in the corner of the image that we were featured on the Racing's Ringer blog.

That son of a bitch is here tonight.

Chapter Fifty-two

After two minutes of craning my neck, pretending I'd recognize the Ringer by the audacity radiating from him, I gave up. I passed Geoff's phone back and paid attention to the speeches, which were legion. Despite my best intentions—and the organizers' best efforts to speed things along—I found my mind wandering.

I wondered if we'd ever know who killed Ellie and Felix or who tried to kill me and Juliana. I wondered if those were the same person. I was ready to hang up my magnifying glass, because I had no ideas. Felix was a good suspect—it was easy to imagine him lashing out at women threatening his domain. But him turning up dead blew that theory.

Scott also seemed like a good suspect—at least to me, though I couldn't pinpoint why. I wondered about Rosalie, who seemed strangely angry. *Could she have killed Ellie? Could I believe that of her? I knew her.* At least, I thought I knew her—but I also thought I'd known Ellie.

I applauded with the rest of the audience as, up on stage, the president of the American Le Mans Series gave way to the president of Kreisel Timepieces.

A few sentences later, I went back to my reverie. Maybe I should be looking at Nash Rawlings or the cousins. Were they the types to commit murder? Who was I kidding? How did I know what "the type" was? *Nice theories, Kate. Maybe you can buy a tin star and play sheriff, too.*

I might not know what a killer personality was, but I knew the people on my short list weren't all sunshine and light. There was also more than meets the eye with our two fans. I couldn't tell if they were happy super-fans or creepy stalker wannabes.

Tomorrow, the racing world and fans would disperse to the far corners of the country, if not the globe. I hoped the off-season would take care of inappropriate attachments, lingering resentments, and homicidal tendencies aimed my way—if they hadn't been dispelled already with Felix's death and Miles Hanson's royal visitation. Tomorrow I'd call the different law enforcement agencies to ask about progress. Otherwise, I decided, it was time to stop worrying.

I felt lighter. My life was turning around. With any luck, Jack would have me back, and I'd pick up a ride for the Daytona 24 in January. Step-by-step, I'd make my mark on the racing world. Second place in the ALMS championship this season was a good start, and we'd get better next year.

With another round of applause, Benny and Jules stepped forward to start the awards process. They went from the lowest, slowest class to the fastest, which meant we started with the GT Challenge class, calling third, second, and finally first place drivers and teams to the podium for their trophies.

Then it was time for our class. Mike and I headed to the stage amid applause from the room and foot-stomping from our three tables. Juliana broke her routine by giving me a big hug before handing over my trophy. Mike and I turned to the audience and raised our linked hands and trophies high above our heads. It felt great. I knew it wasn't first in category, but we'd worked hard and done well. I had the best job in the whole world.

"@katereilly28: So proud to share second place in #ALMS GT honors with Mike Munroe and the Sandham Swift team. Thanks for letting me be part of the fun."

The LinkTime Corvette team accepted first place trophies with short speeches, and then Jack accepted the Founders Cup for the top non-factory-supported entry. I was shocked to see my normally gruff and taciturn boss wipe tears from his eyes as he spoke to the crowd. "I can't tell you what this means to me—then again, you've been through it with me the last couple years. We've had our setbacks." There were a few chuckles around the room, as we all remembered the declining fortunes of the driver I replaced, Wade Becker, before he was killed.

"But I couldn't be prouder of this group of people." He looked to our tables. "The way you came together this year and became a team. You're everything I've hoped for, every one of you. Thank you. Let's do it again next year." Then he pointed to the LinkTime tables in the center of the room. "Except we're gunning for that top spot, so watch out."

Jack returned to the table and passed his trophy around, pausing to lean over Mike and me, a hand on each of our shoulders, and thank us for the effort.

"Did you mean that, Jack?" I asked, looking up at him. "Same again next year?"

"Unless you try to skin me on a new contract, I do. You thought otherwise?"

"I heard a rumor you were looking at other options."

"Fat chance. You two gave this team its best finish in almost a decade."

The relief that swept through me was more potent than the champagne. I felt weightless, giddy.

He gripped my shoulder tighter. "I'm serious about a run at the top spot next year. I think we can do it, too."

"Aye, aye, captain." Mike saluted, making the others at the table laugh.

The rest of the awards passed in a blur, until Mike elbowed me right before the LMP1 class honors.

"And now for the second award voted on by the fans, the Most Popular Driver this year…" Benny fumbled for the right piece of paper.

I felt a quick flutter of excitement, which I quenched, saying to Mike, "No chance at all, with my bad luck lately."

"Kate Reilly!"

Sound receded, and I was frozen in a bubble of shock. *What just happened?*

I looked at Mike, who was clapping, mouthing, "Go! Go!"

I stood up slowly, pausing to be sure my shaking knees would support me. That's when my hearing returned, and the sound of hundreds of people applauding crashed down around my ears.

Walking to the stage, I started to laugh from the absurdity of it all. From delight.

By the time Benny handed me my trophy—a Momo racing wheel on a wood stand, with a nameplate reading "Most Popular Driver" and "Kate Reilly"—I'd gotten my giggles under control. I stared at my name as I moved to the microphone, and for five seconds more as I stood there. I looked up at the quiet room.

"If you Google 'unbelievable' tomorrow, this photo will be the first hit." I paused for laughter. "I'm stunned and honored. Also so proud to be part of such a talented group of drivers and teams. My dream growing up was to drive a great car against tough competition. What I understand now is how important and *fun* it is to have passionate, knowledgeable, supportive fans with us at every turn. Thank you to the fans for this award and for making what I do more enjoyable every single day."

I went back to my seat in a daze, cradling my trophy.

"@katereilly28: In shock still at receiving #ALMS Most Popular Driver award from the fans! Thank you all!"

After the show concluded, the ballroom behind the stage was opened for dancing, and the music trickled out into the banquet area. Champagne and other drinks flowed freely, and people wandered from table to table chatting with friends.

I was hesitant to leave my trophies, but Jack waved a hand and said there'd be someone at the table for a while. "We're not going to tote all this hardware around. We'll keep an eye on it. Go have fun."

I slung my evening purse over my shoulder and headed to Holly's table, stopping to shake hands and accept or give congratulations every few steps. I found Holly just as she left the table for the dance floor.

"Join us, Kate," she urged.

"I will soon. I want to sit in a quiet place for a minute. I thought I'd go look at the displays, go outside for some air. Maybe call Gramps with the news."

"I saw Scott and Juliana heading that way. But sure, you go find your second wind, sugar, then come dance the night away with us. You're the rock star tonight—time to celebrate!" She put her hands in the air and wiggled her butt.

I laughed, promising to see her soon, and headed down the hallway.

Chapter Fifty-three

I rounded the corner to the long entry hall and discovered Juliana and Scott arguing.

"Why can't you—" Scott shouted, gripping her arm.

"I won't have it—let go of me." Juliana couldn't pull away, but slapped him with her other hand.

Scott grabbed her shoulders and shook her.

"Jules!" I started forward, unsure what I could do, besides be a witness to prevent him from doing something else.

He looked at me, turned back to Juliana, and spoke quietly. I was still fifty yards away when Scott shoved her down into a chair against a window. He moved toward me, clenching his hands. His face murderous. One cheek red from her slap. I faltered mid-step, fingers on the clasp of my purse. Then he was past me, avoiding my eyes as he walked down the hall to the banquet.

I exhaled and hurried the rest of the way to Juliana. "Are you all right? What happened?"

She looked disgusted, not intimidated. "I'm fine. He's being a prima donna. If he can't stand the heat, he should get the hell out of the kitchen."

My heart still pounded from observing their altercation, but Jules was cool as a cucumber. I sat down in the chair next to hers. "You're sure you're OK?"

"Takes more than that to rattle me. How about you? What a night!"

"It's been amazing. You were spectacular. Showing them what a pro can do. It's a shame Ellie wasn't here with us."

"Yes." She had an odd tone in her voice. "She wasn't perfect, you know."

"I didn't mean that. I meant I wish she was still alive because then this evening would be pure joy, without the dark cloud over it."

"You'd say the same about Felix, right?" She looked at me sideways, a twisted smile on her lips.

"I don't feel lingering grief about him, but I'm not *glad* he's dead. I know other people are sorry—"

"It's fine, Kate, I understand. Trust me."

We sat in silence. "Jules, I talked with Ellie's husband. He told me about her."

"Her alcoholism?"

"Did you know?"

"Not then."

"Ethan said it was important for her to talk to us, but she never reached me. Did she talk with you?"

"The week before she died." She stood up. "I need a trip to the ladies."

"I could use that, too." I followed her back toward the banquet hall, into a small women's restroom with two sinks in the front half and two stalls in the back. We passed a woman I didn't recognize coming out the door, otherwise we had the place to ourselves.

I refreshed my lipstick in the mirror as Juliana came around and washed her hands, then pulled a complete makeup kit from her purse—which explained why she carried a large leather handbag, instead of a small evening bag. I watched her expertly touch up her face. *I could learn to use those Beauté products from her, too.*

I shook my head. "I'm still so surprised about Ellie. Did she tell you anything about her recovery or how she could function when she was drinking?"

"Not really."

"What would she have to apologize to us for?"

Jules put her hands down on the counter and bent her head. "Lord have mercy, you won't let this go, will you? You always were a terrier."

"I'm sorry, forget—"

"You asked, I'll tell you. She wanted to make amends for betraying me."

"She—what? She wouldn't have—"

Juliana's face twisted. "She *did*. I never had the chance to handle things my own way, she saw to that. She went running straight to Robertson-Kennerly when she found out I'd been diagnosed with epilepsy."

"The job I got that made you quit racing for pageants?"

She nodded and went back to applying mascara with choppy, angry strokes.

"Epilepsy? That was the health problem you had that year?"

She nodded again.

"You couldn't have raced anyway, could you?"

She rounded on me. "I should have been able to make that choice for myself. I'm fine now, it simply took some time to diagnose and balance out my medication."

"So she told them about it and they gave the seat to me."

She slammed the mascara into her purse. "And ruined my racing career."

"But Jules, you couldn't have raced. Not if you were being diagnosed, right?"

"That's not the point!"

I thought it was entirely the point.

"She betrayed me. She kept me from winning that ride, from going on in racing. And then she had the nerve to come crawling to me asking for forgiveness." Juliana faced me, waving her hands in the air as she ranted.

"I'm sure she was sorry—maybe she was drinking back then, and that was why she betrayed you."

"Being weak is no excuse. She'd beaten me. Betrayed me. Then, of course, they were going to pair us in the pits next year. Fucking 'pit princesses' idea. Assholes."

I blinked as she turned back to the mirror and rummaged in her bag. "That would be hard to take."

She applied lip liner, then dug out her lipstick. Our eyes met in the mirror. "You have no idea, little Miss Most Popular Driver, how it felt to be on the outside wanting in. To have lost like that." Her face was bleak.

I reached to touch her. "Jules, I'm so—"

She swept her left hand out to stop me and caught the edge of her bag, sending the contents spilling onto the floor.

I gasped and crouched down to gather the items, glad to help her somehow.

It wasn't until I glanced at the box in my hand that I heard her saying, "No, don't," and "Stop."

A Kreisel watch case, with a clear cover to better display the large, men's watch inside. A race-winner's watch.

Chapter Fifty-four

"Shit," she said. "I knew there was a reason to bring the other purse, not this one."

I felt numb. "Where did you get this, Jules?"

"A boyfriend gave it to me years ago."

I stared at it, pieces falling into place. Juliana was in every location. She knew stories about me from the past. She knew about the hospital visit. She had access to a watch. She was furious at Ellie.

"And then you gave it to Felix?" I lifted my head to look at her.

She nipped the watch out of my hand and tossed everything back in her purse. "He thought he was so clever. So I gave it to him. Then I took it back."

"Jules." I stood up. "What did your mother die of?"

"Heart problems." She stood, thumping her purse on the counter.

"Did she have a prescription for nitroglycerin?"

She didn't respond, but leaned forward and applied lipstick, blotting it with a tissue.

I remembered Juliana speaking to the young pageant girl at the mall event: "Want it, and find a way to be on top."

"This is about winning, Jules?"

"Be the best, that's my motto."

Sorrow washed through me, weakening my knees. I braced myself on the counter. "Were you trying to kill me all along?"

"No, the car, the helmet and suit, the hospital—even all those lovely stories in the right blogging ears—were all diversions." She stowed her lipstick away.

"The car that tried to run *you* down?"

"What car?" She barked out a laugh. "You're the easiest person to fool. All I had to do was sacrifice an old pair of pants and purse to the cause."

"Did you really mean to kill Ellie and Felix?"

"That bitch deserved it. And honestly, what's one less misogynist in the world?" She eyed me. "I did womankind a favor with Felix. He would never let a woman get ahead if he could stop it, not on track, not in the pits. That's unacceptable. Plus he thought he'd try to blackmail me because he saw me put pills in her juice. Did you know nitroglycerin was terribly lethal with his little blue pills?"

"You *killed* him! Womankind doesn't want those kinds of favors."

"Old goody two-shoes, Kate."

I bolted for the door, but she was faster. She bumped me aside, pushing me into the wall, then flipped the lock on the door. I lunged at her, trying to force her out of the way, but she turned and used my momentum to carry us both to the sinks. I hit the counter with the point of my hip, and she slammed into me. I cried out and crumpled over. It hurt like hell.

"Nice try, Kate. But you're not going to beat me. I've come too far to lose now." She kept me pressed against the counter as she reached over to her purse. I bucked against her, moving her back. I was free for a moment. Then she turned and shoved me with both hands.

I stumbled backward on those stupid heels, overbalancing and going down hard on my tailbone against the far wall. My head sounded like a melon thunking against the tiles as I fell. My vision swam, narrowed. I saw black at the edges, and I shouted silently at myself, like I did in the racecar. *Don't pass out, Kate. Focus. Stay awake. Get up and get past her.* My limbs were slow to respond, but I'd kept a death grip on my purse, and my fingers fumbled with the clasp.

Red in my narrowed vision. Then pain as Juliana knelt on my legs. She peered into my eyes, nodded. I got my hand in my purse. Juliana pinched my nostrils closed and raised a cupped hand to my open mouth. Small objects hit my tongue. Some part of my brain shrieked a warning.

I lurched forward. Spit the pills out. Raised my right hand from my purse and shot hairspray point-blank into Juliana's eyes. She fell back with a shriek, rubbing her eyes. Swearing at me. I scooted forward and grabbed, untying the long, black ribbon from her waist. She struck out at me with hands and feet, blind, tears streaming down her face. I stole her trick and sat on her legs. Grabbed one arm. Wrapped the ribbon tight around it and tied a knot.

I scooted two feet away to the metal dividers separating the toilet stalls and wrapped the ribbon around the pillar secured to the floor. Pulled. Juliana's arm was reeled in toward the divider, and she flopped over onto her side on the floor. When she reached her other arm to her bound wrist, I wrapped the ribbon around both wrists together and knotted it again.

She was furious, crying, eyes closed. Stretched out on the floor, kicking. But immobilized. "Don't think this means you're better than me, Kate Reilly."

I slowly got to my feet. My head spun as I stood upright, and I braced myself on the wall until I felt steady.

She kept talking. "You have no talent or style. I will always be better than you. Prettier than you."

I sighed and looked down at my one-time friend. "Give it up, Jules. It's over."

I got past her and wobbled out into the hallway, sinking into a chair across from the bathroom just as Holly and a hotel worker brandishing a large bunch of keys rounded the corner. Three men from hotel security were only steps behind, and I waved them into the bathroom to take charge of Juliana. They also called the cops. I sat with my head in my hands until the police arrived.

As an officer asked me questions to fill in the gaps of my story, Juliana was escorted out of the bathroom, hands cuffed behind her back.

"You might think you've won," she called to me. "But I'll be back."

I marveled at how well she'd hidden her twisted nature under surface charm. "Get some help, Juliana."

"I should have slipped some revenge in your orange juice, too. Maybe next time." She was led away down the hall.

Holly sighed. "She still walks like a pageant queen."

"Thanks for riding to the rescue."

"Not that you needed it, Supergirl. You saved your own skin just fine."

"I guess I did."

Holly raised an eyebrow. "Hairspray, not just for updos anymore?"

I felt a chuckle bubble through the grief and shock. It felt good.

Chapter Fifty-five

I ended up back at the Sandham Swift table in the banquet area. Before I left the hallway, Holly found the Chief Medical Officer for the Series and had him check out my injuries. The doctor confirmed what the paramedics suggested and I knew. I was possibly concussed and definitely banged up, but otherwise fine. I refused all invitations to go to the hospital, and no one insisted.

I was astonished to find, even after spending half an hour with the police—giving them a statement and promising to go to the station to sign it in the morning—I'd only been away from the party forty-five minutes. Our episode in the bathroom lasted a lifetime to me, but only four or five minutes to the rest of the world.

More than one well-meaning person, Stuart included, suggested I might prefer to go home and rest in peace and quiet after the trauma. I told them all the same thing: "I'll be damned if she's going to wreck my celebration." Besides, while I might physically crash from adrenaline, my mind was wired. Sleep wouldn't come soon due to the near-death experience playing on repeat in my head. I might as well be with friends.

I had one other reason for sticking around. I knew the story would sweep through the party and the racing world like wildfire, and I wanted everyone to see I was the last man standing. That was good for public perception of me. It also meant nails in Juliana's coffin. Petty? Probably. But that meant I won.

Fortunately the dining area was subdued. We heard music from the dance floor, as well as the hoots and hollers of the dancers, but it wasn't overwhelming. I held court at our table, an icepack on my head, telling the story over and over.

Zeke must have been in the far reaches of the dance floor, because I'd been sitting there fifteen minutes before he came tearing around the stage.

"You're all right! The story that's making the rounds in there—"

"Believe it," Jack said, as Tom and Leon nodded.

Vicki waved Zeke to an empty chair. "You're going to want wine for this." She nodded at Steve, who poured some and handed it to him.

Zeke sat with a thump, looking from me to Stuart and Mike on either side of me. "It's true? Juliana?"

"Sugar, I'm not sure exactly what you heard." Holly took a slug of wine. "But it would be hard to make something up that would sound more crazy."

"What in hell happened?"

"I have an idea Tom will like," I said. "Zeke, how about an exclusive interview with Juliana's latest—and last—victim? On record, right now."

Tom nodded. "Get your version out first."

"If there's one thing I've learned this last two weeks, it's to control the message. Which reminds me I'll need to call my PR team tomorrow about this."

Zeke was ready with a mini tape recorder. "You talk, Katie-Q, and I'll strike anything you don't want later—you all didn't hear that from a reporter, mind you."

I saw Scott Brooklyn approach and stop two tables away. I stood up. "Hang on, sorry. I owe someone an apology."

I walked over to him. "Are you OK?"

He nodded, his face grim. "I had no idea. She was bossy and demanding, but…"

"But who knew she was psycho? I sure didn't. What were you arguing about?"

"She'd promised to talk to the SGTV producers for me. But she reneged. Laughed at me. I was angry." He raised eyes to mine. "I thought we had a future."

I shook my head. "I need to apologize to you. I thought you were up to no good with her, were trying to use her to get a job. Turns out I had that backward."

He came up with a smile and offered a hand. "How about a truce?"

"A truce." I shook. "Apology accepted?"

"Sure thing. We'll wipe the slate clean, make a fresh start from here."

"You going to be all right?"

He stood and put his hands in his pockets. "I'll be fine. Thanks for asking. I'll see you around, Kate."

I went back to my seat at the table. "I wanted to apologize for thinking he was behind it all. But we've called a truce."

"Good thing, too," Mike said. "Given how our pit reporters are dropping like flies, he might be their senior guy."

"Tell the story, Kate," Zeke prompted.

"After the awards, I headed over to the entry hallway—"

Holly interrupted me. "Shouldn't it start with Ellie two weeks ago?"

"Honestly," I said, "it should start with Juliana's awful mother who drilled into her head she had to win at all costs. To be better than everyone else. That if you didn't win, you hadn't wanted it enough or worked hard enough."

"I've met that mother," Vicki put in, "or her clone, on the pageant circuit."

"There we were, the three of us racing against each other seven years ago, and at the end of the year Juliana and I were up for the same seat. I got it, and she left racing for pageants. I found out tonight that Juliana experienced health issues that year—which turned out to be epilepsy—and Ellie found out and told the team owner."

"Naturally, he gave you the job," Stuart commented.

"Right, but Juliana never knew Ellie told him. Neither did I. But then Ellie found Juliana a couple weeks ago—Zeke, don't print this. Apparently Ellie was an alcoholic for a lot of years, maybe even back to our racing days, I don't know. As part of her recovery, she went to Juliana to apologize for, as Juliana put it, betraying her to the team owner."

I set the icepack down on the table. "I think that tipped Juliana over the edge. She had nitroglycerin from her mother's illness and she spiked Ellie's juice—not mine—at the Tavern."

"She did still try to run you down in Atlanta," Holly reminded me.

"That was a diversion, along with the helmet strap, firesuit, press at the hospital—she must have borrowed Felix's phone for that call. All to make everyone think I was the target, not Ellie."

Zeke looked up from a notepad he'd started scribbling on. "Because there was no 'why kill Kate' that pointed to her."

"Just to other people. But who tried to run her down?" Holly asked.

I shook my head. "No one. She faked that."

Tom spoke. "You can't blame all the stress of the past two weeks on her. I mean, the Ringer, NASCAR fans, that Nash Rawlings guy. Right?"

"She said something about 'stories in the right bloggers' ears,' so I wouldn't be surprised if she planted stories of my early days in racing. But you're right, Tom, I brought most of that on myself."

"Only some," Jack put in. "You brought some on yourself—and learned a damned good lesson. The rest of it was rabid fans and stupid blogs. Everything gets spun out of control too quickly these days."

"It's not hard for someone in the media to drop a word in the right ear, you know." Zeke tapped his pencil on his notebook. "It'd be an easy way for her to try to discredit you—fan those flames."

"Pretty sure she did that. She wasn't after me—not before the end, anyway—in the same way she was after Ellie and Felix, but I don't think she was happy with me achieving more than she did."

"So what about Felix?" Steve Royal spoke for the first time. "I liked that guy."

Vicki punched his arm, and he turned to her. "What? I did."

I laughed. "He didn't like women, Steve. He hated me in particular."

"I didn't know that. Um, what a jerk."

Holly, Vicki, and I burst out laughing.

"He's a keeper," Holly declared. "And so are you." The latter was to Leon, who was refilling her glass of wine.

I went on. "Felix was blackmailing her. Plus, he was in her way. He'd never let her get anywhere, because he didn't think women belonged anywhere in racing—except maybe wearing spandex and holding an umbrella."

"You figured all of this out, how?" Stuart asked.

"I wish I could claim because I'm brilliant. I thought about Juliana…I mean, Felix's father had made him so bitter and I heard other stories of other children warped by their parents' beliefs. But Jules seemed normal, even though stories of her mother were awful. So I wondered—but it was hard to believe she was a killer. I suspected Felix or those bank guys or Scott more than her."

I sighed. "I asked Juliana what Ellie wanted to talk to her about, and learned about the betrayal and the epilepsy—which got Juliana upset. While she ranted, she knocked her purse off the counter, and I picked up a box with a race-winner's watch in it. Everything clicked. She was on the spot, had a watch—from a boyfriend, she said—and she'd just told me about a motive for Ellie. She admitted it all when I asked. Then she locked the door and tried to kill me."

Holly put her hand on my shoulder. "I'd gone looking for Kate, and I could hear her voice, but the bathroom door was locked. I was on the way with keys and help when we found Kate had saved herself with hairspray."

Zeke looked up from his notes. "Hairspray? Are you kidding me?"

"Haven't you taken any self-defense classes, Zeke?" I smiled. "Cops will tell you it's as effective as pepper spray, but legal. I had it with me on purpose."

"A question for the victim then," Zeke said. "How are you feeling?"

I smiled at him. "I'm glad to be alive and glad we all know the truth."

He turned the recorder off with a snap and got up to give me a gentle hug. "I'm glad you're all right, Katie-Q. Take care of yourself, would you?"

"Working on it. Where's Rosalie, anyway?"

He frowned. "Back in our room here. I'll talk to you next week sometime."

"Oy," Leon shouted. "The Ringer. Kate, look."

Five of us pulled out smartphones and called up the site to see a minutes-old post titled "New Beginnings," with a photo of me receiving the Most Popular Driver award.

Tom read it aloud for the rest of the table:

"It's been a crazy night, Readers. I'll pass along details as they become available the next few days, but the bottom line is our assumptions have been turned upside down. Up is down, right is left, and the Ringer is pretty confused. But one thing is clear, we owe Kate Reilly an apology for the harsh things we've said about her in recent weeks. Sure, she's young and still learning, but it's time to admit she's never acted maliciously. Time to admit maybe the Ringer's been a bit of a bully where she's concerned.

"So here's my public apology to Kate—just Kate, not Calamity or Violent—congratulations on your awards and success this year, and good luck in the next season. I hope you're willing to let bygones be bygones with the Ringer, and wipe the slate clean, make a fresh start from here. Signed, the Ringer. P.S. Your dress was fabulous."

Everyone at the table made astonished and gratified noises. I looked across the room and smiled. I'd met the Ringer.

To receive a free catalog of Poisoned Pen Press titles, please contact us in one of the following ways:

Phone: 1-800-421-3976
Facsimile: 1-480-949-1707
Email: info@poisonedpenpress.com
Website: www.poisonedpenpress.com

Poisoned Pen Press
6962 E. First Ave. Ste 103
Scottsdale, AZ 85251